THE SEER'S CHALLENGE

DAPHNE ASHLING PURPUS

ISBN: 0692785833
ISBN 13: 9780692785836
Library of Congress Control Number: 2016916180
Purpus Publishing, Vashon, WA

This novel is dedicated to my family: Pamela, Eric, Kelly, Josie, Jan, and Stephanie.

Other Books in This Series

Dragon Riders
The Egg That Wouldn't Hatch
Dragon Magic
The Dragon Who Chooses Twice
The Girl, the Gryphon, and the Dragon
The Mage's Dilemma

CONTENTS

Acknowledgments   ix
Map of the Four Nations   xi
List of Characters   xiii
1.   Premonition   1
2.   Confrontation   7
3.   Merchant Guild Meeting   11
4.   Lunch with a Mage   19
5.   A New Store   31
6.   Construction   41
7.   Retaliation   55
8.   Injuries   63
9.   Calliope's Rescue   75
10. Bertha's Cave   85
11. Broken Bones   99
12. Disorientation and Dismay   111
13. Discoveries   121
14. Ransom Demands   135
15. Search   147
16. Rodney's Plan   159
17. Illusions   165
18. Consequences   175
19. Inventions   187
20. Mentoring   199
21. Library Expansion   213
22. Energy Grants   223
23. A New Home   235
24. Explosion   245
25. New Beginnings   255

ACKNOWLEDGMENTS

So many people have helped, inspired, and supported me. Once again I'd like to thank the folks at National Novel Writing Month (NaNoWriMo) for all their encouragement and pep talks. This year I participated in NaNoWriMo for the fifth time. *The Seer's Challenge* was written during November 2015.

Next I'd like to thank the members of my Wednesday bridge class, who have been unfailing in their support of my efforts. I also would like to thank my students—both past and present—at Student Link, Vashon's alternative high school, who continue to inspire me with their drive, determination, maturity, and insight in the face of major adversities.

The past year has been a challenging year medically. I would really like to thank everyone at Swedish Hospital and the Arnold Pavilion who have made my journey possible and ultimately very successful. There are too many people to name individually, but I would be remiss if I didn't mention Dr. Karen Hendershott, Dr. Henry Kaplan, and Dr. Vivek Mehta.

In addition I would like to give thanks to some special people, in no particular order: Cynthia Zheutlin, for her gentle wisdom and insight; Nan Hammett, for her friendship and collegial support; Nell Coffman and everyone at Fair Isle Animal Clinic, for keeping my family happy and healthy; Lydia Schoch, for her empathy and encouragement; Anja Moritz, for her wisdom, kind support, and wonderful lunches; Paul Robinson, for his unfailing kindness and assistance; Karen Hain, for her kindness and for keeping my body moving; and Blythe Bartlett, for her support and her eager reading of my novels.

MAP OF THE
FOUR NATIONS

LIST OF CHARACTERS

Al: A Havenshold businessman.

Alma: A Havenshold resident willing to foster Pathfinder students.

Amy: A retired dragon rider bonded to the female green dragon Fern. She's Todd's wife and the mother of Hans, Jake, Emily, Robert, Michael, and Hannah, as well as a foster mother to many young people, including Lucy and Chloe.

Anita: A Havenshold merchant who owns Anita's Second Chance Shop.

Arryn: Sixteen years old, thin and tall, pale with scraggly long brown hair and brown eyes. Her story is told in *The Mage's Dilemma.*

Artemis: A female fox who recently arrived in Havenshold and is bonded to Rya.

Aster: Clyde's daughter. She's bonded with a yellow dragon, Jasmine, and they also have a small female white dog, Sasha, in their bond. The three of them are traveling ambassadors for all of Draconia. The story of their bonding is told in *The Dragon Who Chooses Twice.*

Baron Geldsmith: Known simply as "the baron," he's the richest man in the world. He owns a large estate in Havenshold, managed by his younger son, Lance, and a large mining operation in Forbury. He bonded later in life with a gryphon named Oswald. The story of his early attempt to capture the throne of Havenshold is told in *Dragon Riders*.

Berla: One of Bertha's year old twin cubs.

Bertha: A brown bear who is the seer for the world.

Bill: A Havenshold businessman, George's partner in a coal mining operation.

Boris: One of Bertha's year old twin cubs.

Bruce: A Havenshold resident willing to foster Pathfinder students.

Calliope: The telepathic library cat.

Chloe: A young woman who's the mage for the entire world. She also runs Pathfinder Academy. Her story is told in the book *Dragon Magic*.

Cinnamon: A young brown dragon bonded to Elise.

Clotilda: The queen of all of Draconia. She's bonded to a female purple dragon, Matilda.

Clyde: Rya's uncle, Aster's father, Harmony's son. He's an enormously talented carpenter but the only one in his family without magical abilities.

Dr. Brian: The Havenshold's doctor.

Elise: A dragon rider in training, bonded to the brown dragon, Cinnamon. She is also Patrick's girlfriend.

Emily: The current leader of the dragons and riders as well as the town of Havenshold. She is bonded to the female purple dragon Esmeralda and comes from a large family.

Esmeralda: A female purple dragon who, with her bonded partner, Emily, leads the dragons and riders. She is Matilda's youngest offspring.

Fern: A female green dragon bonded to Amy.

Firebird: A female orange dragon, bonded with Hannah, and the offspring of Fire Dancer.

George Pontsby: A prominent business man who lives on the outskirts of Havenshold.

Gregory: A volcanologist, the son of the baron. He is married to Emily.

Hannah: Emily's sister and the youngest of Amy and Todd's children. She is a dragon rider, bonded to Firebird, and is married to Rupert.

Harmony: A woman with strong telepathic and magical skills. She's Clyde's mother and Aster and Rya's grandmother. She also has a daughter, Mildred, who's an artistic recluse as well as Rya's birth mother.

Hazel Winsong: Chloe's mother, a seamstress, and the organizer of the support group for Chloe's energy net.

Henry Winsong: Chloe's father.

Jake: A dragon rider, bonded to a female brown dragon named Harmony. He is Emily's second-oldest brother and is married to William.

Jaluhz: Draconia's volcano. Havenshold is built on her side.

Jasmine: A yellow female dragon bonded with Aster and Sasha.

Jupiter: A male green dragon bonded to Todd.

King Alfred: The founder of Draconia and the first leader of the dragons and riders who arrived in the world 540 years ago.

Lance: Gregory's younger brother, the baron's second son, who manages the baron's large estate in Havenshold.

Libby: The name the library uses when she takes on human form.

Mac: A kidnapper.

Mary: A Havenshold merchant who owns the yarn and sweater shop.

Matilda: A female purple dragon bonded with Clotilda. Together they rule Draconia.

Munroe: A kidnapper.

Nurse Beatrice: The chief nurse at Havenshold Hospital.

Oswald: A gryphon born with only one wing, which had to be amputated for the sake of his balance. He's bonded with the baron.

Rodney: A red squirrel who is friends with Berla and Boris.

Ron: The owner of a fresh fruit and vegetable cart in Havenshold.

Roy: A kidnapper.

Rupert: A dragon rider bonded with Whipper, a male purple dragon. He's Emily's second in command. He's married to Emily's sister, Hannah.

Rya: A fifteen-year-old girl who recently arrived in Havenshold to be an apprentice to her uncle, Clyde, a carpenter. Her story is told in the book *The Girl, the Gryphon, and the Dragon*.

Sasha: A telepathic white female dog, bonded with Aster and Jasmine.

Sylvester: The Havenshold veterinarian.

Todd: A retired dragon rider, married to Amy, bonded with the male green dragon Jupiter. With Amy they have six children: Hans, Jake, Emily, Robert, Michael, and Hannah. They also have fostered a number of young people, including Lucy and Chloe.

Whipper: A male purple dragon bonded to Rupert. He's Esmeralda's first offspring.

William: A dragon rider, bonded with the male brown dragon Thunder. He is an expert in telepathic communications and is married to Jake, Emily's second-oldest brother.

Zelda Winsong: A dress designer who is Chloe's sister.

— 1 —

PREMONITION

Bertha looked out of her cave entrance at the meadow, which stretched away from the cave and curved down the mountainside to a lovely small river. She loved her home. Her cave was located high in the mountains, above any settled lands. Over the centuries her ancestors had carved rooms and niches in the stone, expanding the original cave so that there was now plenty of room for her and her two offspring. She had her own bedroom, as did her twins, and there was an alcove with a ledge where guests had stayed through the years. The main room held her small kitchen and pantry, as well as a large kitchen table with sturdy benches. The room also had half a dozen large fluffy pillows for relaxing. The walls were decorated with various wall hangings depicting scenes from the surrounding areas. Many of the hangings were gifts to her for help she'd rendered. Some were similar gifts that had been given to her mother and grandmother before her. She treasured each of them, both for their beauty and for the memories the gifts evoked. She really did have a wonderful life and was so fortunate in many ways.

She loved this time of year, with the scent of new life everywhere. The spring wildflowers were just beginning to bloom, a riot of pinks, yellows, blues just beginning to burst forth. The scene was tranquil and calm as the morning sun began to rise behind her cave. She'd looked at this scene many times, over the years, and it always brought her a sense of peace. But not today. She'd woken with a great sense of impending doom, but she had no idea why or where the threat came from. *How can everything look so peaceful when I'm so unsettled?* Bertha thought.

Just then her twins, Boris and Berla, came barreling into the kitchen area behind her, and she turned to watch them. They were nearly full grown, no longer small cubs, but they still acted like juveniles. Boris had very dark brown fur and was slightly larger than his sister, who was also a lighter brown, more like Bertha's own coloring. She smiled as she watched them playing. They didn't have a care in the world, and she really didn't want to have them grow up any sooner than necessary.

It was true that one day Berla would take her place as this world's only seer, and with that responsibility would come worries, at least from time to time, but Bertha didn't plan on passing the reins to Berla for many years. Bertha mused, as she watched her cubs, that she'd carried the burden of being the world's only seer, a seer for the entire planet and the four nations that comprised it, for nearly as long as she could remember.

Her great-grandmother had been the world's first seer, over five hundred years ago when King Alfred and his dragon had been transported here along with the small contingent of dragons and riders, all that remained from a time well into the planet's future. The planet herself had brought the riders back in time to save the world. In addition, the planet had guided King Alfred and his group as they founded Draconia, the fourth nation on this world. Draconia had been established around the volcano, as that land not only suited dragons but was unclaimed by the other three nations, each of which also had magical creatures bonded to riders. Forbury had its gryphons, Granvale had unicorns, and Sanwight had dolphins. Along with the dragons, they formed the protective layer the planet needed. Each of the magical creatures could communicate telepathically with their riders, and in every case the bonded pairs were committed to service, not just to their own nation but to the planet as a whole.

Bertha thought that the planet had been very wise to set this all up, and it was King Alfred who was instrumental in establishing the role of seer after he'd met Bertha's great-grandmother and discovered that she was able to foretell the future, warning about anything that could harm the planet as a whole. She'd even foretold the coming of King Alfred and the dragons, alerting the monarchs of the other nations, so that the transition went smoothly for the riders and their dragons. With the aid of his dragons, King Alfred had helped Bertha's great-grandmother shape the original cave she'd been living in so that it contained its own hidden secrets as well as plenty of room for growing families. He said it was the least he could do if she were willing to become the world's only seer. He wanted her to have a place that was separated from the rest of the world so that her allegiance would be to the planet. Her cave was located high in the mountains above Draconia, near the border with Granvale and not that much farther from the borders of Forbury and Sanwight. It was the perfect location, Bertha thought.

In Bertha's own lifetime, she'd foretold the coming of the asteroid that might have destroyed the planet. She'd then recognized Chloe's gifts and trained her to be the world's only mage. Together they'd come up with a solution, and Chloe's strong magical powers, augmented by the energy net of magic she'd woven from the bonded pairs from all four nations, allowed her to shove the asteroid into a new path, saving the planet.

After that, there had been the evil magician, whom Chloe, with Bertha's help, managed to defeat. And most recently, there had been the matter of Jaluhz, this world's sentient volcano, who'd suffered damage when criminals tried to explore her depths for riches, blowing a large hole in Jaluhz's side and causing the slow release of a large lava stream. Bertha felt a special bond with Chloe because they both were unique in their jobs and both owed their service to the entire planet, rather than just one nation.

There seemed always to be something, Bertha thought, as she watched the twins begin fixing a breakfast of porridge laced with honey. But last night's nightmare had been different. She was uneasy, not even really sure why—but she felt that the very foundation of this world was going to be attacked somehow.

She looked toward the back of the cave and realized that her uneasiness was centered there. At the rear of the cave, there was a hidden room, a room only she could open. King Alfred had brought many scrolls, books, and other items from his time in the future, the wisdom from the world he'd left. He told Bertha's great-grandmother that some of the knowledge had been used to destroy the world he came from. It wasn't the knowledge itself that caused the problems, but the uses to which greedy selfish people had put that knowledge. He felt that one day, some of that knowledge might be needed, and in fact, that's where Bertha found the directions for building the telescope Chloe used to track the approach of the asteroid. That telescope was now housed on the second floor of the library in Havenshold, the town where the dragons and riders lived alongside a community of people who'd chosen to make their homes there.

Bertha was now the custodian of the knowledge from the original timeline, and she sensed that somehow there was going to be a threat to her stronghold. That was why she was uneasy, she realized. She felt as if she was going to be attacked. But she'd never open that secret room. No one could force her.

Just then her musing was interrupted. "Mom," shouted Berla, "breakfast is ready."

Bertha smiled and answered, "Coming."

As the three of them gathered around their kitchen table, Bertha thought again about how lucky she was. She would enjoy the day and would not worry about her nightmare. She'd be given a clear vision when the threat was definite. That's the way her gift worked. Worrying about it prematurely never helped.

Boris said, "Can we go look for honey today?"

Berla nodded and said, "And maybe maple syrup?"

Bertha laughed. "That sounds like a wonderful thing to do on such a lovely spring day. You two made the breakfast, so I'll do cleanup." She gathered the bowls now emptied of their porridge and headed to the sink. "You two, go find buckets and whatever else you think we need. We'll make a day of it."

"Yay," shouted the twins as they raced from the table.

Bertha shook herself and thought, *I'm not going to worry. I'm going to have a carefree day with the twins and let the future wait for now.*

— 2 —
CONFRONTATION

Several days later, while Bertha was doing some spring cleaning inside the cave and Boris and Berla were outside shaking the various wall hangings that adorned the cave walls, she heard Boris shouting, "A man is coming."

Bertha put down her rag and bucket and went outside. They almost never had visitors, and those who did come usually contacted her telepathically before they arrived. She mainly interacted with Chloe or with Emily and her purple dragon Esmeralda, who governed Havenshold. Bertha felt it was polite to be invited to visit, or at least to let her know that some-one was approaching. She was immediately on her guard when she saw the tall man striding across her meadow. He seemed totally oblivious to all the beauty he was walking through as he stomped his big feet on top of the new wildflowers. He had a grim, determined look on his face, and he just brushed past Boris when Boris greeted him.

Boris moved so the he was in front of the man and said again, "May I help you?"

"No," snarled the man. "I'm here to see Bertha. Now, step aside."

Bertha moved out into the meadow as Boris stepped aside and said, "I'm Bertha. What brings you here?"

"I need information, and if you're smart, you'll give it to me," said the man. "I'm George Pontsby, and I know what you have hidden here."

Bertha stared hard at George and said, after a lengthy pause, "I don't know what you mean."

"Oh, yes, you do. I know all about the hidden store of knowledge, and I mean to have it. You can't stop me, so just hand it over now," said George in a steely voice filled with menace. He then walked around Bertha and headed toward the cave.

Bertha put a paw on George's shoulder, which seemed to startle him. She pressed down on his shoulder and said, "You have not been invited into our home. You are rude, and you have no business here. I have nothing that you want. Now, turn around, and leave."

At this last sentence, Bertha rose up on her back legs, standing well over six feet tall, and pressed on George's shoulder to turn him away from the cave. Both Boris and Berla had moved in to stand with their mother.

George nearly lost his balance when Bertha removed her paw, but he quickly regained his composure and said, "I'm a very powerful man. You'd do well to listen to me."

Bertha looked at him and then laughed, with a deep rumbling laugh, which shook her ample belly. Then she said, "Do you have any idea who I am?"

George glared, shook a fist at her, and said, "Oh, I know you're thick with those dragons and their riders, but that won't help you now. I know you're supposed to be some all-powerful seer, but you don't look like anything more than a big bear, and I've killed bears before."

"What?" shouted Bertha, putting her front paws in the air. "Are you really stupid? Don't you know that bears are protected on this planet?"

"I really don't care," snarled George. "You're all just a bunch of animals and nowhere near as important as humans. You may have fooled some stupid people, but I know better."

At this remark both Boris and Berla let out menacing growls and moved toward George, their teeth bared.

George had the good sense to step back as he said, "And keep your brats away from me if you know what's good for you."

He then pulled out a gun and pointed it toward the cubs.

Bertha shook her head and said, with true sorrow in her voice, "Boris, Berla, head into the cave. Take the wall hangings with you, and I'll be right there after I get rid of this vermin."

Boris glared at the man and then reluctantly said, "OK, Mom," as he and Berla did as they were told.

Once they'd left George said, "And just how do you plan to do that? I have the gun after all. Now I want what I came for. Let me into your storehouse of King Alfred's documents."

"Piffle," snorted Bertha. "Your gun means nothing here." And with that remark, she spoke telepathically to George, barging as rudely into his mind as he'd barged into her meadow, saying, *You pathetic excuse for a man. Do you really think your power matches mine?*

George looked startled, and Bertha continued applying pressure to his mind, pushing so hard that he was knocked off balance. As he fell, his gun went off. Fortunately it was aimed at the sky by then and didn't do any damage.

Bertha then stepped over to George and stood on his right arm, causing George to yell in pain as his forearm bone cracked. Bertha picked up the gun, which he'd been forced to drop, and with only a flicker of movement, she broke the gun in half.

"Where's all your power now?" Bertha asked.

"Help me," said George, as he held his broken right arm and tried to sit up.

"Oh, so now you want my help," said Bertha. "Well, you're on your own. You came uninvited. You insulted both me and my cubs. You threatened us, demanding something you don't even know exists. Now, get out of here, and don't ever come back."

George had managed finally to stand up, clutching his right arm with his left. He glared at her and said, "You'll be sorry for this. I have a lot more power than you think, and I can hurt you. You've just made a powerful enemy."

Bertha looked at him, chuckling and shaking her head in wonder that anyone could be so stupid. Then she turned her back on him and headed into the cave. Once inside she told the twins to be careful around any strangers. She knew that they hadn't seen the last of this determined man.

As the three of them rehung their wall hangings, Bertha thought, *So that's the threat. Somehow he's found out about the time travel, the alternate timeline, and the storehouse of information. I'd better let Emily and Esmeralda know.*

— 3 —
MERCHANT GUILD MEETING

The morning sun was shining through the skylight in the conference room at the dragon riders' headquarters. The large round table in the center of the room was bathed in sunlight as Emily and Esmeralda, her lovely purple dragon, entered the room for the merchant guild meeting. Emily, a tall woman in her midforties with short brown hair and intelligent brown eyes, glanced around at those who were already gathered at the table as she and Esmeralda took their places at the table. Usually they enjoyed meeting with the merchants, but today's meeting had a special agenda. It had been called by the only really divisive merchant in all of Havenshold, and in fact possibly in all of Draconia, and Emily wasn't looking forward to having to deal with George Pontsby. As the head of the dragons and their riders, she and Esmeralda ruled Havenshold, so to speak, but most of the time that didn't require more than an occasional bit of guidance.

However, since last fall, when some misguided thugs had set off an explosion in the side of the volcano where Havenshold was situated, resulting in Jaluhz's eruption (Emily still found it rather wonderful that their world had a sentient volcano), George had been a thorn in her side. He and another rancher had owned land right in the path of the trench the dragon riders needed to dig in order to channel Jaluhz's lava across Draconia and part of Forbury so it could enter the sea. George had tried to hold Queen Clotilda and her purple dragon, Matilda—the joint rulers of Draconia—for ransom, demanding prime land in return for allowing the trench to be dug across his property. Thankfully Emily's husband, Gregory, and others had figured out that they could just allow the lava to flow across George's land without a trench since he was situated between two mountain ranges and so called his bluff.

Eventually, a few months ago now, the trench had been built, but George's land became virtually unusable for any ranching or farming. So he'd decided to shift into fabric production, and that was when the real problems began. Today's meeting wouldn't be easy, but waiting wouldn't help, and so Emily stood and called the meeting to order.

"Thank you all for coming," she began, noticing that everyone had availed themselves of the tea and scones she and Esmeralda had set out earlier. "We're here today to try to figure out how to address the issues that have surfaced after the tragic closing of Ingrid's Quilt Shop."

George, a tall heavyset man with receding gray hair and a large paunch, his right forearm in a cast, said, "What do you mean 'tragic'? The woman couldn't make a go of the business. Too bad."

Emily sat down and motioned for the discussion to begin. Mary, the leader of the merchant's guild and the owner of a lovely shop called Sweaters and Yarns, ran a hand through her blond curly hair before speaking. "Ingrid's shop was the major draw for our commercial area. People came from not only Havenshold but indeed from Draconia and the other three nations of our world because of all the lovely fabric she carried, as well as the quilt shows she hosted. She also taught classes, including those for children, and the loss of her shop is hurting all the businesses in Havenshold. Each of us has seen a dramatic drop in income since you, George, forced her out."

"I did no such thing," snapped George, waving his good arm in an angry gesture. "After that damned volcano spilled lava all over my land, I had to find a new source of income. I didn't come bellyaching to any of you. I just looked around and then decided I could make fabric better and cheaper than what you already had. I needed a retail outlet and learned that Ingrid's lease was about to expire, so I stepped in and bought the building from Bob. Then I offered her a new lease, but she turned it down. So that's what happened. It was all business. I have a right to do what I want with my property."

Anita, an elderly woman with nearly snow-white hair and a very slim short build, the owner of Anita's Second Chance Shop, said, "None of us would have been able to afford the lease you offered her, at three times the current rate."

"If you can't cut it, then get out," snarled George. "And I didn't come here to listen to a bunch of complaining and whining. I came here for information about the store of knowledge being guarded by the dragons and their riders. I want that information."

Emily, thankful that Bertha had already contacted her telepathically to explain George's visit to her cave, said, "I have no idea what you are talking about, but we aren't leaving this discussion about the quilt shop just yet." Emily paused before continuing. "Mary, is there any other location available where Ingrid could have her store, because you are right: the loss of the quilt store has had a large negative impact on Havenshold, and we need to see what we can do to help her."

Mary, after taking a sip from her tea, shook her head and said, "Unfortunately there isn't a retail spot large enough for her enormous inventory, and certainly not large enough for exhibits and classes as well. Ingrid is trying to sell out of her home, but she doesn't have the space to display her fabric, so that really isn't working."

As the merchants debated options, Emily listened and took notes before saying, "Remember that the dragon riders do have small-business loans available if that would help Ingrid, or indeed any of you."

"That's the problem with all of you," shouted George, slamming his mug down on the table so hard that it cracked. This brought a stop to the merchants' discussion. As he grabbed some napkins to stem the flow of tea, he continued. "You're weak. You wait for someone to bail you out. No one helped me, and now I'm richer than I was before the lava flowed across my land. If you aren't strong, then you'll fail."

"Ruthless, you mean," said Ron, a man in his early fifties, with graying black hair and a missing front tooth. He was the owner of a fresh fruit and vegetable cart. "What you did may have been legal, but it for sure wasn't right."

"So what," said George. "I'm supposed to be like you. You don't even have a real store. You'll never make any money."

"At least I can sleep at night," said Ron.

"I sleep really well," said George, "and I'm going to sleep even better once I get ahold of the information I came here today for. What about it, Emily? I've been doing some investigating on my own, and I know you riders are hiding something. I've heard stories, and I want access to better technology and techniques for production, and I know you have that."

"I don't know where you are getting your information, George," said Emily, making sure that she made eye contact with him. "We aren't hiding anything. If you need information, why not go to the library? I'm sure Chloe would be happy to help you find whatever it is you think you need."

George gave a sarcastic laugh and said, "That mage! Like Chloe would let go of her power for two seconds. She's as bad as you dragons and riders. I tried visiting the library, and she pretended that she didn't know a thing, but there's something going on, and I'm going to get to the bottom of it. I promise you that."

"Be my guest," said Emily, waving a hand dismissively. "Now back to helping Ingrid."

"I've had enough of this," said George as he stood and headed to the door. "You'll all be sorry that you didn't help me. Just you wait."

"I thought you didn't want help," said Mary in an innocent tone.

George just shook his head and stormed out of the room.

Once he was gone, Ron looked at Emily and said, "I'm afraid he's going to make trouble."

Everyone at the table nodded, and Emily said, "You may be right that he's going to try, but I'll be sure that he's watched. Meanwhile, what can we do for Ingrid?"

The discussion moved back to the suggested options, but no one had any ideas that might actually work. Mary, who'd been doodling on a pad of paper when she wasn't making notes, summed it up as she said, "It's not just that Ingrid lost her store. The second part of this is that George is flooding the market with his fabric, and there is no way anyone can compete with his prices. I've looked at his fabric, and the fact is that it isn't anywhere near the quality of Ingrid's. He's saying that it's better fabric for less money, but the reality is that it's really cheap and flimsy. It won't hold up, and over time, I think his business will fail, but for the moment, there isn't any way to stop him that I can see."

Other merchants nodded, and Anita said, a worried frown creasing her brow, "You know the reason my shop works so well is that the clothes that are made here, from fabric such as Ingrid's, last forever, and so when people outgrow items or want a change, they can bring them to my shop and exchange them for something else. But if the quality of the fabric goes down, well, then guess what—stuff won't last."

"I know," said Emily, sighing. "Well, let's keep trying to come up with ideas and see if we can find a way around George. Maybe instead of a loan, the riders could buy Ingrid's inventory and then resell it at even lower prices to undercut him. I don't know, but we will find a way to stop him."

Mary, looking up from her notes, said, "And the undercutting isn't the worst of it. He's developed some way to manufacture fabric using machines that produce a lot of nasty black smoke. He's also hiring workers and then requiring that they live on his land, in his dormitories, and once they are under contract, he cuts their wages but then demands that they buy their food and everything from him. I talked with a lady who's family is now deeply in debt to him. This just isn't the way Havenshold operates."

"No, it certainly isn't," said Emily, aghast at the news, "and that's the first I've heard of this. Obviously I need to investigate further, Mary. We do have a few labor laws, but I'm not sure what they cover. Normally wages aren't a problem. I'll have to do some research and check this out. If we find that he's employing workers illegally, that might be a way to stop him."

With that the meeting broke up, and as the merchants left, Emily thanked them for coming and asked them to provide her with any information they could, even anonymously, if they were worried about George's retaliations.

Once Emily and Esmeralda were on their own, they walked down the wide hall to their office as Emily said, "You were pretty quiet in there. What do you think about what George is doing? And how could he know anything?"

Esmeralda said, "That man is pure evil. Wish I could just flame him. But seriously, do you think he's found out about the alternate timeline, the way this world was before our sentient planet stepped in and sent the dragons and riders back in time? We've kept that information pretty quiet. I don't see how he could have found out, but if he has, well, that could spell real trouble." Esmeralda curled herself up next to Emily's desk and watched as Emily moved around the large office. Everything in the dragon riders' buildings was built to allow dragons plenty of room to participate in any events.

"I know," said Emily as she sat at her desk after making herself a cup of tea. "I think I need to have a word with Chloe. Maybe I'll head over to the library and see if she's free for lunch."

Just then a young man, tall, slim, with blond hair and deep blue eyes, walked into the office, saying, "So how did the meeting go?"

"Ah, Rupert, just the person I need," said Emily, motioning her second in command to a chair. "The meeting was just about the disaster you predicted. George is definitely up to something, and I need you to find out what."

"Excellent," said Rupert, as a big grin spread across his face, and then quickly, realizing how that sounded, added, "I didn't mean that it's excellent that George is up to something. Just that you have a real job for me. Do you have any idea how boring it is most of the time being your second in command?"

Esmeralda laughed, and Emily thought she'd never tire of hearing her dragon chuckle. It was such a deep melodious chuckle that it always brought a smile to her face and heart.

"I know, you two, that I don't delegate at all well, but with that being said, Rupert, I do need some real sleuthing, as well as some legal research. I think you and Hannah are just the people for this. My little sister—well, she isn't so little, so I'd better say your wife—said something about wanting to be a dragon rider lawyer, so she can start training."

"She's been doing a lot of reading in her free time," acknowledged Rupert, "and Chloe's gotten her some great resources. Hannah has a real knack for all the legal terminology, which just seems like so much jargon to me."

"We're going to need that skill," said Emily, and she went on to tell Rupert what Mary had said about George's employment practices.

"That's nasty," said Rupert.

"And I'm hoping illegal as well," said Emily. "But there's more and this could be a lot worse."

Emily went on to explain how George had demanded so-called hidden information, stating that he knew the riders were keeping secrets.

Once she explained this, Emily said, "We need to know what he knows, or suspects, and how he's getting access to rider information. But we can't let him know that we're looking into him. Can you do that?"

"Yes," said Rupert, "and I'll ask Jake for help as well, since he supervises all the rider training."

"My brother will be able to help, I'm sure, but the fewer people who know, the better, OK?"

"Right," said Rupert. "I'm on it."

With that he eagerly bounced out of the office, not noticing the smiles on both Emily's and Esmeralda's faces.

"And I'm off to the library then," said Emily. "Catch you later."

— 4 —

LUNCH WITH A MAGE

Chloe—a young woman in her midtwenties, tall and thin with midlength dark red hair, blue eyes, freckles, and fair skin—spent her morning in her office, touching base with her Pathfinder students before they took off for the summer. She was not only the world's only mage, but she was also the head of Pathfinder Academy, a job she just loved. It did her heart good to see students who were not interested in or suited to following a traditional path strike out on their own and forge their way.

She looked around her office, located just off the library's main room, and realized she was definitely in need of some tea. She walked over to the small kitchen area in the far corner of her office and, using some of her magic, heated up a mug of tea. She brought it back to her desk and sat, pulling the folder for the next and final meeting of the day. This meeting was with Arryn, and as Arryn walked into Chloe's office, Chloe couldn't help but notice how much better she looked than when she'd been rescued from a really horrible situation just a short time ago. She was sixteen years old and would always be thin and tall, but at least she wasn't unnaturally thin. Her color was also much better, her naturally pale complexion set off by her brown hair and brown eyes. Most importantly, there was a real sparkle in her eyes now, a sparkle due in large measure to having a really good place to stay, fostering with Amy and Todd (retired dragon riders and Emily's parents); a girlfriend, Rya, who was apprenticing as a carpenter with her uncle Clyde; and a real desire to become a librarian, the path she'd chosen at Pathfinder.

"How's it going?" said Chloe after she indicated that Arryn should sit.

"Really well," said Arryn, with enthusiasm. "But I wanted to talk to you about summer."

"Sure thing," said Chloe, and then she smiled as she noticed Calliope jumping from Chloe's desk, where she'd been acting as a paperweight to all Chloe's files, into Arryn's lap. The library cat—as Calliope (a lovely calico cat, mostly white but with orange, brown, and black spots) labeled herself—had really taken to Arryn, putting her stamp of approval on Arryn's choice of professions.

As Arryn petted Calliope and Calliope's purrs grew almost deafening, Arryn said, "Well, you know that Rya's going to Bertha's for a month to study her powers as nature's empath."

"Yes," said Chloe.

"Well, I thought that since she'd be away and since she was studying, well I'd really like to work in the library, if that's OK," said Arryn in a rush.

Chloe laughed and said, "Of course it's OK. The library is always open, and you know that Libby would unlock her doors for you even if it weren't. That's one of the many advantages to having a sentient library who can look after herself."

Arryn gave a wry smile and said, "Yeah, that's true. Well, I don't know why, but I just have this feeling that the library is going to grow soon."

"Grow," said Chloe in a puzzled voice.

"Yeah, sounds weird, I know," said Arryn.

"Not entirely," said Chloe. "After all, I've shared with you what the library looked like when I first came to Pathfinder and how part of my mage training was changing the inside so that it better fit our needs, adding offices for William and Gregory, a lab (which was first used to build the telescope and then turned into a teaching lab for students), an astronomical observatory on the added second floor, and finally my own apartment in the back. I'd say that Libby has changed quite a bit, even though her exterior remains the same."

"Well, I'm getting the impression that this change is going to have more to do with the library contents. I'm not sure, and maybe I'm just hoping, but I want to spend the summer making sure I'm really familiar with everything that's already here. That way I can also help people when they do come in, not that we get a lot of people, but I'd like to see that change as well," said Arryn.

"I like your thoughts," said Chloe as she picked up Arryn's paperwork and looked it over before she continued. "I know you said that you wanted another year at Pathfinder, but, you know, you really could graduate by the end of summer if you do this."

"I'm not in a hurry," said Arryn quickly. "And I have so much to learn." She paused and looked down at Calliope. Then she added softly, "And Rya still has a number of years on her apprenticeship so…"

Chloe smiled and said, "I get it, but hear me out. What I'm proposing is that you study this summer with Libby helping. That should make you qualified by summer's end to be a librarian apprentice, and I'd also like to make you my assistant principal in training."

"What," exclaimed Rya. "Really?"

"Before you get too excited, you might want to talk with Rupert, who's in the same position with Emily. You'll be getting a bunch of boring paperwork. In addition, I'd like you to help with any students who might need library resources because I too am hoping to build that part of our studies for any who are so inclined.

"Then next year you would not be a student, but instead an apprentice working toward your master library apprenticeship, which in turn would be followed by becoming a full librarian. It will take you about the same length of time as Rya's apprenticeship, if that's any help," Chloe concluded.

"Oh, that would be perfect," said Arryn, blushing slightly.

"But I don't want you here all the time. Not that we don't enjoy having you here," she said as she glanced from Calliope to Shosty, the library dog, a small tan dog with a white underbelly and a tail that curled nicely above his back, who was now asleep under Arryn's chair.

Chloe continued, "I know you are also working with Todd on his inventions and that both of you really enjoy doing that."

"Yeah," said Arryn with enthusiasm. "Do you know what he's working on now? He's trying to make a longer-lasting solar battery."

"Goodness," said Chloe. "What for?"

"That's the great thing about Todd," said Arryn. "He really doesn't care or plan how he's going to use it. He says when the need arises, he'll be ready."

Chloe laughed and said, "That's Todd all right."

"And I also learn so much from Amy," continued Arryn. "I'm getting to be a pretty good cook, or so she says."

"Keep at it," said Chloe, a bit wistfully. "That's something I never was interested in or showed any abilities for, but it's really important."

Arryn nodded and then said, "But more than that, and the household management skills she's taught me, it's her way with people. I'm learning so much about how to listen, how to hear between the words. I don't know if she even realizes what a gift she has, but I've been observing how she interacts in a lot of different situations, and I'm realizing that I need those skills too as a librarian, so that I can really understand what people want, sometimes even when they don't."

"That's very perceptive of you," said Chloe. "I've learned a lot from her as well. Like you, I was one of Amy and Todd's fosters, and like you, since I wasn't a dragon rider, I got to foster with them for six years. I suspect she's always had empathic abilities, but certainly raising six children and a number of fosters as well, not to mention being married to Todd, her abilities and people skills have reached a level that few could achieve. I'm glad you've picked up on that as those skills can't really be taught, but they will serve you well in all aspects of your life."

"Definitely," said Arryn. "So while Rya's away, I want to study in the library, as well as continue helping Todd and Amy."

"I think that's an excellent summer plan," said Chloe.

With that, Arryn gently lifted Calliope and placed her back in her favorite spot atop Chloe's papers, scooted her chair back carefully so as not to bump Shosty, and stood. Of course once she'd managed this, Shosty jumped up, so he could say goodbye. Chloe walked around her desk and gave Arryn a hug, saying, "I'm glad you'll be around this summer."

Once Arryn had left, Chloe resumed making notes on her file. She was just finishing that up when Shosty raced out of her office to let her know that they had another visitor. Calliope merely lifted her head as Emily walked into the office. "Hi there," Chloe said, smiling as Emily entered. "Great idea about having lunch. Thanks for your telepathic invitation. I'm swamped with end-of-the-school-year paperwork and can really use a break."

"I really appreciate your seeing me on such short notice. I've had a difficult morning and also needed a break," said Emily as she moved over to the comfy chair near the couch. She flopped into the chair and sighed. Calliope jumped off Chloe's desk, where she'd been holding down some papers, and plopped herself in Emily's lap.

"What am I missing?" said Shosty as he came barreling around the corner, sliding through the door into Chloe's office.

Chloe and Emily laughed, and Emily said, "Hi, Shosty. My how you've grown!"

"Thanks," said Shosty, standing as proudly and tall as only a puppy could.

You're such a showoff, said Calliope telepathically, so both Emily and Chloe could hear.

Chloe stood and moved from her desk to the couch, using a hand to slip her midlength dark red hair behind her ears as she sat. Shosty jumped up into Chloe's lap, which Calliope hissed at briefly but then allowed. Chloe looked at Emily and said, "So it sounds as if you've had a tough day so far. How about we start with lunch, and then you can tell me all about it."

"Sounds like a plan. You know, you may be half my age, but you always seem to know what I need," laughed Emily.

"Hey, you're only forty-three! Don't make it sound as if you are ancient. And I am a mage after all. Now, how about some vegetable soup and bread, with herbal tea, as well?"

Before Emily could do more than nod, the lunch appeared on the table in front of them. Emily smiled and said, "It doesn't matter how many times you 'magic' up something, it always amazes me."

"Better than eating what I could actually cook," said Chloe. She shooed Shosty off the couch as Emily lifted Calliope down to the floor; Chloe made sure they each got treats before she handed a bowl of soup over to Emily.

Once each of them had taken the edge off their hunger, Emily said, "So how's the winding down of the school year going? Another successful year at Pathfinder Academy, I'm assuming."

"Yes, it's been a great year for all nine students, and in fact all of them have elected to stay for another year, which pleases me. It gives them more time to pursue their chosen fields, and at least by now, all of them have chosen a field. That process took longer for some than others, but that's fine."

Chloe stopped to drink some tea and then asked, "But what about you and your morning?"

Emily proceeded to relate all the events from the merchant's meeting, as they had happened. Once she was finished, Chloe just stared at her for a few minutes and then said, "What do you think George really knows? And how?"

"That's the real worry, of course," said Emily, frowning. "I really thought we'd kept knowledge of the time travel and alternate world pretty quiet. People in general really don't need to know that humans nearly destroyed this planet and it was only saved when the planet herself stepped in and tossed the few remaining dragons and riders back in time to try things again and do a better job."

"I agree," said Chloe. "And Bertha, as our world's ursine seer, has guarded all the knowledge from that time, releasing only what we need to know when we actually need it. She's a wise old bear, and our world is now on a very different path from the destructive, polluted one seen in the purple dragons' memories."

"Having seen those images that Esmeralda and Matilda hold, I never want to experience anything like that," said Emily with conviction, "and we have to do everything we can to protect our world and all the life on it. From the little bit we know about that alternate timeline, its failure was caused by greedy people just like George."

"First off, we need to find out where he's getting his information," said Chloe.

"I've already asked Rupert to start investigating," said Emily. "And I've asked him to get Hannah to look into George's employment practices."

Chloe chuckled and said, "Nice that she wants to be a lawyer. And nice also that you can keep it all in the family! Guess that's what comes of having such a large family, with five siblings, three of them also being riders."

Emily nodded. "Yes, and I know I can trust them, as well as all their respective spouses. Rupert is going to talk with Jake, as I seem to remember that George has a son who is friends with some of the riders who are in training."

"And there are only a very few nonriders who know about the time shift, and none of them would be likely sources either," said Chloe.

"I was so startled when George started demanding information that I didn't even know how to respond. We've never had a threat like that. I was so glad that Bertha had alerted me to his appearance at her cave last week."

"She told me as well, and I've been talking with Libby, but I don't want to panic yet. I think the first step is to try to stop George's own move toward making fabric. That sounds problematic on a number of levels," said Chloe.

"We've gotten a number of reports about black smoke rising from his plant already, and certainly that has to stop," said Emily.

"And the abuse of employees," added Chloe. "That is definitely not how our world works."

"I sure hope we can do something to stop him," said Emily.

Just then a tall, thin woman with short, dark red hair that had turned mostly gray came storming into Chloe's office, shouting, "You have to do something!"

She stopped as soon as she saw that Chloe wasn't alone and then said, "Oh, sorry."

"Hi, Hazel," said Emily.

"Mom," added Chloe, "what do I have to do?"

Hazel looked at them both and then sat down on the couch next to her daughter. "This whole business with Ingrid just has me so upset. And if having a daughter who's the world's only mage isn't worth something, then what's the point. Can't you just whip her up a store with your magic?"

"Please, Mom, have some tea, take a deep breath, and tell me what's got you going now," said Chloe, passing a cup of tea to Hazel.

"Well, you know how that George Pontsby shoved her out of business. If that weren't bad enough, he's flooding the market with lousy second-rate fabric, and now your sister, Zelda, can't get fabric for the dresses she's designed. She's refusing, and rightly so, to use George's stuff because she says if she's going to put all the effort into designing clothes, she's not going to use shoddy materials. Her seamstresses all have complained about George's stuff, saying that it doesn't lay right."

"OK," said Emily, "but can't she still get her fabric from Ingrid?"

"Ah, now you've hit the problem," said Hazel. "Because Ingrid lost her store, she has nowhere to display her fabric. It's all crated up, and so no one can decide what to pick, as they can't see it. That's why I said you should just magic her up a store," concluded Hazel with a smug look.

"Mom, you know I can't do that. I can only use magic in very specific circumstances when regular means won't work."

"Yeah, like cooking," said her mother with heavy sarcasm in her voice.

"Actually, yes," said Chloe with a smile. "You of all people should know how much damage I could do if I did the actual cooking."

"But…," said Hazel.

"Hold on, Mom," said Chloe, raising a hand to slow her mother down. "We were just talking about finding ways to stop George, so how about trying to help us do it without magic."

Emily spoke up now. "Hazel, you're saying that the demand for Ingrid's fabric is still as strong as before, right? That the designers, like Zelda, and the seamstresses want her fabric. It isn't just the quilters?"

"Right," said Hazel. "Everyone who sews used to use Ingrid's fabric. Now, I guess those who are on really tight budgets are switching to George's, but anyone who's making anything they want to last or that they really care about is finding George's fabric too flimsy to use."

"I did have a thought," said Emily, "but I'm not sure how it would pan out. I need your ideas."

"Shoot," said Hazel as she reached for a chocolate chip cookie from the plate that had just appeared on the table.

"I was thinking that the riders' business-loan fund could simply buy Ingrid's fabric outright and then let it be resold at less than what George is selling his for."

"Brilliant," said Hazel, "but your fund would take quite a hit financially."

"Let me worry about that," said Emily. "One of the things that George was ranting about that really got my goat was that the riders help too much, helping the weak. But I don't see it like that, and neither do any of the other riders. We take the planet's mandate to us to care for all life very seriously. So if we do this, not only can we help Ingrid and all those needing fabric, but we can taunt George."

"OK," said Chloe, "sounds great. So what's the problem?"

"We're back to the problem Hazel mentioned earlier. We don't have the space in the headquarters for a store as large as Ingrid would need, and there isn't anywhere in the business district that does either. Buying the fabric but keeping it in crates wouldn't help anyone. Ingrid needs a storefront, and that's where I need the help."

Chloe and Hazel were quiet, furrowed brows on both of them indicating that they were thinking hard. Finally, Hazel said, "I've got a bit of an idea, but I don't know."

"Go ahead, Mom," said Chloe, nodding at her mother.

"Well, now that Zelda's got a place of her own, ever since the divorce really, my house has felt just way too large for just me and your grandma. And she's getting to the point where she can't manage stairs anymore. I'm thinking of moving."

"That's a big decision, Mom," said Chloe. "That home has been in the family since the first rider."

"I know, but what use is it? Maybe Zelda might want it eventually, but she's not showing any signs of settling into the kind of life where she'd need it. And you are very happy with your apartment at the back of the library. I can't see you wanting it either."

Emily said, "What if we found you a small house, suitable for you and your mother, but you didn't give up ownership of what you have now? At least for the moment. Chloe's right. This is a big decision, and I wouldn't want you to regret it down the road."

"Well, something needs to happen now to stop George and help Ingrid," said Hazel.

Chloe said, "Hey, where's Ingrid living now? Doesn't she have that cute little purple house on the edge of town?"

"Yes," said Hazel. "So?"

"What about a house swap? The second floor of your house would be easy to make into living quarters, and the main floor has such wonderful big rooms that it wouldn't take much to put in shelving for fabric. She could then live above her shop, if that appealed to her. Then you and Grandma could move into her home, which is only a one-story house."

"Gads," said Emily, "that might really work. We need to talk to Ingrid. Nothing can happen without her."

"Yes, but we also need to keep it all quiet. George can't get wind of it," said Chloe.

"And there will be a fair amount of work needed to redo my place to make it into a store, even if the basic layout is good," said Hazel.

Emily said, "Let me contact Ingrid this afternoon and see what she thinks. And, Hazel, maybe you can start packing?"

"Definitely," said Hazel with enthusiasm.

"I'll come over after work and help you, Mom, and I'm sure Zelda will as well."

"And I think your dad will help also. Maybe he'll bring Todd."

Emily laughed. "Those two will love to work on the renovations. My dad likes nothing better, and I think he and Henry make a good team. Gregory will help also, and I'm guessing my brothers as well. Don't worry; we'll have lots of help for you, maybe even more than you want."

Everyone stood and Emily said, "I'll let you know what Ingrid says as soon as I know anything."

"And no matter what," said Hazel, "I do think it's time for a move, so I hope Ingrid likes the idea, but otherwise, I'll be looking for somewhere to take Mom and me."

Chloe gave her mother a big hug and said, "It will all work out! And thanks so much, Mom, for the great idea."

— 5 —
A NEW STORE

Emily decided to walk to Ingrid's house. She thought that bringing Ingrid to her office might set off speculations, so she took a chance at finding Ingrid home. Emily left the library and headed down Main Street. She quickly reached the edge of town and turned right. It didn't take her long to reach Ingrid's home, which was actually just outside the business zone. Emily's first impression of the house was that it was really cute, with pink shutters on the windows and a pink front door to set off the purple house.

Emily walked up three steps to the front door and knocked. Ingrid answered the knock, and Emily thought how stressed she looked. Her short blond hair was disheveled, standing up in the back a bit, and her eyes had deep dark circles under them.

"Hi, Ingrid," said Emily. "I wonder if I might come in and talk to you for a bit."

Ingrid stood aside to let Emily in the door as she said in a listless voice, "I guess."

Ingrid led Emily into the kitchen area, and they sat at the table. "Sorry, I should have offered. Would you like some tea?"

"No, I'm fine," said Emily, "and I'm here to let you know what some of us have been thinking, which may help you out a great deal."

"Oh?" said Ingrid, her voice rising in a question, and for the first time she looked as if she might be a bit interested.

"First, I don't know if you are aware of the reaction to the loss of your fabulous shop, but it has hit a lot of people really hard."

"Hasn't done wonders for me either," said Ingrid wryly.

"I know, and in addition, people are really upset by what George has done and continues to do. So several of us put our heads together."

Emily went on to relate the information from the merchants' meeting, followed by her conversation with Chloe and finally Hazel's determination to get Ingrid's fabric back on the market.

"I hadn't really realized that the closing of my shop was affecting so many," said Ingrid in an amazed voice. "I have heard from my suppliers, and they're being hard hit as well. But what can I do?"

"Thanks to a suggestion of Hazel's, I think we may have an idea if you're willing," said Emily. She proceeded to explain about the house swap.

"But Hazel can't do that," protested Ingrid. "Her house is so large and beautiful. It's worth a lot more than mine."

"I know and I'm suggesting that the house stay in Hazel's name, at least for the moment. But she is right that it's way too big for just her and her mother, and her mother is having trouble with stairs, and they were looking for a smaller place even before your shop got closed."

"It's too generous," said Ingrid, shaking her head.

"Don't forget that her daughter Zelda is one of the designers who's having a hard time now that your fabric isn't available. And Hazel herself, as well as her mother, is involved because if garments aren't being made that will need their beadwork, then they also are out of luck."

"Well...," said Ingrid hesitantly.

"Please say that you'll try it," said Emily. "I know we can do this, and by having the dragon riders' fund underwrite it, you can sell fabric way below cost, which we hope will put George out of business."

"That's scary in itself," said Ingrid.

"How so?" asked Emily.

"I don't know if you realize just how nasty he is. He decides what he wants, and nothing will stand in his way. I tried to raise the funds to buy the building or else pay his outrageous rent, but he made it very clear with a number of not-so-veiled threats that I didn't have any option except to leave."

"You should have reported him," said Emily firmly.

"He never said anything in front of witnesses or put anything in writing, so it would just have been his word against mine. He's definitely smart and devious, as well as ruthless," said Ingrid sadly.

"Well, now that we know, I'll be sure you're protected. So what do you think?"

"I miss my store, and I'd really like to try it, if Hazel is sure," said Ingrid, with longing in her voice.

Emily laughed and said, "She's already packing. I'll let her know that we have a plan. And I've got trusted people, mostly my family, to call on to make it all happen. Let's just keep this quiet and not tell anyone else until you're ready to open again."

"The longer it is before George finds out," said Ingrid, "the better."

"Well, then, I'd better get things moving (pun intended). And just let me know when you need help."

They both stood and walked to the front door. "Please thank Hazel for me," said Ingrid. "I can't believe what a generous offer she has made."

Emily gave Ingrid a hug and said, "We all want your quilt shop back! It was always such a fun place, so bright and cheery.

Lots of people enjoyed it, not just quilters or seamstresses. And the likes of George have to be stopped. Hang in there, and you'll be back in business before you know it."

Emily walked back to her office with a spring in her step. As she walked, she contacted Chloe telepathically. *You can let your mom know that Ingrid has agreed. She almost didn't because she thinks Hazel is being way too generous, but honestly, she looks a wreck, and she really needs her store back.*

I suspected as much, answered Chloe. *And my mother is beside herself with joy, not only by the prospects of moving Grandma to a smaller place, but because there's nothing she likes better than helping, especially when it's her plan.*

Emily laughed. *I know, and she is an excellent organizer, so we'll let her run with it. I'll alert my family, so they'll be prepared when she contacts them.*

That evening Chloe, Emily, and Ingrid gathered at the large kitchen table in Hazel's home to discuss what needed to be done, both to turn Hazel's home into a store and to accomplish the house swapping. Hazel had set out a plate of chocolate chip cookies and mugs of tea.

Once everyone was comfortable, Hazel began. "First of all, Ingrid, are you truly OK with letting me and my mother move into your lovely home?"

"Oh, yes, Hazel," said Ingrid. "But I can't believe you'd be willing to part with this lovely home."

Hazel smiled and said, "I'm definitely ready for a smaller place, and my mom needs to be somewhere without stairs. She's in her room upstairs right now, and honestly, she spends most of her time there because she finds it too hard to go up and down the stairs. We've turned a couple of bedrooms into a suite for her, and I take her meals to her and sit with her when I can, but it's far from ideal."

"I understand," said Ingrid.

"So this will really help both of us," said Hazel. "Now what we need is your input about turning the main floor into a store. I don't know anything about that. Would you like a tour?"

"Yes," said Ingrid with enthusiasm. "This is really a wonderful opportunity for me, one that I never expected to have."

Hazel stood and said, "Well, let's get started then."

The other three women also stood and let Hazel lead the way. Emily pulled out a pad of paper and pen, so she could take notes.

"Obviously this is the kitchen," began Hazel, "and it is a large room. I'm not sure if you'd need such a big kitchen down here. Certainly we'll have to put a kitchen on the second floor when that is converted to your living quarters."

"Oh my," said Ingrid, evident dismay in her voice, "that seems like a lot of work."

Emily laughed and said, "My dad will be thrilled!"

Chloe nodded and said, "As will mine. Don't think about the work that needs to be done. Instead, just dream and let us know what your ideal store would be like. We'll let you know if anything you ask for is not feasible."

"OK," said Ingrid, "if you're sure."

As the other three women nodded, Ingrid went on, "Well, all I'd really need in the store is a small space with a table and a few chairs where I could make tea for customers."

Hazel smiled and nodded, saying, "That's what I figured. And much of this kitchen could be moved upstairs, so no worries there."

Hazel then turned and moved toward the dining room. "As you may have observed already, the main floor has four main rooms. In addition to the kitchen, there is the dining room here, then the living room, and finally a family room. All four rooms are about the same size. And between the living room and family room, there is the front foyer with a small hallway, which allows access to all four rooms, as well as the staircase to the second floor."

Ingrid nodded and then said, "Which direction does the house face? I didn't notice when I arrived."

"The front door, living room, and family room are on the north side of the house with the kitchen and dining room facing south," said Chloe.

"Hmm," said Ingrid, and the other three women were quiet to allow her time to think. Finally Ingrid said, "I'd like the family room to have space to hang quilts, so I can have my exhibits the way I did before, if you remember."

"Wonderful," said Emily. "I don't sew, but I used to love to see your exhibits, and you had some really unique ones."

"Since that room is on the northeast side of the home, it will get the least sun exposure, so if possible, maybe," said Ingrid a bit hesitantly, "maybe some large picture windows could be put in so that the exhibits could be seen by those who walk past?"

"An excellent idea," said Emily as she made more notes.

"If the exhibits were to hang around the edges of the room, with a few big pieces hanging near the windows, then there would be space in the middle for my classroom," continued Ingrid.

"The students could then be inspired by the exhibits," said Chloe.

Ingrid nodded and moved back toward the living room before saying, "The main cash register should be in here, and then both this room and the dining room are going to need a lot of shelving for all my bolts of fabric."

"How do you envision that layout," asked Chloe.

Ingrid smiled and said, "Rather like the stacks in your library, Chloe. If you remember my former store, there were aisles of shelving, and I then arranged the fabric by type and topic."

Hazel said, "Yes, it was wonderful! I always knew just where to go for my favorite fabrics. And I loved how you had the cutting table and checkout surrounded by a row of notions and two long rows of your brightest colored fabrics. It made the store so inviting."

"Thanks," said Ingrid, as Emily scribbled more notes.

"Anything else?" asked Chloe.

"Is there a restroom on this floor?" asked Ingrid. "I'll need a customer restroom and don't really want people going up to my apartment."

"There is," said Hazel, "along the hallway just past the stairs before you get to the kitchen."

Ingrid nodded and said, "Oh, of course! I remember now."

Emily consulted her notes and said, "Well, I think this is enough to start with."

Hazel headed toward the stairs and said, "Would you like to see upstairs?"

"Oh please," said Ingrid, and the four women headed to the second floor.

As they reached the landing, Hazel said, "There are four bedrooms up here and two bathrooms. My bedroom has its own bathroom, and I've now given that to my mom. Shall we go say hi?"

Ingrid nodded, and Hazel led the group toward the main bedroom. She knocked on the door and waited for her mother to say, "Come in."

They walked in and saw that what used to be the main bedroom had been turned into a large sitting room. Chloe's grandmother was sitting in a comfy chair, with an afghan over her legs. Chloe ran over and gave her grandmother a hug and said, "You're looking very comfy, Gran."

Julia smiled and said, "Good to see you, Chloe. And you too, Emily." She nodded toward Emily. "And, Ingrid! Wonderful that you'll have a store again. I've missed yours. Will you have space to display some of my beadwork?"

Ingrid smiled and said, "Of course, Julia. Just as I did before."

Julia nodded and said, "And you're really going to let Hazel and I have your cute home?"

"Most definitely," said Ingrid. "I think I'm getting the better part of this deal."

"Never," said Julia. "I'm so looking forward to not being confined as I am now." Then after a moment she said, "Oh, don't get me wrong. Hazel and my granddaughters have done everything they can to make me comfortable, but I'll be one hundred two this fall, and I don't get around as easily as I used to."

Emily put a hand on Julia's thin shoulder and said, "You really are a remarkable woman and an inspiration to us all. I will consider myself very lucky if I'm even half as sharp as you are if I live to be as old."

Julia chuckled and said, "Don't worry, young one. You will I'm sure."

Hazel said, "Well, we need to see the rest of the house, Mom, and you need your rest, so we'll say good-bye for now."

After the other three women had said their good-byes, Hazel showed them the rest of the second floor. She said, "I thought that you'd probably like the large bedroom, and in fact you might like the suite just as it is, so you could use the large bedroom for your living room."

Ingrid nodded, and Hazel went on. "And the bathroom off that room already has plumbing, so the bedroom next to it"— here Hazel moved to the room Julia was using as her bedroom— "could become your kitchen with a small eating area."

Hazel then led the women across the hall to the other two bedrooms, which had a bathroom between them. "These were Chloe's and Zelda's bedrooms, but you could take your pick, and then maybe the other one could be a dining room, if you entertain, or a den or whatever you'd like."

Ingrid walked around with an expression of wonder on her face. The other three left her to imagine how things might be, and finally, Ingrid nodded decisively and said, "Hazel, your ideas are great. I'd like the living room and kitchen as you suggest and between them, if possible, an eating area with a midsize table. I don't entertain much, so I really don't need a full dining room.

"And then I'd like the larger of the two bedrooms—was that yours, Chloe?"

As Chloe nodded, Ingrid went on, "I'd like that for my bedroom and the other, Zelda's old bedroom, for a study. It's nice that the bathroom can be accessed from either room. That makes things very convenient."

Hazel nodded with approval, and Emily made more notes, which she'd give to her dad. Then they all headed back downstairs, heading again for the kitchen. They sat, and Hazel refreshed the tea mugs as she said, "Now for the actual swapping of houses: I'd really like to do that as soon as possible."

Ingrid looked over at Hazel and said, "You want to be gone before the construction begins!"

Hazel's eyes twinkled, and she said, "Living through construction is never fun. And I think you should be onsite so that you can keep an eye on things and also give your input when needed."

"That makes sense," said Ingrid.

Emily smiled and said, "And honestly, Julia doesn't need to hear all the noise that my dad is going to make as he rips into things."

Chloe smiled and said, "Mom, would you like me to arrange the logistics of the move?"

Hazel winked and said, in a conspiratorial voice to Ingrid, "Never turn down a mage's offer of assistance." Then she turned to Chloe and said, "That would be wonderful."

Chloe laughed and said, "OK, no worries. School is out for the summer, and I've got plenty of time. Why don't you ladies work in your respective homes, marking items to be moved, especially furniture. Ingrid, I'd think that your new apartment will be about the same size as your current home, so you can no doubt bring all your furniture if you want it. Mom, you're going to have to decide what will fit and what won't."

Hazel nodded and said, "I've already been doing some of that and maybe tomorrow." She turned to Ingrid. "I could come over and get a tour of your place?"

"Definitely," said Ingrid. "How about nine o'clock?"

"Works for me," said Hazel.

"And I'll ask Rupert and Hannah," said Emily, "if they can help you both with packing."

"Thanks," said Ingrid.

"That would be very nice," said Hazel.

With that the gathering broke up. As Hazel saw the other three to the front door, she said, "Emily, will you talk with Todd and my ex and see when they want to come over to plan things?"

"Certainly," said Emily, "and with any luck we can have you both moved by the end of the week."

— 6 —

CONSTRUCTION

Early the next morning, Emily, Esmeralda, and Chloe arrived at Hazel's to meet with Todd and Amy (Emily's parents), Harvey (Chloe's dad), and both Hazel and Ingrid to discuss where the renovations would begin and how the swapping of houses would proceed. Todd and Harvey discussed all the things that Ingrid had asked for the night before, walking through both floors of the house, talking between themselves, muttering at times, as the rest of the group waited in the kitchen.

Finally, after an hour of planning, the two men returned to the kitchen as Todd, grinning, said, "This is going to be a lot of fun!"

Hazel said with a smile, "If that's the case, I want to move now."

Todd nodded and said, "That's definitely the first step. We stopped in to say hi to Julia, and I really don't want her here when we begin the demolition of the home she was born in."

Amy spoke up then and said, "I have a suggestion. Why don't I ask Julia if she'd be willing to come stay with us for a day or two. We have plenty of room, and I could look after her, leaving you (Hazel) and you (Ingrid) free to supervise the actual move. We could even start today."

"Oh, that would be so kind of you," said Hazel.

"I'll go up and ask her now," said Amy, "and if she agrees, I'll help her gather a few things together. Meanwhile, you guys can plan just how you want to shift the heavy stuff."

"Nice move," said Emily, smiling.

As Amy stood and left the kitchen, Hazel looked at Ingrid and said, "Are we rushing you?"

Ingrid shook her head and said, "Definitely not! And I don't really have a lot of things to move, other than the store, of course. I do have a lot of shelving and a great deal of fabric. But I don't want the fabric here during the construction phase. I couldn't keep it clean and free of dust."

Chloe said, "We'd thought about that," as she looked at Emily, who nodded, before Chloe continued, "and we also want it in a secure location."

"Yes," chimed in Emily. "I'd thought at first about letting you have some of the dragon riders large tents, but they wouldn't be secure enough, I'm afraid."

Chloe got up from the table and went to the kitchen window to look out into the backyard. She saw that it was secluded and private and that there was a large, flat, grassy area that was big enough for several of Emily's large tent.

Chloe turned back to the group and said, "Unless," and she grew thoughtful before continuing, "unless I could devise the right spell." She grew silent again, and the others waited.

Finally, she said, her eyes bright with excitement, "Yes, I can do it; I'm sure. I'll put wards around any tents to repel anyone who does not have the password, and I'll also cloak the tents with an invisibility spell."

"Really?" asked Ingrid.

"I promise," answered Chloe. "Your fabric will be as safe as if it were in a sealed vault. And I can also adjust any other climate considerations you might have."

"Thank you," whispered Ingrid.

"Great," said Emily. "So first, let's get Jupiter and Fern here, Dad, if your and Mom's dragons are willing to help."

Todd nodded and paused before he said, "I just sent them the message. They're on their way."

Ingrid looked at Todd in amazement and said, "How did you contact them?"

Todd grinned and said, "With telepathy. Jupiter and I are never really apart, and neither are Amy and Fern, and over the years, as Amy and I have grown closer, we've developed secondary bonds with each other's dragons, so the four of us are a solid unit."

Ingrid just shook her head and said, "I never imagined."

Just then they all looked up to see two gorgeous green dragons landing in the backyard.

Todd smiled and said, "They're ready."

Emily looked at Ingrid and said, "So do you want to return to your place and organize your fabric to be moved? I'll have Rupert and my sister, Hannah, meet you there to help."

"It all sounds too wonderful to be true," said Ingrid as she stood. "Thank you all so much!"

"You don't need to thank us," said Todd. "Harvey and I are thrilled to be allowed to do this, aren't we, Harvey?"

"Definitely," said Harvey, who then quickly added, as he looked at Hazel, "not that I'm glad to be demolishing your family home."

Hazel chuckled and said, "Don't worry, Harvey. I do understand, and I'm glad that you'll be a part of this shift. Our marriage wasn't wonderful, in large measure because of me, but I hope that we're now becoming good friends."

Harvey looked surprised but pleased as he nodded and said, "I hope so too."

With that, Ingrid left, eager to begin the move.

Emily took charge again and said, "I'll have a few dragons and their riders here to set up the tents, so they're ready when the fabric starts arriving. Now, what about the furniture? If we could get Ingrid's furniture out of her home, then there would be space to move what you want, Hazel."

Just then, Amy and Julia walked into the kitchen, Amy carrying a large suitcase and saying, "I'm going to take Julia to our place now."

"How?" asked Todd. "I don't think you can walk that far, Julia, can you?"

Julia smiled and gave Amy a conspiratorial grin before saying, "Amy has promised me a ride on Fern. I've always wanted to ride a dragon!"

Hazel looked at her mother in surprise and said, "Are you sure?"

"Most definitely," said her mother. "While I was never chosen to be a dragon rider, our family has a long and illustrious history as dragon riders, and my mother was bonded with a lovely green dragon."

Hazel went over and gave her mother a big hug and said, "Well then, go for it! You are amazing!"

Amy added, "Don't worry; Fern and I will take good care of her, Hazel. And, Todd, I'll have Fern join Jupiter at Ingrid's once we've gotten Julia home. Fern said that was the plan."

Todd nodded and went with Amy as Amy helped Julia out to the backyard. Julia watched as Fern lay down in the grass, stretching out a leg. Amy lifted Julia and then carefully carried her as she herself walked up Fern's outstretched leg. Amy then placed Julia on Fern's back in front of her own seat. Todd handed up Julia's suitcase just before Fern stood.

Everyone else had come out into the backyard to watch as Fern gently took flight, going just high enough to clear the house and the neighboring trees. Then she circled the home again, so Julia could get a good look before moving off toward home. Todd and Amy's house was within easy walking distance, but not if you were over one hundred years old.

The remainder of the day was filled with making the swapping of houses a reality. Emily drafted several more riders and their dragons to help set up the tents. Then she arranged a two-way ferry routine, bringing Ingrid's fabric, shelving, furniture, and possessions to Hazel's and taking Hazel's furniture and possessions back to Ingrid's. At both houses, since the weather allowed, Emily had the riders place the furniture in the respective backyards, so that there would be less chance of mixing things up.

Once all the items had been shifted to their new locations, Hazel went to her new home, and Ingrid, to hers so that they could each oversee the placement of items. Chloe was at Ingrid's new home when Ingrid arrived and was not surprised in the least that Ingrid's first concern was for her fabric. The two women went out to the tent that had been set up and walked into it.

"Wow," said Ingrid. "I had no idea that it would be this big!"

Emily joined them and said, "I had the riders put the shelving on the ground on the tarp that I had them lay, and then stack the bolts of fabric on top. I figured that would get the fabric farther away from the ground and protect it better."

Ingrid stepped over to the piles of fabric and said, "That was a great idea. Moisture or humidity will damage fabric faster than you might imagine."

"It shouldn't have to be here long," said Chloe. "If I know my dad and Todd, they'll make short work of the renovations. But while the fabric is here, I can magically adjust the humidity inside the tent, so there's no chance of damage."

"Please," said Ingrid, "if it's not too much trouble."

Chloe laughed and said, "Nope, it's really easy. Now, why don't you head into the house with Emily and tell the riders where you want your furniture, and I'll be in as soon as I secure this tent."

"Come on, Ingrid," said Emily, touching the young woman on her arm. "I've told the riders in both homes that you two are to have beds ready for sleep before they can leave, even if everything else doesn't get done."

Chloe smiled as she noticed Ingrid give one last look at the fabric before she followed Emily. Once they were gone, Chloe cast a spell to govern the humidity. She then exited the tent, fastened it shut, and put several spells on it to ward off any intruders, whether four-footed or two. Satisfied with her work, she then went inside the house long enough to be sure Emily didn't need her for anything before she headed over to her mom's new house to check in with her.

Todd and Harvey arrived back at Ingrid's new place first thing in the morning, and they were not surprised to find the front door standing open in welcome, as Ingrid, a mug of tea in her hand, walked through the rooms of the main floor, pacing off distances and talking to herself.

Todd said, "Hi, Ingrid. How did you sleep?"

"Oh, good to see you," said Ingrid, a bit distracted, and then she went on. "Well, it was really late when I finally called it a day, but I slept pretty well. It's always hard in a new place, and I also kept thinking and planning as I lay in bed, which didn't help at all. On top of that, I kept hearing strange noises. I guess that's just from being in a new place."

Harvey and Todd both chuckled, and then Todd said, "Well, we're here to begin. I've been trying to figure out the best way to do this quickly and still allow you to live here. I think Harvey and I have come up with a plan, and we'd value your input."

"Sure," said Ingrid, "although I should let you know that I know nothing about construction."

Harvey laughed and said, "Neither did I until I started help-ing Todd. You'll learn fast I'm sure."

"What I really want to run past you, Ingrid," Todd said, "is the overall plan of attack. What we think would be best would be if we moved the refrigerator and stove up to the second floor and positioned them where you will ultimately want them for your kitchen area. If we do that, making them functional, then you'll have everything you need to live on the second floor, even if the bathroom sink has to double as a kitchen sink for the time being."

Ingrid nodded and said, "I'm fine with that."

Todd continued, "Once that is done, which Harvey and I think we can manage today, we'll move on to making the first floor into your store. Finally, once your store is complete, and you'd even be able to open it for business, then we'll manage the final phase of making your apartment into a proper home."

Ingrid smiled and said, "I like your plan, and I'll do whatever I can to help."

"Thanks," said Todd.

And with that the renovations began. Harvey and Todd were able to set up Ingrid's temporary kitchen upstairs that day as he'd hoped. From Ingrid's perspective, the next two weeks passed in a blur of activity. In addition to Todd, who of course organized the renovations, and Harvey, his right hand, Emily's mom, Amy, kept the crews plied with food. Hazel also stopped by and helped Amy or anyone else once Julia was settled in their new home.

Jake and his husband, William, showed up regularly to help with the interior renovations. Jake didn't have as much time to give as William did, since Emily's next-to-oldest brother was in charge of the three classes of dragon rider apprentices, but William was his own boss, and with his office located in the library, only Chloe would notice if he wasn't there. William's work in telepathic communications frequently took him out of the office and into the field to explore other telepathic beings so that his absence was definitely not something that anyone would remark on. Since both Jake and William were riders, that meant two more dragons, Harmony (a lovely warm brown dragon) and Spruce (William's deep green dragon), to assist with transport, bringing in needed building materials and supplies.

Chloe stopped by one evening and smiled at the gathering of dragons. Hazel came outside as Chloe walked up and Chloe said, "Well, Mom, you always wanted a dragon rider in the family. Looks as if you have more dragons than you know what to do with."

Hazel laughed and said, "It's funny how things worked out. And honestly, I'm so proud of you that it doesn't feel as if we've lost out at all. Sure, our family came here in the time shift, and we had many generations of riders, but you know what, we never had a mage. No one did. And now you are the only one. That's pretty darned special."

"How's Grandma adjusting to her new home?" Chloe asked.

"She's in her element," laughed Hazel. "When the riders aren't needed here, they're over at our new home helping to set things to rights there. They are all deferring to her, asking her what she thinks, and she just sits in a chair in the center of the room and lets them know how a home ought to be set up."

"Do they listen?" asked Chloe.

"Sometimes," said Hazel, "and the funny thing is that she doesn't seem to care whether they agree or not."

After four weeks Todd pronounced the renovations complete, and then everyone pitched in to help Ingrid set the store up. Chloe had asked a couple of the Pathfinder students who were studying art to make a banner to hang over the front door, as well as various signs to guide shoppers through the four large rooms on the main floor. There was plenty of room for all the fabric, and Ingrid's tables and sewing machines were set up in an alcove Todd designed for the classroom. Ingrid still had the quilts from the show that had been hanging in her old store, and so those were rehung now in the newly designed gallery.

The day before the opening, a reporter from Havenshold's weekly newspaper was invited for a preview. The reporter was shown through the new store and given the information about the sale prices for the grand opening. The article would appear three days after the store actually opened, but Ingrid didn't want to chance George finding out ahead of time. She'd already told both Chloe and Emily that sometimes, late at night, she'd gotten the feeling that someone was watching her. She'd never seen anyone, and she hoped it was just her unfamiliarity with her new living space, but it did make her uneasy.

Amy, Hannah, and Emily helped Ingrid set up her new home on the second floor. As they'd planned at the beginning of the remodel, the existing four bedrooms and two baths had been modified according to Ingrid's needs. Todd and his crew had used the largest bedroom for a great room with Ingrid's living-room and dining-room furniture. They'd then turned the smallest bedroom into a functional kitchen, leaving Ingrid with a bedroom for herself and a guest bedroom or study, depending on her preferences. Amy supervised the decorating, including painting the walls, after she'd visited Ingrid's small home to see what her preferences were. Ingrid was so busy setting up the store that the others really wanted to surprise her.

Chloe helped her mother and grandmother move, and she was relieved that Hazel seemed enchanted with the way Ingrid's house was done. Hazel had always gone for neutrals, so Chloe wasn't sure how she'd take to a house painted in bright colors, but Hazel seemed ready for an adventure.

"And after all," said Hazel, "I can always paint later. Grandma seems happy to be in a green room, and I love the blue master bedroom. I may be the only one I know with a pink living room and an orange kitchen, but it is all very cheery and inviting."

Chloe gave her mother a big hug and said, "You really are wonderful, Mom!"

Hazel looked surprised by her daughter's reaction, but also very pleased.

The morning of the opening was a glorious spring day. Summer was nearly upon them, and that seemed obvious on a day that was both warm and breezy. Hazel went through the business district of Havenshold, putting up flyers announcing Ingrid's grand opening, and soon people were flocking out to the edge of town to see the new store.

"Wow," was the general response as people walked through the new space. Once the shoppers noticed the sale prices, they began grabbing bolts of fabric off the shelves and lining up to have their fabric cut. Ingrid had more than she could handle, but Hazel and Zelda, who couldn't wait to get into the store, quickly stepped behind the counter and began cutting as well. Chloe, who'd taken the morning off, manned the cash register, and soon they were all working in sync so that customers were served quickly and efficiently.

However, Chloe noticed that no one seemed ready to leave even though they had their purchases. They just seemed happy to have Ingrid's Quilt Shop back in business. Emily had also taken the day off to be at the opening, and she wandered easily through the throng of shoppers, listening to the comments, noticing who was there, and keeping an eye out for anyone who seemed unhappy. She was very pleased to note that everyone was really happy, both with the store and their purchases.

Everything was going all fantastically until late afternoon when George came storming into the shop. As soon as he walked in, the conversation in the store stopped. He walked all the way through, glaring at everyone and everything. When he saw the sign with the reduced prices, his jaw dropped open, and then he started shouting.

"You can't do this," he yelled.

Emily immediately stepped toward him and said, "Can't do what, George?"

"These prices," he spluttered. "There is no way you can make money selling at these prices."

"But that's our worry. What if we don't care about making money?"

"You have to care," he shouted. "What other point is there to being in business?"

"Again, not your problem. Ingrid is entitled to run her shop any way she wants. She isn't breaking any laws, and look," said Emily, pointing to the shoppers, who were still very quiet but smiling, "her customers are happy."

"Of course they're happy," snapped George. "They're stealing fabric. But others won't be happy."

"What others?" asked Emily innocently. "Aren't you the only other person selling fabric in Havenshold?"

George turned bright red in the face and snapped, "You'll be sorry. You can't do this to me."

"Is that a threat?" asked Emily.

"You're damned right it is," said George.

Emily lowered her voice to a near whisper and said, "Be careful how you throw threats around, George. You could get yourself in trouble if you don't watch out."

George looked around the room and seemed to realize that everyone there had heard him. He turned and stormed out of the store, slamming the door behind him.

As soon as George had left, everyone in the store cheered loudly. Soon they were shouting, "Hooray for Ingrid," and "Ingrid's the best."

Once the customers had left, Emily helped Ingrid close the shop. Ingrid was both excited and terrified. "It was so good to be open again, but what about George?" she asked.

Chloe was also still there, helping Amy and Hazel shelve bolts of fabric, as there hadn't been time during the day to put them back. "I agree with Ingrid that George is a problem. However, I think I have an answer. I'll weave a protection spell over the entire house, the way I did earlier with the storage tent in the backyard. I'll need to put it on at the end of each day and then remove it the next day when you open, but it will cause anything George does to backfire on him. At least you'll be able to sleep in peace, knowing that you are safe."

"You can do that," said Ingrid.

"I certainly can," said Chloe. "The only thing I can't control is what happens during the day, so we need to have some sort of presence here to watch the customers just in case George slips in something nasty when you are open."

Emily nodded and said, "I'll make sure we have at least a couple people here ostensibly helping you, Ingrid, during the day, so don't worry about a thing. But Chloe's right. There was quite a crowd here, and it would have been easy for someone to slip in something damaging without being noticed."

"Once I put the spell on, you won't be able to leave your home or have anyone in. It's a bit of a pain, but hopefully we won't have to do this for too long."

"Well, at the moment, I'm so tired that finding myself dinner and crashing into bed are about all I'm good for, so the restrictions don't seem onerous at all," said Ingrid. "And maybe I won't keep feeling as if someone is watching me, the way I have over the last few weeks."

"At least you and your store will be safe," said Emily, "while we deal with George."

Amy and Hazel came up to the front, and Hazel said, "We've gotten all the bolts of fabric put away, so they'll be in the right spot for tomorrow."

"Thank you both so much," said Ingrid.

"Hey, don't thank us," said Amy. "It's been really fun, and we're planning to be back tomorrow if that's OK."

"That would be wonderful," said Ingrid.

With that Amy, Hazel, Emily, and Chloe prepared to leave, after arranging to be back at nine the next morning, an hour before the shop opened. Once outside, Chloe put her protection spell on the entire house, saying, "Let's see what George makes of that."

— 7 —

RETALIATION

Chloe and Emily arrived at Ingrid's Quilt Shop at nine the next morning as promised. They walked up to the front door, and Emily said, as she looked around the front yard, "What are all those rocks doing? They weren't here yesterday."

Chloe smiled as she undid the protection spell and then said, "Someone tried to throw rocks through Ingrid's windows. Somewhere in Havenshold he or she is sporting bruises."

"What?" said Emily, bewilderment in her voice.

Just then Ingrid came outside and said, "I was wondering why you two were just standing here."

Chloe laughed and pointed at the pile of rocks. "I'm guessing you didn't hear a thing last night."

"No, I slept very soundly," said Ingrid, "for the first time since I moved in."

"Well, as I was just saying to Emily, someone tried to smash your windows. But my protection spell is set up so that whatever harm people try to do to your home rebounds on them. Whoever did this would have discovered that the rocks flew back and hit them instead of hitting the windows."

"Fantastic," said Emily. "That's true justice."

Chloe nodded and said, "Judging by the number of rocks, the perpetrators obviously didn't believe what was happening, and I suspect got quite mad."

"So we need to keep our eyes out for someone with a bunch of fresh bruises," said Ingrid.

"Right," said Emily, "but I'm guessing that George didn't do this himself. He's too smart for that. Still, it's nice to know that you're safe, Ingrid."

"Yes," said Ingrid, who was still staring at the pile of rocks, "I don't think I really realized what lengths someone might go to in order to shut me down."

Chloe looked at her and said, "Please don't worry. Both you and your store will be protected, and just remember how many people are thrilled to have you open again. Havenshold really needs your shop, and they've already shown you what most people think."

"I know," said Ingrid, "and I'm grateful for their support."

"Now, what can we do to help you open for the day?" asked Emily as the three women entered the shop.

The second day was even more successful as the word was spreading that Ingrid was back in business. In fact, Ingrid sold so much fabric that her shelves had some bare spots. One customer in particular had not just bought a yard of this or a half yard of that, but rather bought the entire bolt of fabrics she liked.

Once the shop was closed for the day, Ingrid said, "I really need to contact my suppliers and start restocking."

"That's a nice problem to have," said Emily.

"Yes, but what about the cost?" asked Ingrid. "I've sold a lot in just two days, but since the prices are so low, it won't cover replacing the fabric."

"No worries," said Emily. "I told you that the dragon riders' funds would cover this until we can get George sorted. Can you have your suppliers send me their bills? I'll see that they are paid promptly."

"I don't see why not," said Ingrid.

"May I make a suggestion," said Chloe. Both women nodded, and Chloe said, "We don't want George to know what's happening, so would it work for you, Emily, to set up an account for Ingrid, one that was anonymously funded, and then have Ingrid pay directly? That way George wouldn't be able to find out how Ingrid is managing this."

"Great idea, Chloe," said Emily. "I hadn't thought of that, but even if we asked the suppliers to keep a secret, well, not everyone is good at that, and George might be able to bully information out of them."

Once they'd decided on the mechanics involved in getting Ingrid more fabric, Chloe and Emily left, with Chloe again putting a protection spell over the house.

Soon an easy routine developed around keeping Ingrid both safe and open for business. Amy and Hazel were thrilled to be able to spend the time in the quilt store, and they proved to be excellent at keeping an eye out for trouble. Hazel caught one lady who was carrying a bottle of ink. Just as the woman took the cap off the black ink bottle, Hazel asked her what her favorite fabric was and so startled the woman that she spilled the ink all over herself.

Hazel escorted the woman to Emily's office, and Emily questioned her. "Why did you want to destroy fabric?"

"I don't," said the woman, sobbing loudly. "But I had to. I'm in debt to George Pontsby, and he told me that he'd cancel my debt if I helped him out. And if I didn't, he'd foreclose on my home. My husband just died, and I really don't know what to do."

Emily handed the woman a handkerchief and then gave her a glass of water before continuing. Once the woman had calmed down a bit, Emily said, "First, you can always come to me if you are in trouble. You may not be aware of it, but the mission of all dragons and their riders is to help all in need. I'm sorry for your loss, but please don't fall into George's traps."

"Thank you, ma'am," said the woman. "I had no idea that's what you did, honestly."

"Not a problem," said Emily. "Tell me, did George give you anything in writing to prove that he'd cancel your debt?"

"No," said the woman, misery filling her voice.

"Were there any witnesses to his request and promise?" continued Emily.

The woman sighed deeply and said very quietly, "No."

"Don't worry," said Emily. "I do believe you. But I do wish we had proof. Obviously if I confront him, it will just be his word against yours."

"I'm so sorry," said the woman.

"You felt trapped, and I get that," said Emily. "And thankfully Hazel stopped you so that there was no damage, or else we'd have a bigger problem. But we have to get you out from under George's thumb."

"I don't know how that's going to happen," said the woman miserably. "He holds my mortgage."

"I think that you're going to find a hidden bag filled with your husband's life savings, a bag with more than enough to pay off the mortgage so that you own your home free and clear."

"But...But we never had that," said the woman.

"Your husband kept it as a secret, and you've just now found it," said Emily with a smile on her face. "Do you think you can make George believe that?"

"I'm not sure," said the woman.

"Well, you need to. And we need to make sure that there is a witness or two when you give George the full amount owing on your home. Do you have any family? What about friends?"

The woman thought for a minute or two and said, "Maybe my sons—they work in Alfredsville, but they're coming this weekend to see me."

"Perfect," said Emily. "Once George is paid off, we'll see about helping you to pay back your husband's stash, but don't worry about that now."

"Why are you being so nice? I nearly ruined a bunch of fabric," said the woman.

"You didn't ruin it, and you were being coerced by a very nasty bully, someone we really want to stop. As long as this isn't something you make a habit of, we'll say no more about it," said Emily.

Once they'd settled on all the details, Emily let the woman leave. Rupert then came in and said, "I've got something to report."

"Excellent," said Emily.

"First, I've discovered that George has a son who is good friends with some of the newest rider apprentices. The son, Patrick, hangs around the headquarters a lot. I don't know that's where the leak is, but it seems a good place to start. I've tried to befriend him, but he's really cautious around both me and Jake."

"Is Patrick close to his dad?" asked Emily.

"That's a good question," said Rupert. "I think he's more afraid of his dad. And I noticed this morning that Patrick has a black eye."

"Now, that is interesting," said Emily and explained about the rocks at Ingrid's a few days earlier. "Does Patrick have friends, other than the rider apprentices?"

"I haven't found that out yet," said Rupert.

"Well, keep digging, and good work," said Emily. "And what's Hannah uncovered?"

"Sadly, Draconia doesn't have a lot of laws governing hiring people. Hannah says that laws usually arise when there are problems so that an impartial ruling can be made. I'm not saying that there have never been disputes, but apparently there haven't been enough consistently to have laws formed."

"Well, this may be the situation that causes that to happen," said Emily. "We may need to involve Queen Clotilda and Matilda, but let's wait a bit on that. Can Hannah find anything on basic rights to shelter, food, and so forth?"

"She's looking, and she's trying a number of different angles, so let's hope so. She's also attempting to meet with some of his employees to talk with them, but so far she hasn't found anyone who's willing to talk."

"I think you should ask her not to approach anyone yet," said Emily. "It could be dangerous for both Hannah and anyone who actually is seen talking to her. We'll have to find a way to protect any informants before we take that route."

Rupert gave a big sigh of relief and said, "Thanks, Emily. I thought the same, but Hannah said I was just being an overprotective husband."

Emily laughed and then said, "So I can be the overprotective sister instead, huh? Still, I want to wait. If we could find anyone who is a former employee, that would be very helpful."

Rupert stood and said, "OK, I'll get Hannah onto that and then see if I can talk to Patrick's friends in the compound. He seems close to two of the apprentices, and I think Jake is going to find an excuse to have me help with an aspect of their training, so I can get to know them better."

"Excellent plan," said Emily. "Keep me posted, and meanwhile, no one is to do anything that might alert George to our investigation."

Before Emily headed home for dinner and a quiet evening with Gregory, she decided to stop in at the library and catch up with Chloe. She arrived at Chloe's office to find Chloe working on paperwork, with Calliope and Shosty helping. Chloe, looking up as Emily walked in, said, "Saved from my paperwork! I've been taking so much time off to help Ingrid that I've really gotten behind. I'm going to take a bunch of this home tonight to get caught up, but I'd really like a break. How about some tea?"

"That would be great. Gregory's expecting me home for dinner soon, so I can't stay long. But I thought we should catch up."

Over tea, Emily brought Chloe up to date not only with the ink-wielding woman but also with Rupert's investigations and Hannah's discouraging information.

"Well, I'm actually not surprised that Draconia doesn't have labor laws because thankfully our culture—and I think this is true for the other three nations as well—hasn't developed a large legal body. But at the moment, some laws would make it easier to prosecute George," concluded Chloe.

"But if we had a lot of laws, then we'd have tons of lawyers, judges, courts, and so on, so I guess I'm glad overall that we don't," agreed Emily.

"What normally happens in cases like this is that someone complains, and then you or Clotilda are called upon to decide. But for that to happen, we need to have someone—or even better, several someones—to complain. Then you can rule as the head of Havenshold, and then George can appeal to Clotilda when he doesn't like your ruling. But none of that can happen without a complaint, and it appears, especially after the information you gathered from that poor woman with the ink, that George has a stranglehold on his employees."

Emily stood and put her tea mug in the small sink in the corner of Chloe's office. Then she said, "Well, we'll figure something out, I'm sure, and hopefully before George strikes back."

"I hope so too," said Chloe. "It would be nice to get this all resolved so that I didn't have to keep putting protection spells on Ingrid's. Actually, when I get a moment, I could try making a spell that renews itself. Maybe Libby could help me with that."

"Having a sentient library who can turn herself into a woman you can chat with is certainly handy," said Emily. "And I'd be interested in seeing what she thinks about our George problem as well, especially his apparent knowledge of the other timeline."

"You're right," said Chloe. "I really need to talk with her. I'll get myself invited to breakfast with her tomorrow, and then when I arrive at Ingrid's, I'll update you."

"Excellent," said Emily. "Have a nice evening of paperwork."

— 8 —
INJURIES

Once Chloe was showered and dressed for the day in purple slacks with a green top, she, Calliope, and Shosty headed to the connecting door with Libby's apartment, knocked, and entered when they heard the cheery, "Come in."

Shosty bolted through the door as only a puppy can and raced right over to Libby. Libby, when she was in human form, appeared as an elderly lady, a bit plump, with white hair that occasionally stuck out and green twinkling eyes. This morning, she was dressed in a long skirt and a knitted green sweater. And as was usual with her, she was knitting, but she quickly put her knitting on the nearby table and patted her lap so that Shosty could jump right up and snuggle.

"Well, it's good to see you all," said Libby as Chloe and Calliope followed Shosty into the room and then sat across from Libby on the couch.

That dog is the limit, said Calliope.

Libby laughed and said, "Don't worry, Calliope. I have plenty of love for you, too. And what about breakfast?"

"Food," said Shosty, who could communicate both telepathically and with human speech but who usually chose the latter simply to irritate Calliope since she was limited to telepathy only. He hopped down from Libby's lap, his long curly tail wagging frantically.

"Yes, food," said Libby as she conjured up oatmeal and a cinnamon roll for Chloe and food bowls for both Shosty and Calliope.

"Thanks, Libby," said Chloe as all three of them enjoyed their food.

"So what can I help you with?" asked Libby once everyone was finished. Shosty was again nestled in Libby's lap, and Calliope was in Chloe's.

Chloe proceeded to tell Libby all about George Pontsby, and when she'd finished, she said, "Our main worry is his apparent knowledge of the time travel and the alternate reality. He seems determined to discover knowledge from that time, and we know that most of that would only harm our world, at least if it's used for personal gain."

"Hmm," said Libby thoughtfully. "And you think that he's using his son's friendship with the younger riders to discover information?"

"That's our current hypothesis. We can't think of any other way for George to have found out."

"Well, Bertha has released some of it as we've needed it, such as the telescope plans when the planet was threatened by the asteroid."

"True," said Chloe, "but I don't think that George is interested in things like telescopes. He seems to be looking for some kind of machines that can be powered by burning coal. Or maybe there are even worse options, but he's really polluted the air around his so-called fabric factory."

"Yes, that's what I was afraid of. He's not interested in using the thermal energy from the volcano? Jaluhz provides most of the energy for all four nations, after all."

"I know," said Chloe, "but he seems to have a grudge against the dragon riders, and after all they're the ones who trade the thermal energy for the good of all Draconia."

"Why does George care where he gets it?" asked Libby.

"I'm not sure, but apparently at the merchant's meeting, George ranted about weaklings who couldn't take care of themselves and how the riders just helped those who couldn't survive on their own."

"That's so sad," said Libby.

"I know," said Chloe. "He has no concept of compassion or working together. After all, what Emily has set up for Ingrid benefits many people, not just Ingrid."

"He's obviously very selfish and greedy."

"But what are we going to do about his knowledge of the alternate reality?" asked Chloe. "Should we alert Bertha?"

"Have you talked with Aster yet?" asked Libby. "She is Draconia's historian, after all, and she knows better than any of us what information is available more readily, say in books in the library."

"No, I haven't. She and Jasmine are off helping the smaller communities in Draconia. But maybe I should ask Emily to recall them, at least for a bit. I know they are fantastic ambassadors for the dragons and riders, but your point is well taken," concluded Chloe.

"And don't I remember that Rya is supposed to head to Bertha's in a week or so for more training?"

"Yes, and I think Harmony is planning to take Rya, but maybe Aster and Jasmine could go as well, making it a family outing with Aster's grandma and cousin," said Chloe.

"I just have a feeling that it would be good to have Aster and Jasmine there," said Libby. "So see if that would be OK with Emily."

"I will," said Chloe. "And do you think we should contact Bertha ourselves before then?"

"No, she's enjoying spending time with her kids, if you can call Berla and Boris kids since they are now full-grown bears! And I don't think George is an immediate threat, so just keep an eye on him," said Libby. "Bertha has already told us about George's threatening actions when he came to her cave, so she's aware of his intent. She really doesn't need anything more."

Chloe nodded and then shifted Calliope off her lap as she stood. "Well, thanks for breakfast. I'd better head out to Ingrid's and remove the protection spell. Oh, that reminds me. I know how to make a protection spell, but is there a way to make it more permanent and allow Ingrid to go in and out, even opening the store?"

Libby thought for a moment and then said, "I can't think of a way to do that and still give her full protection. After all, as you told me, one of her customers was caught trying to do damage. A spell wouldn't be able to tell the difference between people. If we were sure that George would act directly, then I could help you design an anti-George trap, so to speak. But he's demonstrating that he's going to use third parties to do his dirty work."

Chloe shrugged and said, "Yeah, that was the conclusion I came to also. I guess I'm just going to start and end my workdays at Ingrid's until this is sorted. Talk to you later!"

During Chloe's lunch hour, she headed over to Emily's office and asked her about bringing Aster and Jasmine back. "I think we need our resident historian," said Chloe, and she shared Libby's ideas.

"Hmm," said Emily, rifling through some papers. "It looks as if it will be about two weeks before I can bring them back. If

Harmony and Rya are going to see Bertha anyway, why don't I have Aster and Jasmine meet them there?"

"Yes, I think that would be fine," said Chloe. "Libby didn't think there was any immediate urgency. Bertha is uneasy, saying that something will happen, but she also doesn't seem to think it's imminent. And I know Harmony wanted to have some time with Rya as they travel to Bertha's even if it doesn't take more than a day. Rya's been working so hard with her uncle Clyde on her carpenter's apprenticeship that I think Harmony is planning a bit of time off for Rya before she begins working with Bertha."

"How's Rya doing, now that she doesn't have to communicate with Jaluhz to save Havenshold from imminent disaster?" asked Emily.

Chloe laughed and said, "She's doing fine, as far as I know. Her empathy with the planet, especially her ability to foretell the weather, is a big help in the construction business, but since the weather is something she's been able to predict easily since she was little, it isn't a big deal for her. And she's a born woodcarver, as well as carpenter. I really think her ability to feel the natural world is a major asset. She's able to sense the nature of the wood when she's carving. Anyway, the animals she's carved out of wood, including a figurine depicting Artemis, seem almost alive."

"Her bond with that lovely fox is unique. I mean, each nation has its bonded pairs—be it dragons and riders, gryphons and riders, unicorns and riders, or dolphins and riders—but no one has bonded with a different species except for Rya with Artemis," said Emily.

"Well, our world only has one mage, only one seer, and now only one nature empath, so I guess it's fitting that she should be part of a unique bonded pair," said Chloe. "Anyway, I'd better get back to work. I'll let Harmony know that Aster and Jasmine will meet them at Bertha's cave."

After Ingrid's store had been open for two weeks, Emily heard that George was really angry. Apparently he hadn't been able to sell any fabric, and now he was having to lay off his workers. Emily met with Hannah and Rupert to discuss this development.

"So, Hannah," said Emily, "if George has laid off workers, does this mean we might get someone to testify to his business practices?"

"I'm hoping so," said her younger sister. "But apparently he's allowing his workers to live in his substandard housing for the moment at least, so maybe they'll still be afraid to say anything in case they lose their housing."

"Is there any hope that we could get them different jobs?" asked Emily.

"I'm looking into that," said Hannah. "Unfortunately these workers aren't actually trained for making fabric the way Ingrid's suppliers do, using hand looms and so on. George went to some of the really small villages and offered jobs to those who couldn't find work at home. He's moved them away from family and friends and then taught them to run these machines he's designed. That's all they know."

"And they can't go back home," added Rupert, "because there's no work there either."

"How many workers are we talking about," asked Emily, "and what kind of work had they tried to do at home?"

"There are about twenty total," said Rupert, "and they came from family farms where there were too many hands already."

"Farms," said Emily thoughtfully. "I wonder if any of the large ranches in and around Havenshold, like the baron's place, could use some extra hands. If they each took a few, maybe we could get them all placed."

Rupert smiled and said, "I'll ask around."

Hannah said, "If they do get new jobs, then I'm sure I can get at least some of them to talk to me. Also, the word is spreading that George is really upset by the protection charm on Ingrid's shop."

Emily laughed and then said, "Well, if he weren't trying to damage it, he wouldn't know that there was a protection charm."

"True," said Hannah. "His knowledge damns him, but it's not good enough evidence."

When Chloe arrived at Ingrid's the next morning, she discovered a young man screaming, with his arms covered in burns. Running over to him, she saw that there was a burned-out torch and some charred wood next to him. Her first concern was obviously to get medical assistance, so she called telepathically to Emily. *I need help now for a young man who's been badly burned.*

Esmeralda and I will bring Dr. Brian right away, Emily responded.

While Chloe waited, she did her best to comfort the young man, covering him with a blanket and talking to him. "What's your name?" asked Chloe.

"P-P-Patrick," said the man.

"Help is on the way," said Chloe.

"I didn't want to do this," said Patrick. "But I knew my dad was really upset by this shop, and he was taking it out on everyone."

"Don't talk now. Just rest, and we'll get your burns treated. That's the most important thing at the moment."

Just then Esmeralda swooped down from the sky with Emily and Dr. Brian on her back. As soon as she'd landed, Dr. Brian jumped down, carrying his medical bag, and stepped over to Patrick.

He examined the burns, cut away the fabric of Patrick's shirt, and said, "I need to get him back to the hospital, so we can treat him."

"Esmeralda will fly the two of you back," said Emily. "I'll stay here with Chloe."

Once Esmeralda had headed back to the dragon riders' complex and the hospital, Emily said, "Do you know what happened?"

"I think so," said Chloe. "That's George's son, Patrick, and he said that his father was so upset by the business he was losing to Ingrid's store that he was making life miserable for everyone. So I think, but I'm not sure, that Patrick decided to take matters into his own hands and destroy the store."

"Oh dear," said Emily.

"Yes, and remember how I said that whatever anyone did to the house would just bounce back onto them? Well, he tried to start a fire, and the fire attacked him instead. He's really lucky that he hadn't gotten a large fire going, or it would have killed him," said Chloe.

"This is really going to anger George," said Emily. "Let's hope that Patrick isn't too badly injured. Still, he brought it on himself, as tough as that sounds. Imagine having a father like George."

Just then, Ingrid came out and said, "What happened to that young man? I didn't like to come out when you were tending to him, but I can't help but wonder if I'm somehow responsible."

"You aren't," said Emily. "He brought this on himself."

"And without my protection charm, things might have been a lot worse," said Chloe. "He might have burned down the house with you inside it."

Ingrid turned white as a sheet, looking as if she might faint. Emily had her sit on the front porch and was glad when Amy and Hazel arrived. Once Amy and Hazel learned what had happened, they took charge of Ingrid, getting her inside, plying her with hot sweet tea, and reassuring her that this was definitely not indicative of the way most people felt about either her or her shop.

Finally, when Ingrid was calmer and ready to open for the day, Emily and Chloe made their way out of the store.

"Well, I need to get back to the library," said Chloe to Emily as they reached the road. "I'm meeting with several students, but please let me know when you hear anything about Patrick's condition."

"I will," said Emily. "I'll stop at the hospital to see what the prognosis is, and then I have to find George and tell him what's happened."

"I sure don't envy you that task," said Chloe.

"No, but it's my responsibility."

When Emily reached the hospital, she talked with Nurse Beatrice, who just shook her head at the way this injury had happened. "Dr. Brian has sedated Patrick," Beatrice said, "and the burns have been treated. Patrick will heal, but there will also always be some scarring. Have you told his father?"

"That's where I'm headed now," said Emily.

"Good luck," said Nurse Beatrice.

Emily found Esmeralda, and they flew out to George's property. "It's easy to spot his place by the big black smoke cloud billowing from that tower," said Esmeralda.

"We really have to do something about his pollution," said Emily. "I know that some people do burn small amounts of coal for heat in the winter, but nothing on this scale. But we can't deal with that now."

"Shall I land in the front yard?" asked Esmeralda.

"Yes, let's get this over with," said Emily.

As Esmeralda landed George came out of his house and yelled, "So what are you doing on my property? I didn't invite you. Come to gloat?"

Emily got down from Esmeralda and said, "I'm sorry, George, but I have some bad news."

"What kind of news?"

"Patrick is in the hospital. He's been badly burned," said Emily.

"How did that happen?" asked George. "Did one of your dragons attack him?"

"No," said Emily. "Actually, he did it to himself. He was trying to burn down Ingrid's Quilt Shop. He thought that would help you."

"What!" shouted George. "I didn't ask him to do that."

"Maybe not, but he knew you were upset. What he didn't know is that there's a protection spell on the house, so whatever anyone tries to do rebounds on the perpetrator. So the fire he tried to set on the house burned him instead."

"So this is all your fault after all," shouted George.

"No," said Emily. "No one asked him to burn the house down."

"I don't care," said George. "If it weren't for you, none of this would have happened, and I'd still have my business. You're trying to ruin me, but you won't succeed."

"No one is trying to ruin you, George, and I'm very sorry that Patrick is hurt."

"Get out of here," snarled George. "I need to get to the hospital."

"Again," said Emily, "I'm so sorry that Patrick is hurt."

With that, Emily leaped onto Esmeralda, and they flew back to the riders' compound.

Chloe spent the day meeting with students. The school year was nearly over, and she wanted to document their studies and start the plans for next year. It was always an exciting time of the year and one she looked forward to.

When it was time to head back to put the protection spell on Ingrid's shop, Chloe decided that she'd take Shosty on his walk as well. "Keep an eye on the library while we're gone, Calliope."

Don't I always? Calliope answered.

It was a lovely early summer day, and Shosty was excited to be going on such a long walk. He had to sniff every bush and tree along the route, and Chloe enjoyed his enthusiasm and company. They'd nearly reached Ingrid's when suddenly Shosty growled. George stepped out from behind a large shrub and said, "You won't be putting any more spells on anything."

He then raised his rifle and fired directly at Chloe. Shosty charged at George as Chloe put up a hand to deflect the bullet. George gave Shosty a vicious kick, sending him into a tree. Shosty hit the tree with a loud thump, and the little dog crumpled.

George turned back to face Chloe, who'd turned to see Shosty, and he swung his rifle, hitting Chloe in the side of the head with a resounding thud. Chloe fell not far from Shosty, with blood oozing from the side of her head.

"That'll fix you busybodies," snarled George as he quickly fled the scene, leaving both Chloe and Shosty unconscious.

— 9 —

CALLIOPE'S RESCUE

As Chloe was struck, Calliope, sleeping in Chloe's office in the library, woke and gave an unearthly yell. Then she raced out of the office and ran around the library, looking for anyone who would help her, hopefully someone with telepathic abilities.

She tried William's office first, but he'd already left for the day. Then she ran toward Gregory's office, only to run smack into him.

"Whoa there, Calliope," said Gregory.

Calliope then raced for the front door, then back to Gregory, and then back to the door because she knew Gregory couldn't understand her telepathy. He had limited abilities and could understand Esmeralda when she spoke to him, but then that was because he was Emily's husband.

After Calliope had run back and forth several times, Gregory finally said, "If I didn't know better, I'd say you wanted to go out the door."

Thank heavens he got that much, thought Calliope as she continued to run to the front door.

When Gregory reached the door and opened it, Calliope ran outside, down the steps, and then looked back at Gregory. She then ran up the steps and back down again, turning toward

Gregory again. *Come on, figure it out. You're smart. You know all about volcanoes. Can't you understand a cat?*

Gregory scratched his head and finally said, "You want me to follow you?"

Yes, of course, thought Calliope as she then ran farther down the road.

"OK," said Gregory. "Lead on."

Calliope then ran as fast as she could, and soon Gregory was jogging to keep up. They had nearly reached Ingrid's Quilt Shop when Calliope turned into the bushes and used her loudest voice to get Gregory to follow.

But Gregory had no trouble sensing what Calliope wanted, and as soon as he stepped through the bushes, he saw Chloe and Shosty lying in the underbrush, both of them unconscious and blood seeping from Chloe's head.

Calliope sat between the two bodies and looked at Gregory, willing him to do something.

"Good thing you know what's going on, Calliope," said Gregory as he knelt beside Chloe. She wasn't bleeding badly, but she obviously needed immediate medical attention.

"Calliope," said Gregory, "wait here while I see if there's anyone at Ingrid's who can contact the hospital. Damn! Times like this I sure wish I were telepathic."

Me too, thought Calliope as Gregory took off at a run for Ingrid's. He wasn't gone long before he returned with Hazel.

Now, that's a lot of help, thought Calliope. *Hazel is no more telepathic than you are.*

As if Gregory could sense her thoughts, he said, "I found both Hazel and Amy there, and Amy has already called Emily telepathically, so they'll get medical help here soon, but someone had to stay at Ingrid's in case Chloe's attack is a prelude to another attack on Ingrid's, and Hazel wouldn't stay since it's her daughter who's injured."

OK, makes some sense, I guess, thought Calliope.

"Oh, Chloe," said Hazel as she knelt beside her daughter.

Gregory looked up and waved as he sensed Esmeralda's approach. For the second time in one day, she was carrying both Emily and Dr. Brian. Esmeralda landed in the road, and Emily and Dr. Brian pushed through the bushes. As they approached the injured pair, Calliope said, *Thank heavens, someone who can understand me.*

Emily looked at Calliope and said, "I understand you're the heroine in this scene. Thank you so much."

I knew the minute she was hit. And Shosty too.

"Well, I'm really glad you were able to get Gregory to understand," said Emily, bending down to pet Calliope.

Dr. Brian looked up from his patients and said, "It looks as if Chloe was battered with something hard, enough to break the skin but more importantly enough to knock her out and, I suspect, give her a concussion. Also, she has a head wound that I suspect is the result of being grazed by a bullet. Shosty was also struck hard. I suspect he was kicked, as it looks as if he might have fractured ribs. I need to get them both back to the hospital."

I won't leave them, said Calliope. *You can't make me.* She promptly sat on Chloe's chest.

Dr. Brian smiled and then said, "Calliope, I may not be telepathic, but I've been around enough bonded pairs that I know you are going too. And give me some credit. I'm keeping Shosty with Chloe. Once we get to the hospital, I'll send for Sylvester to help with Shosty, as he's a lot more knowledgeable about dogs, but I won't send Shosty to the animal clinic."

Well, I should hope not.

Emily laughed but did not pass on Calliope's remarks.

"Will my daughter be all right?" asked Hazel with obvious concern in her voice.

"I will know more once I get to examine her properly. Let's just get them back to the hospital," said Dr. Brian.

Gregory and Emily helped Dr. Brian onto Esmeralda and then lifted up Chloe, followed by Shosty. Calliope climbed up one of Esmeralda's front legs and then sat on her head.

"You better be good, cat," said Esmeralda, but there was obvious kindness in her voice.

Just don't drop any of us, Calliope answered.

"I've never dropped anything in my life," said Esmeralda.

Esmeralda then took off for the hospital, with Hazel following as quickly as she could on foot.

Once they were gone, Emily and Gregory examined the area where they'd found Chloe and Shosty.

"Look here," said Emily. "Drag marks."

"Yes," said Gregory, and then he walked out to the road before continuing, "and there's some blood here."

"It looks as if they were attacked on the road and then dragged out of sight."

"I agree," said Emily. "And I'm sure this is George's work. He was pretty upset that the fire his son tried to start backfired. He knows about the protection spell."

"What do you want to do now? Your mother is still at Ingrid's, keeping an eye out."

"Let's head over there, and I'll see about getting some backup for her, someone to stay the night on guard," said Emily.

They walked into Ingrid's to find the shop empty except for Ingrid and Amy.

"How's Chloe?" said Amy as Emily and Gregory walked in.

"Both she and Shosty are unconscious. Esmeralda has just taken them with Dr. Brian, and of course Calliope, to the hospital," said Emily.

"Calliope is the real hero in all this," said Gregory. "I've never seen her so upset, and I felt really helpless when I couldn't understand her."

Amy laughed and said, "I'd say she got her message across. And thank heavens she's linked to Chloe, and apparently Shosty as well, or those two might have lain hidden in the bushes for hours."

"I'll say," said Ingrid. "I would have wondered why Chloe wasn't here to put on the protection spell, but after this morning's incident, I really thought that George would give up. They could have spent the night in the bushes."

"Well, I don't think we can leave you without some protection, so I've asked Rupert and Hannah, along with their dragons, Whipper and Firebird, to come and spend the night here. They are happy to help and will be here in a few minutes."

"Is that really necessary," asked Ingrid.

"Yes," said Gregory and Emily in unison.

Amy put a hand on Ingrid's shoulder and said, "I agree, and besides, it's better not to argue with these two."

Emily smiled and said, "Got that right. Anyway, this attack on Chloe and Shosty was brutal. I'm going to have riders out looking for George, but we can't take any chances. And now, we need to get to the hospital and see how Chloe and Shosty are doing."

Rupert and Hannah walked in just then, and Emily said, "Have you heard anything?"

"No," said Hannah. "We did stick our noses into the waiting room, but Nurse Beatrice chased us out, saying that when she knew something she'd let people know. But she's being very kind to Hazel, so we figured we'd better get over here."

"Well, we're going back and sit with Hazel as support," said Amy. "Chloe's one of our fosters, so no way am I not going to be there."

Emily said, "Thanks for being willing to stay here tonight."

"I suspect with Whipper and Firebird outside no one will try anything, but we're going to keep a close eye on everything anyway," said Rupert.

With that Emily, Gregory, and Amy left.

As they walked back to the rider complex, Amy said, "I can't believe that George would do this."

"I can," said Emily. "He was really angry when I told him about Patrick. And on George's side, I don't think he sent Patrick, although I'm sure he would have thought what Patrick wanted to do was a good idea."

"I suspect that Patrick has been bullied by his father all his life," said Gregory, "and always wanted his father's approval."

"That's kinda what Rupert felt also when he was investigating Patrick's friendship with the rider apprentices," said Emily.

"It's very sad," said Amy.

The three of them walked through the front doors of the hospital and into the waiting room. Hazel was sitting there alone, although Nurse Beatrice had gotten her some tea.

"Any word, Hazel?" asked Amy after she gave Hazel a hug.

Hazel just shook her head.

Emily and Gregory sat down on one side of Hazel, and Amy, on the other. No one felt much like talking, but it was nice to have the small support group for Chloe and Shosty.

They'd been there for over an hour when Dr. Brian finally came into the waiting room. Hazel jumped out of her chair and said, "How is she, Doctor?"

"Still unconscious," said Dr. Brian. "And so's Shosty. I have determined that they both have pretty severe concussions, so my guess is that they will be unconscious for a while. There is some swelling of the brain tissues, and that needs to subside."

"Can we see them?" asked Hazel.

"Yes, one or two at a time and for short visits," said Dr. Brian. "And do talk to them. It's been shown that people, and I'm hoping dogs as well, do hear even when we think they can't. So let them know you're there, and then just make small talk."

Amy and Hazel went in first. Emily and Gregory waited for their turn. Amy came out after about five minutes and said, "Dr. Brian is pretty fantastic. He's managed to put two beds together, and he's got it made up as a double with both Shosty and Chloe in it. I think he's right that they are supporting each other. And Calliope is nesting between them, refusing to move."

"Sounds like Calliope," said Emily.

"I also saw Sylvester, and while he's hopeful for Shosty, he does say that this is a bad injury, especially for a puppy. In addition to his concussion, he also has three cracked ribs, as Dr. Brian had surmised. Apparently all anyone can do now is just wait."

"Well, we aren't going to wait on finding George," said Emily. "He's got a lot to answer for."

Nurse Beatrice came in and said, "Dr. Brian is going to allow Hazel to spend the night in Chloe and Shosty's room, so I think you should wait until tomorrow for any visits."

Emily nodded and said, "You're right, of course."

Nurse Beatrice said, "I'll be sure to get word to you if there's any change in either of them. Whoever would hurt our mage deserves anything you want to do to him. And to kick a puppy like that—well, I just can't say how much I want that guy caught."

"We certainly agree with you," said Gregory.

"How's Patrick doing?" asked Emily.

"As well as can be expected," said Nurse Beatrice. "He's going to have a lot of scarring, but if the burns don't get infected, he should make a full recovery. He's not going to be as handsome as he was since some of the flames hit the side of his face, but arsonists can't expect sympathy."

"I agree," said Amy, "but I also think that Patrick's had a tough life with George as a father."

"Oh, don't get me wrong," said Nurse Beatrice. "We're giving him the same care we would give to any patient, and honestly, he does seem very remorseful. One of his friends came by, and I heard him saying that this was all his own fault, so hopefully he's learning something as well. He's only fifteen, and it's a shame to see him in so much trouble, as well as pain."

"Well, we aren't doing anything," said Emily, "until he's healed. Then we'll have to see how things play out."

"See you in the morning, then," said Nurse Beatrice.

Once they were outside, Emily said, "I need to stay here and organize a search for George."

Gregory said, "I knew that was coming, but you haven't had any dinner. None of us has, I suspect."

Amy said, "I'm heading home to Todd, who hopefully has made our dinner. But I'm not sure that there's enough for two more. Sorry."

"No worries," said Gregory. "I was thinking of picking up something for us at the cafeteria, if that's OK with you, hon. Then I'll bring it to your office, and we'll eat on the run as we organize the search. I can help with the ground crew at least."

Emily nodded and said, "I could really use your help, and it would be wonderful to have you searching. And yes, if you don't mind getting us something—I'd like veggie soup and a sourdough roll—that would be excellent."

"Well, then, I'll leave you two to it," said Amy and gave them each a hug before heading home.

Gregory walked into Emily's office a little later carrying a large tray with lots of food on it. He set it on the desk as Emily looked up from her notes. "Here we go," said Gregory as he moved the bowls off the trays.

They ate in companionable silence, both of them really hungry. Then once they'd finished, they reviewed the strategy Emily had devised to hunt for George.

"I've already sent riders to his property," said Emily, "but no one is there. Even the workers have cleared off."

Emily's older brother Jake walked into the office then and said, "Several riders report seeing George riding away from Havenshold and into the mountains. He's going to be really hard to find there."

"OK," said Emily. "Let's call it a night now and rethink things in the morning. That terrain is extremely rugged. Please thank everyone who was searching."

"Will do," said Jake.

— 10 —

BERTHA'S CAVE

The next morning found Emily back at her desk just before sunrise. She'd stopped off at the hospital only to find out that Chloe and Shosty were both still unconscious. Emily hated feeling helpless, and she knew she couldn't be of any help to the injured at the hospital, so she headed across the rider courtyard to the building where her office was. There she found a stack of reports on the search for George, and just as she started to look through them, Rupert walked in.

"George has run off," said Rupert as he flopped down into his chair next to Emily's desk. "All the information we've gathered indicates that he's headed deep into the mountains."

"Yes, I'm seeing that as well from these reports," said Emily. "Apparently he's left his son too."

"And all the workers either have been run off or have taken off once he left," said Rupert. "Hannah's going to try to track some of them down to see if they'll testify against him, but right now, we can't find them either."

"And we have no idea what his next move will be," said Emily.

"That's the worrying part, all right," said Rupert. "I'm sure he's going to do something. Why try to take out Chloe if he didn't have plans for something else?"

"Well, it could just be revenge," said Emily, "but I agree with you. I think it's more."

"Do you think it's time to let Bertha know about all this," said Rupert. "I know Chloe was going to handle that, but now..." Rupert left his sentence unfinished, but Emily knew they were both wondering if Chloe would recover, and if so, what effect the concussion might have on her abilities as mage.

"Chloe's plan was to have Aster and Jasmine talk with Bertha when Harmony and Rya went to Bertha's cave for Rya's training. If I talk with Harmony, that could still happen," said Emily.

"Shall I see if I can find Harmony and ask her to stop by?" asked Rupert.

Emily thought for a few moments and then nodded. "Yes, would you please?"

"I'm on it," said Rupert as he stood and turned to leave the office. "Anything else?"

"Not at the moment," said Emily. "I'm afraid this turn of events has rather taken me aback."

"You're not alone in that," said Rupert. "Everywhere I go people are asking after her, talking about how horrible the attack was. And it isn't just riders either. In fact, I think the nonriders seem even more shocked. Chloe's done so much for not only Havenshold, but all of Draconia and indeed our entire planet. It's amazing, and she's ten years, at least, younger than I am."

"I know," said Emily. "She seems much older, and she's so capable that it's hard to see her lying helpless."

"Folks are asking after Shosty as well," said Rupert, "remembering how you gave him to Chloe as an eight-week-old puppy at the celebration to mark Chloe's work with Jaluhz and the lava flow."

Emily laughed and said, "Little Shosty was so excited, and having a dog who can speak out loud, as well as telepathically, well, he just seemed a natural for Chloe and the library."

Rupert nodded. Both of them were quiet for a bit, and finally Rupert said, "They have to be OK! They just have to be."

Then he turned again for the door. "I'll find Harmony—Aster and Rya's grandma, not Jake's dragon," he concluded with a smile.

Emily tried working on her paperwork after Rupert left but found that she didn't do much except push papers around. She thought about going over to the hospital again or even just taking a walk, but she knew the first idea was pointless. If there'd been any change, someone would have told her. And the second idea of taking a walk might mean a delay in finding out anything when there was a change.

Gregory stopped by midmorning. "Just can't seem to focus on anything," he said as he dropped into Rupert's chair.

"I know," said Emily. "Any change?"

"No," said Gregory, "I stopped on my way over here. The waiting room is filling up with people, though, keeping vigil with stories about Chloe. A lot of folks are sure pulling for her."

"It may be just as well that George has absconded. I think if he were still in Havenshold, we'd have to worry about a lynch mob. Chloe is loved by nearly everyone," said Emily.

"Hazel hasn't left Chloe's room, apparently," said Gregory, "and now both Zelda and Henry are there as well. I think your mom is checking on Hazel's mom from time to time to be sure she's holding up. Otherwise, she and your dad are looking after Ingrid and her shop, with Jupiter and Fern on guard duty."

"That sounds like them, and certainly Jupiter and Fern will be excellent deterrents. No one is going to mess with those green dragons," said Emily. "And I'm worried about what George might do now. He obviously has an agenda."

Both of them looked up as there was a knock on Emily's door. Emily said, "Come in."

A woman with short silver-gray hair and brown eyes walked into Emily's office, saying, "Rupert said you wanted to talk with me."

"Yes, Harmony," said Emily, "and thanks."

"I'll head out now," said Gregory, "so you two can talk. Do you want me to bring you lunch later?"

"That would be nice," said Emily as she also stood and hugged him.

"Hi, Harmony," said Gregory, shaking her hand as he headed for the door.

"Good to see you, Gregory," said Harmony as she moved toward Emily's desk and Emily motioned to her to have a seat in Rupert's chair.

Once Gregory had left, Harmony said, "Now, what can I do for you? Does it have something to do with the terrible attack on Chloe and Shosty?"

"In a way," said Emily, who then proceeded to tell Harmony all about George and his talk about secret knowledge. When she finished, she added, "We think that Bertha needs to hear about this, and I've asked Aster and Jasmine to head to Bertha's cave once they finish their current assignment."

"And Sasha," said Harmony with a smile.

"Yes, of course," said Emily. "I can't forget to include that little white dog—she's certain that she's a vital part of their bond, and I know she's right. She's just so small that I tend to forget her. Anyway, I understand that you are planning to take Rya and Artemis to Bertha's. When are you leaving?"

"Rya and Clyde have just finished work on their current project, so Clyde said we could leave whenever we wanted. My son is going to miss having his niece around, and I don't think he's happy about this, but he does know that it's in Rya's best interest to learn about her empathic abilities from Bertha."

"Could you leave as soon as tomorrow?" asked Emily.

"Certainly," said Harmony, "and we can go directly there. I had thought about camping along the way, just to give me some quality grandma time, but I can do that another time. If we leave first thing in the morning, we'll be there easily by late afternoon."

"That would be perfect," said Emily, "and while you might not get time with just Rya, you'll soon have both of your granddaughters together, as Aster said they could be there by late tomorrow night."

"Oh, that's wonderful," said Harmony. "I haven't seen Aster since the celebration over the lava solution a few months back. When she's done at Bertha's, will she be coming back to Havenshold for a bit? If so, I could let Clyde know that he might be losing a niece for a month, but he'd have a daughter for a visit."

Emily smiled and said, "Yes, you can tell Clyde that. Aster, Jasmine, and Sasha do deserve a break before I send our roving ambassadors off again."

Harmony stood and said, "Well, then, I'd better get home and pack."

Emily also stood and came to give the older woman a big hug. "And thanks for talking with Bertha. I think that hearing about Chloe from you will make things a bit easier, although I know she's going to be devastated."

"You'll let Aster know as well? I can't communicate telepathically with you, but I can with Aster, and I too want to know how Chloe and Shosty are doing," said Harmony.

"For sure," said Emily.

The next morning, true to her word, Harmony and Rya and Rya's bonded partner, Artemis, left Havenshold. Rya and Harmony wore backpacks, and Artemis had a small saddlebag arrangement across her lovely orange fox body. They moved along at a good pace and soon entered the more mountain-ous region surrounding Havenshold. After stopping for a pic-nic lunch, they hiked farther, and by midafternoon they were approaching the glen in front of Bertha's cave.

"Who's that?" asked Rya, pointing to several men coming out of Bertha's cave.

Artemis let out a growl and started toward the men. Rya said, "Artemis, no," but that didn't stop the fox.

Harmony said, "I don't like the looks of them. And where's Bertha?"

The men looked over at them, and the tall, heavyset leader said, "Get them! Don't let them get away."

Two of the men raced toward Harmony and Rya, waving sticks. Before Harmony and Rya could move, they were sur-rounded. Artemis tried to jump on one of the men and did succeed in biting him in the leg before the man clubbed her. Rya ran to help Artemis, grabbing onto the man's arm, but his partner swung his club and landed a hard blow on Rya's leg. Harmony could hear the crack of bone, and that propelled her into action. Unfortunately she was no match for the men, and before she knew it, she too had been hit across the legs.

The leader said, "Put them out of action. We can't have them raising the alarm."

The men were only too happy to oblige, and soon Artemis, Rya, and Harmony were lying unconscious on the ground, hav-ing been badly beaten. Then the leader called to his men and said, "OK, let's get out of here. We need to make sure we're gone before that bear comes back. When she finds out we've captured her kids, she's going to be plenty mad."

With that the men left.

In a nearby area, there was an artist's cabin, and the woman who lived there felt the attack on Harmony. The cabin was the home of Mildred, Harmony's estranged daughter, who had been allowing some telepathic communication with both Rya and Harmony, but who refused to see them. She hadn't seen Rya since she gave her up for adoption fifteen years ago, and she hadn't seen either her mother or brother for twenty-six years, since she herself was twenty-seven.

But she felt pain and a telepathic connection with her mother, a connection that was quickly severed by unconsciousness. She knew that her mother was traveling with Rya and Artemis to Bertha's cave, and that wasn't far from her cabin, so she grabbed her pack, dumped out her paints, brushes, pencils, and tablets, filled it with rags, bandages, and water bottles, and headed out.

She walked quickly through the woods, being careful at the same time to listen for any intruders. She didn't see or hear anyone, and soon she was at the small stream running through the glen in front of Bertha's. Mildred had never met Bertha, but she knew where she lived, and she was well aware of the fact that bears were a protected species. She also knew that Rya was going to study with Bertha, and Mildred had debated going to see Rya in person while she was here. Somehow meeting her daughter seemed slightly less daunting than meeting her mother. But now, it seems, she had no choice. And who could hurt anyone without angering Bertha? None of this made any sense.

Mildred crossed over the small stream, stepping on the large stones that had been placed for that purpose, and strode into the glen. At first there didn't seem to be anyone there, and then Mildred noticed the bodies lying on the ground in front of the cave entrance.

She ran across the glen and soon discovered her mother, Rya, and Artemis. They were all unconscious, and as she examined them, she discovered that both her mother and Rya had legs that looked sure to have been broken, given the unnatural position they were lying in. She also suspected her mother had a broken arm. Both of them had numerous bruises and small cuts. Artemis looked to have a broken tail, as if someone had swung her around by it.

Mildred walked into Bertha's cave, calling out to the bear, but there was no answer. That didn't really surprise Mildred; if Bertha or her cubs had been here, no one would have been able to hurt Harmony, Rya, and Artemis. But Mildred was surprised by the destruction that had been wrecked inside the cave. There was broken furniture, honey and flour spilled everywhere, and a water barrel overturned.

Mildred's first concern was to tend to the injured. She wasn't sure if she should move them or not. She wished she knew more first aid. She did know that she'd have to try to splint any broken limbs before she moved anyone.

She went back outside and, using her water bottle, tried to bathe Harmony's face to see if she could awaken her. She was relieved when her mother groaned and opened one swollen eye.

"What happened?" asked Harmony groggily.

"I don't know," said Mildred. "I heard your cry for help, and when I got here, I found you three, unconscious and injured."

"You heard me? Telepathically?" said Harmony, trying to make some sense out of all this.

Mildred took a deep breath and then said, a bit hesitatingly, "Yes...yes, Mom."

"Mildred?" said Harmony, and even through her pain, her joy radiated.

Mildred could only nod as she noticed the tears in her mother's eyes. Then realizing that it was getting on for nightfall, she said, "I have to help you, but I'm not sure how. I think that both you and Rya have broken legs. Artemis appears to have a broken tail. I think you're right arm is also broken, and I'm sure I'm not supposed to move anyone with broken bones and head injuries."

"Where's Bertha?" asked Harmony.

"She's not here, and neither are her cubs," said Mildred.

"Her cubs...," said Harmony. "That man said something. I can't quite remember. What was it? Something about Bertha's cubs. I think he and his men have kidnapped them."

"Kidnapped them?" said Mildred with incredulity in her voice. "Do you know how big they are now?"

"Oh yes," said Harmony, "about full grown, but they're also young, and I suspect they were tricked."

"We need help," said Mildred, looking around the glen as if help would suddenly materialize. "I don't know what to do."

"Aster, Jasmine, and Sasha are on their way here," said Harmony. "We were supposed to meet them here. Can you reach Aster telepathically? I don't think I have the strength."

"I can try," said Mildred. "You know that I can only really reach you and Rya, but I can hear Aster when she reaches out to me. I also need to see if I can waken Rya and Artemis."

Mildred moved away from her mother and took her wet cloth to Rya and then Artemis. She was relieved when both of them showed signs of waking. But as soon as Rya was awake, she started crying in pain, so Mildred wasn't convinced she'd done her any favors.

Artemis tried to move over to Rya, and Mildred said, "I think you should stay still, Artemis."

"She needs me," said Artemis.

"We need help for all three of you," said Mildred. "Can you communicate with Aster or Jasmine or Sasha?"

"Sometimes," said Artemis, "if they are close."

"Well, they should be reasonably close. Shall we try together?"

"You're Mildred, aren't you?" said Artemis.

"Yes, I am. My cabin isn't far from here, and I heard my mother's cry," said Mildred.

"OK, let's try," said Artemis, as she tried to hold her head up and then gave up the effort and lay back again.

Both Mildred and Artemis concentrated on calling Aster while Harmony drifted in and out of consciousness and Rya cried in pain. After about fifteen minutes, by which time Artemis had also lost consciousness again, Mildred could hear the beating of wings. She looked up as a gorgeous yellow dragon, who was probably about seventeen feet in length, swooped down from the sky and landed near them. Aster jumped down, holding Sasha in her arms, and then she put Sasha down, and the two of them ran over to Harmony.

"What happened?" asked Aster.

Mildred related what she knew. Harmony woke up at the sound of Aster's voice and said, "I'm glad to see you."

"Oh, Grandma," said Aster. "I'm so sorry. You look dreadful."

"I don't feel so hot either," said Harmony.

"We'll get you back to the hospital in Havenshold," said Aster. "I have to contact Emily."

Emily, Aster called telepathically.

Aster? What's wrong?

Grandma, Rya, and Artemis have been attacked. My aunt Mildred found them, but we really need help.

"Tell her that I think both Mom and Rya have broken legs; Mom also probably has a broken arm, and I think Artemis's tail is broken. In addition, all of them have concussions," said Mildred.

Aster nodded and relayed that information.

Esmeralda and I will be on our way with Dr. Brian. It will take us close to a half hour to reach you. I'll also get Rupert and Whipper, Hannah, and Firebird to help with the transport, said Emily.

OK, but hurry. Rya's awake now and really in a lot of pain. I suspect Grandma is as well, but she keeps drifting in and out of consciousness. Artemis is being brave, but she hurts too.

Do you know how to make temporary splints for broken arms and legs? asked Emily.

I haven't done it for real, said Aster, *but I do remember the first-aid class I had as a rider. I'll try.*

We'll keep in contact once we're airborne. Hang in there.

Aster turned to Mildred and said, "Emily suggested that we try to splint the broken limbs. Have you ever done that?"

Mildred shook her head and said, "No, unfortunately."

"Well, we need some strong straight branches and some material we can tear into strips. Let's see what we can find," said Aster.

Jasmine said, "I'll get the branches. We can't leave the injured alone."

Sasha said, *I'll watch over them.*

"Good girl, Sasha," said Aster. "Mildred, let's see what we can find in Bertha's cave. I'm sure she wouldn't mind."

"Bertha's cave has been ransacked," said Mildred as she and Aster entered.

"Gads, so it has," said Aster. "Bertha won't like this. She always keeps the place so tidy."

"There's some bedding on the ledge over there," said Mildred.

"That's where I always slept when I was here, and I expect Bertha had it made up for Rya," said Aster.

The two of them grabbed the sheets and blankets and headed back outside just as Jasmine was landing, with her claws holding onto several small trees.

"Nice to have a dragon around," said Mildred.

"Of course," said Jasmine, who promptly proceeded to rip the smaller branches off the tree trunks.

Once the trunks were bare, Aster measured the lengths against Harmony's left leg and Rya's right. Jasmine then used her teeth to bite the trunks into the appropriate lengths. One of the smaller lengths was just right for Harmony's arm.

"Now comes the hard part," said Aster. "We have to pull on the broken legs to make the bones snap back into place, and that's not going to feel good at all."

"Here," said Jasmine, holding out a couple smaller branches. "Make them bite on something before we pull. Then I'll hold them while you two pull on the ankles. Let's start with Rya as I think once we have her splinted, she'll be in less pain. I hope anyway."

Following Jasmine's instructions, Mildred and Aster pulled hard on Rya's leg until the broken bones were in a straight line. Thankfully, Rya passed out at the beginning of the process. Aster and Mildred strapped the tree trunk to the leg and then moved over to do the same thing to Harmony. Harmony also passed out and so didn't feel it when they set her arm.

"Now, what about Artemis's tail?" asked Jasmine.

"Hmm," said Aster. "I think a really small splint should help."

As they were finishing up splinting Artemis's tail, they heard dragons overhead.

Esmeralda and Emily landed with Dr. Brian, who said, "Let's hope that these injuries stop soon. Not that I'm not grateful for the transport," he quickly added.

Dr. Brian checked out all three patients and said, "Nice job of splinting. I think surgery will be required once we are back, but at least they are safe to transport now."

Rupert, Whipper, Hannah, and Firebird arrived then, and Emily set about allocating who would carry whom. "I'll take Artemis," she began until Artemis set out to howl.

"OK," she said, "Hannah, can you take both Rya and Artemis?"

"Certainly," said Hannah.

"And, Rupert, can you and Whipper take Harmony?" asked Emily.

"For sure," said Rupert.

"Finally, Mildred," said Emily. "First, it's a pleasure to meet you. Sorry it's under these circumstances, but we're sure glad you were here."

"Thanks," said Mildred as she glanced in awe at the four dragons.

"I know you are a recluse, but would you like to return with your mother and daughter?" continued Emily.

Mildred nodded and then said, "Yes, I would. I think it's long past time."

"Excellent," said Emily. "Aster, I'm sure you want to take your aunt with you and Sasha on Jasmine."

"Definitely," said Aster, who motioned to her aunt to come over by Jasmine, so she could help her up.

"That just leaves us, Dr. Brian," said Emily. "Ready for a return on Esmeralda?"

"For sure," said Dr. Brian.

It took a few minutes to get the injured situated on their respective dragons, but soon all four dragons were again in the air, flying back to Havenshold.

— 11 —

BROKEN BONES

The flight back to Havenshold was hard on the injured even though the dragons did their best to fly as smoothly as possible, and Dr. Brian was relieved when the courtyard in front of the hospital came into view. Nurse Beatrice came running out as soon as she saw the dragons landing. She called out to Dr. Brian, "Guess what! Both Chloe and Shosty are now awake, and Chloe keeps saying she has to help Bertha."

Dr. Brian said, "She's not helping anyone right now."

"I told her that, and her mother is doing her best to keep Chloe in bed and flat."

"And now I have three more patients who need to be in surgery," said Dr. Brian. He thought for just a few seconds and then said, "Nurse, will you please get the injured into surgery. I'm sure Emily, Rupert, and Hannah will help you."

As Emily nodded, Dr. Brian went on, "And will you find Sylvester and let him know that I'd like to have him check Artemis out and then deal with her broken tail."

"Right away, Doctor," said Nurse Beatrice.

"I'll go check on Chloe and Shosty, and I'll be in surgery by the time you have the patients prepped. I think we should start with Harmony as she's more badly injured."

Nurse Beatrice nodded and then began directing the riders to the stretchers she'd gotten ready.

Dr. Brian headed directly for Chloe and Shosty's room and soon discovered that Chloe was doing her best to fend off her mother and get out of bed. But he smiled to see that Chloe was no match for a determined Hazel.

"Now, what's this I hear about you getting up?" said Dr. Brian as he came into the room.

"I have to," said Chloe. "Bertha's in real trouble. She's the one who woke me. I could feel her telepathic cry to me, but I can't reach her."

Dr. Brian grabbed his stethoscope and a small flashlight and headed to the bed where Chloe and Shosty were. He was amused to see that it wasn't just Hazel who was trying to restrain Chloe. Calliope was sitting right on top of Chloe's chest refusing to budge. Shosty was next to Chloe, and Dr. Brian thought that he looked in fine shape, tail wagging, as he tried to lick Chloe.

"Let me check you out first," said Dr. Brian. "I don't have a lot of time as I now have more patients in surgery, so please cooperate."

"If you must," said Chloe.

Dr. Brian listened to Chloe's heart and took her pulse. He checked her eyes and was relieved to see that the pupils were now normal. "How's your head feel?" he asked.

"Fine," snapped Chloe.

"Don't try to fool me, young lady. How does your head really feel?"

"It hurts a lot," said Chloe with reluctance.

"I'd be very surprised if it didn't," said Dr. Brian. "And you, Shosty," he said as he moved over to the puppy, "how are you feeling?"

"I want to get that man," said Shosty.

"I'm sure," said Dr. Brian, "but I asked how you're feeling."

"My head hurts, but I'm hungry," said Shosty.

Just then Emily walked into the room, saying, "I thought you might need some help with a difficult patient, Dr. Brian."

"Thanks," he said, "and I do have to get into surgery. OK, Chloe, here's what's going to happen. You will stay in bed—"

Chloe started to protest. "But I—"

Dr. Brian held up a hand and said, "No buts about it. You may try sitting up, although I suspect your head won't like that, and you may have tea and broth. Neither of you will have any solid food until you demonstrate that you can handle the broth."

"Broth," said Shosty. "Growing puppies need more than broth."

"I can see that I have two difficult patients," he said with an amused chuckle. "Anyway, Chloe, you mentioned trying to reach Bertha telepathically. I don't want you trying any telepathy or other magic."

Chloe began, "But I—"

"Again, no buts," said Dr. Brian. "To be honest, we aren't sure how this concussion will affect your mage abilities, but I am certain that you could do harm, both to yourself and your abilities, if you push things too soon. Both of you have nasty concussions, and those take time to heal. As long as you have the headache, no reading, no multitasking, no exercise, and definitely no magic. Is that clear?"

Tears formed in Chloe's eyes, and she said, "Clear."

Emily said, "We've got the instructions, Dr. Brian, and we'll see that they both obey them."

"Good, and after I'm done with surgery, I'll come back and check on you both," Dr. Brian said as he hurried out of the room.

Emily pulled up a chair next to Chloe as Hazel handed her daughter a handkerchief. Calliope jumped off Chloe's chest but sat on the bed right next to both Chloe and Shosty. Hazel helped Chloe sit up a bit and then positioned pillows behind her head and neck.

"What about Bertha?" said Chloe.

"Let's start with that," said Emily. "You say that Bertha contacted you?"

Chloe began to nod and then winced as pain shot through her head. "Yes, I heard her crying in my head."

Hazel chimed in. "All of a sudden Chloe was yelling something about getting to Bertha. And Shosty also heard it, as the two of them woke together."

"And when was this?" asked Emily.

"Right after Dr. Brian left," said Hazel. "Nurse Beatrice came running in to see what had happened, and she was upset that she couldn't bring Dr. Brian in to check on them, but she did insist that Chloe stay in bed until he returned."

"OK, so that was after the attack on Harmony, Rya, and Artemis, so we do need to find out what caused Bertha to cry out then," said Emily. She then proceed to tell them the little bit they did know, about the attack and the ransacking of Bertha's cave, as well as what Harmony heard about kidnapping Boris and Berla.

"How do you kidnap full-grown bears?" asked Chloe.

"That's what we said also. However, they are still young, and so they must have been tricked somehow," said Emily.

"Is this George again?" asked Chloe.

"We're assuming so. We'll get more details once we can talk with Artemis, Rya, and Harmony, but certainly I can't think of anyone else who'd do this," said Emily.

Sylvester entered the room then, carrying a tray with a tea mug and two bowls of veggie broth. "Glad to see that you're awake," he said as he put the tray down on a table near the bed. "I'm helping out Nurse Beatrice, as she's in surgery. And Dr. Brian asked me to check on you, Shosty."

Sylvester examined Shosty and found a number of sore spots but nothing major. "You do need to take it easy," he said to Shosty. "No running or jumping until I give you the OK."

"But I'm a puppy," said Shosty. "That's what puppies do."

Don't I know it, said Calliope.

Sylvester laughed and said, "Well, you can still lick, but no chasing Calliope. If you want to get off the bed, ask Hazel or Emily to lift you down. Do you understand?"

"Yes," said Shosty, looking as sad as his happy face could.

Emily asked, "How's Artemis?"

"She's doing pretty well," said Sylvester. "Her tail is broken, and it looks as if she was swung by it, which is horribly cruel, but I've splinted it and wrapped it well, and she's a lot more comfortable. She won't leave Rya, but that didn't surprise me."

Emily handed the mug of tea to Chloe and said, "Thanks, Sylvester."

"You're welcome," he said, "and I'll be at the nurses station in the hall if you need anything else. I told Nurse Beatrice that I'd stay until she was out of surgery."

After Sylvester left the room, Hazel took one bowl of broth and helped Chloe with it. Emily picked up Shosty and put him on the floor in front of the other bowl, and soon both patients were enjoying their nourishment. Once they were finished and Shosty was back on the bed, Emily said, "What can either of you remember about your attack?"

"I don't remember a thing," said Chloe. "The last thing I remember was leaving the library with Shosty to walk to Ingrid's shop. Then I woke up here screaming about Bertha."

"I think that's pretty normal," said Hazel, "after a concussion. You may remember more later, but you also may never remember that period of time."

"It's all so frustrating," said Chloe. "And what about Bertha? She needs help."

"Don't worry," said Emily. "I've already sent dragons and riders out to search, but you know how difficult that terrain is."

"I remember the attack," said Shosty, sounding very important.

"You do?" asked Emily. "What do you remember?"

"We were nearly at Ingrid's when this man came out from behind a tree. He was waving a rifle, and Chloe said, 'George, put that down.' But he didn't. I tried to bite him, but he kicked me, sending me crashing into a tree, and I fell. That's all I remember," said Shosty. "I'm sorry, Chloe; I should have protected you."

Chloe reached over and petted Shosty and said, "I think you were really brave. Thank you."

Shosty then proceeded to lick Chloe's face, and she laughed before she groaned, "This head."

"OK, take it easy," said Emily. "And I'm not sure, but based on what Gregory and I found when we examined the scene, you and Shosty had been dragged into the shrubbery after you were attacked. If Calliope hadn't gotten Gregory to find you, things could have been a lot worse."

Chloe reached over for Calliope and said, "I'm so lucky to have you. Thank you for being such a clever cat."

Certainly better than a dog, said Calliope with an air of superiority.

"Better take that back," said Shosty.

"Now, listen, you two," said Chloe. "I'm lucky to have both of you, so give it a rest."

"Well, at least we know it was George who attacked you," said Emily. "Not that there was much doubt."

"I think we'd better let Chloe and Shosty rest now," said Hazel.

Emily stood and said, "Right you are. And, Hazel, I think you need to go home for a bit as well."

Hazel nodded and stood, giving Chloe, Shosty, and Calliope each a kiss and saying, "Calliope, you're in charge of these two now. I'll be back in the morning."

I can handle them, said Calliope, and Chloe relayed that comment to her mother, who wasn't telepathic.

Hazel laughed and said, "I'm sure you can."

Emily and Hazel headed out together.

Emily returned to the hospital the next morning, and she'd barely gotten into the waiting room when she heard shouting. Following the voices she arrived at the room where Rya, Artemis, and Harmony were located. Harmony was doing the shouting.

"I want to go home," said Harmony.

"Well, you can't," said Dr. Brian in his calmest voice. "You have a badly broken leg, which is encased in plaster that's barely dry. You have a broken arm as well, also in a cast with a sling. You will be staying here for at least another twenty-four hours, and then you'll have to go somewhere where you can be looked after."

"Looked after?" shouted Harmony. "I've been looking after myself for seventy-eight years. I'll manage just fine. I want to go home."

"Mom, please," said Mildred.

"Don't 'Mom' me," said Harmony. "I've been on my own for years, and I like it that way. I want to be in my own home."

Rya and Artemis were watching this altercation with smiles. Clyde had an expression of incredulity on his face, and finally he said, "Mom, you can come stay with me. Aster and Jasmine will be home for a bit, and they can help me look after both you and Rya."

Harmony looked around the room. Not only was Dr. Brian there, but both Mildred and Clyde. She hadn't had both of her children in the same spot since Mildred left home so long ago. Aster was there as well, and the three of them were ganging up on her.

"Clyde," said Harmony, "thank you, and that is very sweet of you, but I can't come to your home now. I need to be in my own space, my own home. And I have to look after all my animals. They depend on me."

Emily poked her head into the room and said, "Hey, I could hear you all the way out at the front door. Glad to hear that your lungs are in good shape."

Harmony looked a bit embarrassed. She said, "They're all ganging up on me."

"Oh, are we?" said Dr. Brian. "How are you planning to get around? If you had just a broken arm or just a broken leg, maybe. But with both, crutches aren't an option. You're going to need help."

"You can just make this a walking cast," said Harmony. "I've seen them."

"Eventually," said Dr. Brian, "but not for quite a long time. This break is a nasty one, and you can't put any weight on it at all for at least eight weeks."

"Eight weeks," wailed Harmony. "How am I going to manage?" Tears began to seep from her eyes.

"Exactly what I've been saying," said Dr. Brian. "You're going to need a lot of help."

"And it makes sense to have us together, Grandma," said Rya.

"You get crutches, at least," said Harmony.

"I know. I'm really sorry you had your arm broken also," said Rya.

"Well, I'm glad you didn't," said Harmony.

"And what about my tail," said Artemis.

"Yes, dear, I'm sorry for that also, but at least you can walk," said Harmony.

"OK," said Dr. Brian. "Let's leave it for now. I'm keeping both Rya and Harmony here until at least tomorrow morning. And Artemis will be staying as well because she needs to be with Rya. So please, just think about things, Harmony. And the rest of us will as well. We'll find a solution that will work for everyone, I'm sure."

Harmony looked a bit sheepish and said, "I know I'm being unreasonable. But I just want to be home."

Dr. Brian smiled and said, "I've heard that already today, from another stubborn patient."

"Chloe?" asked Emily.

"Yes," said Dr. Brian, "and she and Shosty are being released but only under strict guidelines, and Hazel is going to keep track of them."

"Chloe gets to go home," said Harmony.

"Now, don't start again," said Dr. Brian. "We'll talk about it tomorrow. Please, just rest and try to stay calm."

With that Dr. Brian left the room, and Emily said, "I'll leave you now to get some rest as well. Mildred, it's so good to have you here."

"Thanks," said Mildred.

"I just can't believe it," said Clyde. "The attack was vicious and hurtful, and I know we are all worried about Bertha, Boris, and Berla, but I feel so lucky that Mildred was able to get to Mom, Rya, and Artemis so quickly and that our family is all together again."

"Well, enjoy it, and I'm really glad to see you three looking a whole lot better than you did yesterday," she concluded, looking at the Harmony, Rya, and Artemis.

Emily then walked down the hall to Chloe's room, where she found Chloe sitting in a chair, fully dressed, with Hazel packing up the few things she'd brought for Chloe.

"I hear you get to go home," said Emily.

"Thank heavens," said Chloe.

"But Dr. Brian has given her a detailed list of dos and don'ts," said Hazel, "and I'm going to make sure she follows them."

"Libby will also," said Chloe, resignation in her voice.

"Yes," said Hazel, "I couldn't tell Dr. Brian about Libby. I know most people don't know that the library is actually alive. I let him believe I'd be staying with Chloe. But the fact is that Libby will know if Chloe tries any magic. I wouldn't be able to tell—well, unless she used magic to make food."

"I'm sure Libby will provide whatever Chloe needs," said Emily.

Chloe stood, looking a bit wobbly.

"Do you two want some help back to Chloe's apartment?" asked Emily. "I'd be happy to accompany you."

"That would be nice," said Hazel. "I think Chloe could use an arm, even if she won't ask for it."

"Mom, I'm fine," said Chloe.

"Why don't I just walk next to you, then," said Emily as she winked at Hazel.

The five of them headed out of the hospital, Calliope racing ahead and saying, *No running, now,* to Shosty.

Chloe called after her and said, "Don't tease him, Calliope. And remember, he's only a puppy, so he won't be able to resist temptations the way you can."

"I'll be good, because I'm going to stay right next to you. No one's going to attack you again if I can help it," said Shosty.

It didn't take long to walk to the rear of the library, where Chloe's front door was. Hazel helped her to settle on the couch, with both Calliope and Shosty in her lap.

Libby walked through the connecting door and said, "So the patients are home, are they?"

Hazel smiled and said, "Thanks, Libby, for being willing to look after my very stubborn daughter."

"My pleasure," said Libby with a twinkle in her eyes.

"Well, I'm going now, dear," said Hazel as she gave Chloe a kiss. "I'll be back later to check on you."

"Thanks, Mom," said Chloe. "Thanks for everything!"

Once Hazel had left, Libby and Emily sat down across from Chloe, and Libby said, "I have managed to get ahold of Bertha."

"Oh, good," said Chloe, relief evident in her voice. "How is she?"

"Not well at all," said Libby. "She tracked the kidnappers for a while, but then lost all traces of them. She has no idea where Boris and Berla are, and she can't sense them telepathically, which isn't promising."

"What does that mean about their condition?" asked Emily.

"It could be several things," said Libby. "I couldn't sense Chloe when she was unconscious, for instance, and I'm amazed that Bertha could blast through that. However, I suspect that, one, Bertha's cry was primal and deeply felt and, two, that Chloe and Shosty were about to wake on their own, although I can't know that for sure.

"It could also mean that the twins have been doped, which might explain how they were kidnapped in the first place.

"And finally, of course, they could be dead."

"Yes," said Emily, "but let's hope that George still needs them alive to get Bertha to open up the vault in her cave."

"Agreed," said Libby.

"So what can we do now?" asked Chloe. "We have to help Bertha."

Libby nodded and said, "I'm trying to keep her calm, not an easy thing to do with a distraught mother, especially one as large and overprotective as Bertha. She's still hunting for Boris and Berla, and I understand that. However, if she doesn't return at least once a day to her cave, she won't know if George leaves any demands. So far he hasn't done anything except kidnap

Boris and Berla, but I can't imagine he'll wait long. Those two will be a real handful if they wake."

"We have to save them," said Emily, "and I do have dragons and riders searching, but what we really can't do is give George the information he's seeking."

"I know," said Libby, "and I've reminded Bertha of that. After all, she's the planet's only seer, a position handed down through the female line of her family, and she has a link to the planet, similar to that of the riders and their dragons, to protect the planet and all on it.

"However, at the moment, Bertha isn't thinking at all clearly. I understand that, but I'm not sure I'm getting through to her."

"Well, I'm just hoping that we can find her kids before any decisions have to be made," said Emily. "Now I'm going to leave you, so Chloe and Shosty can rest, and I'll be back later."

"Thanks, Emily," said Chloe.

"I'll keep an eye on them and be sure they get food and so on," said Libby.

— 12 —

DISORIENTATION AND DISMAY

Berla opened her eyes and began to panic. She couldn't see anything, and at first she thought she'd gone blind. Then she realized that she was just in a really dark place, but she had no idea where. She tried to reach out with her mind to first her mother and then her brother, but she couldn't contact either. Now she really did begin to panic. All her life she'd had her mother and Boris just a thought away. As she'd grown older, she sometimes chaffed at the constant presences, wanting a bit more independence, but having it snatched away was terrifying. Had they been killed? Why else couldn't she contact them?

Then Berla heard a faint groan. "Who's there?" she asked.

"Berla?" said a soft voice, which she realized was her brother.

"Boris?" she answered. "Where are you?"

"I don't know," answered Boris, "and I can't reach either you or Mom with my mind."

"I know," said Berla, whimpering a bit. "I'm so scared. What happened?"

"I'm not sure," said Boris, and he started to move toward the sound of her voice. "Keep talking, so I can find you."

Berla answered, "I thought both you and Mom must be dead when I couldn't contact you. At least you're alive, so maybe Mom is too."

Just then Boris bumped into her right leg, and soon they were hugging each other. Then they tried to sit more comfortably, although they'd discovered that there were manacles attached to their legs, and the manacles had long heavy chains, which kept them from moving too far. In fact, Boris's chains were extended nearly to their full length once he reached Berla.

Berla said, "Why don't we move partway to the place you were originally, and that way, we'll each have some slack in our chains?"

"Good idea," said Boris.

"How long have we been here, I wonder," said Berla once they were as comfortable as possible.

"More to the point," said Boris, "how did we get here and why? What's the last thing you remember?"

"That lovely honeycomb, just sitting out on the large log," said Berla. "And we were so hungry as it was nearly lunchtime."

"Yeah," said Boris, "it seemed too good to be true."

"We should have remembered Mom's warnings," said Berla. "If something seems too good to be true, then it probably is."

"My head feels as if it's stuffed with cotton," said Boris. "I can't think. I can't sense anything. How do people live like this?"

"I know," said Berla. "Maybe if you've never been telepathic, you don't know what you're missing, but I do and I don't like it." Her voice started to rise in panic as she continued, "And what must Mom be thinking? She must be worried sick. I'm sure she's been calling us for lunch, and we don't know how long we've been here or where here is."

"That honeycomb must have been drugged," said Boris.

"And who would want to hurt us?" said Berla, after she took a deep breath and tried to calm herself. "Bears are a protected species in all the nations. What does someone want with us?"

"Good question," said Boris. "I've no idea."

"But what if it isn't us?" said Berla.

"What do you mean?" asked Boris, in a puzzled voice.

"Well, it's obviously us, but what if we're only a—how does Mom put it?—a means to an end," said Berla.

"What end?"

"Think about it," said Berla, trying to sound calm and logical. "Mom is the planet's only seer. She's pretty important, and I know she is guarding stuff in the back room of the cave. She's just started my training, as one day, a day a long way from now, I hope, I'll be taking over for her, and once she showed me a hidden room in the back of the cave."

"Really?" said Boris. "That sounds pretty neat."

"Yeah," said Berla, "and pretty important. And Mom would guard it with her life. But what could make Mom give up its secrets?"

Both bears were quiet for a minute, thinking, when suddenly they looked at each other and said, "Us!"

Berla nodded and said, "Right. If she thought it was the only way to save our lives, she'd probably cave in."

"You know how she protects us," said Boris, "how she hovers over us, to the point of driving us nuts."

"She is so maternal that she's really overprotective," said Berla. "She loves us more than life itself."

"So if we're in danger," continued Boris, "she'd do anything to save us."

"And we fell right into the trap," cried Berla. "It's our fault that Mom is now in this mess."

Boris nodded and said, in as brave a voice as he could muster, "So it's up to us to save ourselves and protect Mom."

"But how?" said Berla, pulling on the chains that were fastened to her ankles.

"Yeah, how?" echoed Boris.

The two of them sat in the dark, trying to think of something, but no ideas came to them. The chains had metal ankle cuffs, which were securely fastened to their back legs, and as far as they could discover, the other end of the chains were bolted to the cave walls.

"Let's try to explore this cave," said Boris, after they'd sat for what they thought was about half an hour. "I know we can't go far, but your chains seem to be fastened on one side of the cave and mine on the other, so let's see how big this cave is."

"Good idea," said Berla, "and it's getting a bit lighter in here, which must mean we've been here all night and the sun is now rising."

Each of them moved slowly toward their respective chain ends. They didn't have far to go, but they did discover large buckets of water next to each of the chain ends.

"At least we won't go thirsty," said Boris as he drank heavily from his bowl.

"That's something," said Berla as she followed suit with her bucket.

They then continued exploring and discovered that the chains were about ten feet in length, and while they could move toward the source of the light, they couldn't get even halfway to what was probably the cave entrance. The cave they were in seemed to be at least thirty feet across in every direction.

Finally, tired and discouraged, they met again at the only point in the cave where they could be next to each other.

"That didn't help much," said Boris.

"And I'm getting sleepy again," said Berla.

"The water," shouted Boris, "they must have drugged the water. How stupid can we be?"

Berla nodded and then fell asleep before she could say anything. Boris looked at her for a few moments before he too was sound asleep.

It was hours later before they woke. They were both groggy and still unable to communicate telepathically.

Berla said, "We must have been out for nearly a day. Look— the cave is just starting to get light again, so it has to be morning."

Boris shook his head, trying to clear it, and finally said, "And I'm hungry, thirsty, and I have to pee."

Berla nodded and said, "Me too."

They searched the cave again, this time looking for a suitable place to pee. As they were looking, Berla said, "And promise me, no more eating or drinking. That has to be how we're being drugged."

"Agreed," said Boris, miserably.

After they'd found a low spot where they could relieve themselves, they again spent time yanking on the chains where they were bolted to the wall, but they were unable to get any of the bolts to loosen.

"They used four bolts with a metal plate to fasten these," said Boris finally when they were back in the spot they could both reach.

"Someone is really serious about keeping us here," agreed Berla.

"Had your water bucket been refilled?" asked Berla.

"Yes," said Boris, "and there was a smaller bucket with honey as well."

"Same here," said Berla, "so obviously someone came in here while we were asleep."

"It was really hard not to eat that honey," said Boris. "I'm so hungry."

"Listen," said Berla, "we have to get rid of the honey and the water, so they think we've eaten it. Then we have to pretend we're asleep, so we can see who comes in."

"That's a good idea," said Boris, as he sat up a bit straighter. "It would help to have something to do so that we could feel as if we were helping to get back to Mom."

"I don't know how long it will take for whatever drug they gave us to wear off. It obviously not only sedates us but steals our telepathic abilities. But once we have those back, we can definitely do something to alert Mom," said Berla.

"We can dump the water in the spot where we peed, so that's pretty easy, but what about the honey?" asked Boris. "If we just dump it, they'll see it, whoever they are."

"I have an idea there," said Berla, "but it's pretty gross. We need to dump the water as you said, and after that put our honey in the same spot and then," she paused and shuddered before continuing, "then I'm afraid we need to poop on the honey to cover it up."

"Ugh," said Boris, "that's really gross."

"I know, but no one will think to dig through bear scat to search for fresh honey," said Berla. "Can you think of anything else?"

Boris shook his head and finally said, "No, I can't. Let's just do it and try not to think about how good that honey would taste."

Once that very distasteful task was completed, the bears again returned to the spot where they could be together. "Now we just have to wait," said Boris.

"And we'd better be really quiet," said Berla. "After all, we're supposed to be in a drugged sleep."

Boris nodded, and they settled themselves as comfortably as they could and kept watch.

Many hours later as the sun was sinking, Berla and Boris started to nod off in earnest when they heard someone entering the cave. They feigned real sleep with eyes closed as they heard the person walking toward Berla's food station. Squinting, they peeked over at what was obviously a large, heavyset man carrying two buckets. He poured one into Berla's water bucket and the other into her food bucket.

As he turned back to the entrance to the cave, Berla and Boris quickly shut their eyes. Soon the man was back, and he repeated the same procedure with Boris's food station. He glanced over at the bears, who pretended to be sleeping, but he did not seem to realize their deception. Then he walked quickly out of the cave.

After about a half hour, Berla said very quietly, "He never came anywhere near us."

Boris nodded and said, "I don't know what we thought we could do, but certainly we can't do anything if he doesn't come within reach."

"And how long will it be before this blasted drug wears off, so we can contact Mom?" asked Berla. "How long can we go without any food or, more importantly, water?"

"I don't know," said Boris in a voice laden with discouragement.

As the two bears sat and worried, they became aware of a scurrying sound. "What's that?" whispered Berla.

"I don't know," Boris whispered back.

They both peered into the deepening gloom of the cave, barely able to see anything as the sun was nearly set. Suddenly they saw a red squirrel standing right next to them.

"Rodney," said Berla.

The squirrel, who was indeed their friend Rodney, chattered away, waving his front paws at them.

Boris looked at Rodney and said, "We can't talk with our minds. Someone drugged us and chained us here."

Rodney walked around them, before running up Boris's chain. He returned and chattered again.

Berla said, "I sure wish we spoke squirrel, Rodney. We never had to before as we could talk with you like this, and then we could read your answers telepathically, but now—"

Berla broke off as a small sob escaped from her. Both she and Boris were losing hope.

Rodney chattered again, shaking his head at them and then nodding and pointing toward the cave entrance. He then ran that way, came back to them, and pretended to be presenting them with something.

Boris and Berla were watching, and finally Berla said, "You can go get help?"

Rodney nodded frantically, letting them know that he was planning to do just that.

Boris said, "Find our mom. She'll know what to do."

"And, Rodney," added Berla, "can you let her know that we were drugged and that's why we can't contact her?"

"Yeah," said Boris, "and we aren't eating or drinking what they bring us now." Boris explained how they were dealing with the water and food, before concluding, "So we're both really hungry and thirsty, but we still must have some of the drug in us as our heads are still fuzzy."

Rodney nodded again and then raced up to each of their shoulders, one at a time, and gave them each a lick on their cheeks. Then he ran down their bodies and headed for the cave entrance. Before he was completely out of sight, he turned and waved to them and then darted outside.

Berla looked at Boris and said, "Well, he's smart, and he's a good friend. I bet he can find Mom and let her know what's going on."

Boris agreed and then said, "We might as well sleep for real now. Maybe we'll forget how hungry and thirsty we are."

— 13 —

DISCOVERIES

Chloe woke the next morning feeling much better. Her headache was nearly gone, and she had gotten an excellent night's sleep now that she was back in her own space, sleeping in her own bed.

"I feel great," said Shosty. "Can't I jump and run?"

Chloe laughed and then said, "You know the answer to that. Not until Sylvester gives you the OK."

As she lifted Shosty off the bed, he complained, "But my head doesn't hurt at all."

"That's a good thing," said Chloe, "and mine barely hurts. We've got to see Dr. Brian and Sylvester at ten, so try to be a bit patient."

What a whiner you are, said Calliope.

"Don't stir him up, Calliope. And think how you'd feel if you couldn't jump or run," said Chloe.

That will never happen, said Calliope confidently.

"I hope not," said Chloe.

Chloe picked out a pair of blue slacks and a pink sweater to wear and then showered and dressed.

"Shall we breakfast with Libby then?" asked Chloe once she was ready.

Definitely, said Calliope.

Libby was really happy to see them all and to hear how good Chloe and Shosty felt.

"That's excellent news," said Libby as she used her magic to provide breakfast. She made pancakes for Chloe and kibble for Shosty and Calliope.

"Yes," said Chloe, "but I'm worried about my abilities. What if I can't do my mage stuff? I haven't had even a hint of a telepathic thought since Bertha basically rammed her way in."

"Let's not cross that bridge until we have to, if we ever do. I for one think your abilities will return," said Libby.

"But what if they don't," said Chloe, sounding scared and miserable.

"If they don't, then they don't," said Libby. Then she held up a hand to forestall Chloe's next statement and went on. "Don't forget that you are more than just a mage. Gregory chose you to take over Pathfinder Academy from him, and you have made and continue to make a tremendous difference to those who attend."

Chloe said, "Maybe, but—"

"There's no maybe about it. Gregory was right that there are young people who either aren't chosen at a dragon hatching or who graduated from the required schooling and have no idea what they want to do with their lives. That's why he started Pathfinder, and that's what you handle so masterfully. You help students find their own way, students who aren't in the mainstream, students who frequently are at odds with their families, sometimes even totally rejected by them."

"Yeah, maybe," said Chloe. "But I'm our world's only mage. I have more responsibilities, not only to Draconia, but Forbury, Granvale, and Sanwight as well."

"True," said Libby. "But you know I've been here a lot longer than you. King Alfred built the library when he and the dragons arrived back in this time frame well over five hundred years ago. You've been a mage for—what?—eight of those years, including your training."

Chloe said, "Yeah, but—"

Libby interrupted again. "You are filled with lots of buts today. You've saved our planet from an asteroid; you've dealt with an evil magician; you've figured out how to help us live with an active, sentient volcano, among other things. You've already done more than most people do in their entire life, and you're just twenty-three."

"I guess," said Chloe, staring at her hands, which she was twisting in her lap.

Libby laughed and said, "So I don't think it's likely that you will lose your magic, but if you do, that just means other opportunities will be available to you."

Then, noticing the tears streaming down Chloe's face, Libby said, "Please, dear, don't jump ahead. You need to go slowly and not anticipate the worst. If Bertha were here, maybe she could foretell what lies ahead for you, but I can't and you shouldn't try either. Take each day as it comes," Libby concluded, handing Chloe a lovely purple handkerchief.

Chloe took the handkerchief and said, "I know, and I'll try. And it doesn't help that I'm so worried about Bertha."

"So am I," admitted Libby. "I can't reach her either, so that has nothing to do with your abilities. It's nearly time for you to go see Dr. Brian. Why don't you head over there and let him look at you. And then talk with Emily. She may have more information."

Chloe stood, placing Shosty on the floor, and said, "If nothing else, this little guy wants the all clear to jump and run."

Libby laughed and said, "I bet he does. And, Calliope, are you going to keep watch on the library? I've missed having you the last couple of days."

Definitely, said Calliope. *And I've missed a lot of naps as well.*

Shosty and Chloe walked to the hospital and entered to find Nurse Beatrice at the front desk.

"Good morning," said the nurse. "Dr. Brian is waiting for you in his office."

"What about me?" said Shosty.

"Don't worry, you silly puppy," said Nurse Beatrice. "Sylvester is there also. Glad to see both of you looking much more like your usual selves."

Chloe and Shosty walked over to the door to Dr. Brian's office and knocked. When they heard his "come in," they entered.

"Well, you two are looking much better," said Dr. Brian, as he motioned Chloe to a chair.

Sylvester came over to Shosty and said, "How are you, young man?"

"I'm fine," said Shosty. "Can I run and jump again?"

Sylvester laughed and said, "Let me check you over while Dr. Brian talks with Chloe, and then we'll see."

Sylvester lifted Shosty up onto the examining table as Dr. Brian said, "And how are you, Chloe?"

"I got a really good night's sleep in my own bed, and now my headache is nearly gone," said Chloe.

"Good," said Dr. Brian, and he came over to check her vitals and look at the stitches on her incision, where the bullet had grazed her.

"I don't like having a shaved spot on the side of my head," said Chloe, "but I guess you had to shave it to stitch it."

"Yes, I did, and believe me, we shaved as little as possible," said Dr. Brian, "but it would have been worse if the bullet had penetrated. Did you block it?"

"I don't remember," said Chloe, "but Shosty said the rifle was aimed for my heart, so I must have."

"You're very lucky," said Dr. Brian as he finished his exam. "I think you're through the worst of this. I'm going to let you go back to work as long as you don't spend a lot of time reading and as long as you take frequent breaks."

"What about magic? Telepathy?"

"You may gently try some," said Dr. Brian. "I'm at a disadvantage here since I'm not telepathic. Often wish I were, but there it is. So I'm not sure what it entails. But on the theory that it's like rehabilitating an injured muscle, I'd say take it easy, and don't expect to be up to full speed all at once."

"Got it," said Chloe.

"And if your head starts hurting more, then stop and come see me immediately," said Dr. Brian.

Sylvester came over to Chloe then after putting Shosty on the floor. "The same goes for this fellow. He can do limited—did you hear that, Shosty?—limited jumping and running but nothing taxing."

"Yeah," said Shosty.

"Limited," said Sylvester firmly.

"I got it," said Shosty.

"OK, then," said Dr. Brian, "it looks as if you guys are set to face the world. Emily is with Harmony and Rya now, and she asked if you'd join her there. I'll be down in a bit to release them both."

"Thanks, Dr. Brian," said Chloe, "and Sylvester, for all your care!"

Chloe and Shosty walked down the hallway to Harmony, Rya, and Artemis's room. As they entered, they saw that not only was Emily visiting, but that Mildred, Clyde, and Aster were also there.

Clyde was saying, "You have to come home with me, Mom. We've been over this. Mildred is staying with us as well."

Emily raised a hand and said, "Could you guys wait a few minutes here so that I can question Harmony, Rya, and Artemis about their attack? Then I'll get out of the line of fire."

"Sorry, Emily," said Clyde, looking embarrassed. "She's just so stubborn."

Harmony looked as if she were going to start in again, so Emily forestalled it by saying, "Harmony, can you tell me about the attack on you? I'd really like descriptions of the men involved."

Harmony was quiet for a minute, gathering her thoughts and looking at Rya and Artemis. Then she said, "There were three of them, weren't there?"

"Yes," said Artemis, "and the big fat one hit me first, knocking me out. Sorry. I couldn't stop him."

Rya rubbed Artemis's fur and said, "You tried, which was really brave of you." Then Rya looked at Emily and said, "After that guy hit Artemis, he grabbed her by the tail and swung her around over his head and let her fly. Artemis hit a tree and then fell to the ground. It was horrible."

"I'm sure," said Emily, as she took notes in her notebook. "What happened next?"

"It all happened so fast," said Rya. "I don't really remember a lot. There were two other guys, both really tall and skinny, but they had heavy sticks."

"Yes," agreed Harmony, "all three guys had brown hair, on the long side. The heavy one actually had his tied into a ponytail."

"So how old were they?" asked Emily.

"I'd say that the heavy one and one of the skinny ones were in their forties. The other skinny one...I don't know, but he seemed older. He was the one who was obviously in charge."

Emily looked at Chloe and then said, "None of them sound like George."

"And the one who was in charge was the one who talked about Boris and Berla," Harmony added.

"So George didn't do this," said Chloe.

"But George shot you," said Shosty firmly. "I know that was George."

"Hmm," said Emily. "And we still haven't heard what the kidnappers' demands are."

"It would help if we could find Bertha," said Chloe.

"Yes, it would," agreed Emily. "Can you three remember anything else?"

Harmony shook her head and said, "I can't."

"Neither can I," said Rya.

"And I was out for the count," said Artemis.

Emily chuckled as she put her notebook away. "Well, I'm just glad that you are back here and that you will all heal from your injuries."

"If I can get home," said Harmony.

"Well, you can't," said Clyde.

"Grandma, please," said Aster.

Just then a tall, muscular man with silver hair, brown eyes, and a tanned complexion came into the room followed by a tawny wingless gryphon. He said, "Do I get a vote?" as he walked over to Harmony and kissed her on the cheek.

"Baron," said Harmony, smiling broadly. "And Oswald. How did you two get here?"

"A little bird," the baron said with a wink at Emily, "told me about your injuries. Oswald and I left Forbury even before you were on your way to Havenshold from Bertha's cave."

"I ran really fast," said Oswald with obvious pride in his voice. "We just got here and came to see you first off."

"Thanks, Oswald," said Harmony, reaching out with her good arm to ruffle his fur.

"Baron," said Clyde, "can you talk some sense into my mother. She thinks she can be on her own in her own house."

The baron looked down at Harmony and said, "Well, obviously that isn't going to work."

"See...," said Clyde.

"We told you," said Mildred.

Harmony said, "But—"

The baron held up his hands and said, "Hang on. I said she couldn't be on her own. I didn't say she couldn't go home."

"What?" said Aster.

"Harmony will not rest at your home, Clyde, no matter how you try. She'll be worried about all her rescue animals," said the baron.

Chloe added, "In addition, as I discovered last night, sleeping in one's own bed is really therapeutic."

"Precisely," said the baron. "But, Harmony, you can't manage on your own. That's why Oswald and I are here. Your home is, after all, on my Havenshold property and isn't that far from my home. Lance won't care if his dad is here longer than I normally visit, and I can keep an eye on you."

"Me too," said Oswald.

Harmony smiled and said, "You sure I won't be too much trouble for you? What about your home and business in Forbury?"

"Don't you worry about a thing. Henry's an excellent second in command and quite able to look after things in Forbury for a while," said the baron. "It will be nice to spend some time with Gregory and Emily as well. I often have wished that my sons weren't so far away, and I expect we'll get a chance for a good visit."

"If you're sure," said Harmony.

"Definitely," said the baron. "I'd like to look after you." Then he turned bright red with embarrassment.

Harmony blushed and then looked at her family. "So, I'm going home," she said.

Clyde threw his hands up and said, "You win. But we'll be by to see you a lot, just so you know."

Mildred looked at her mother and said, "Is there room in your home for me to stay? I could help."

"That's really sweet of you, Mildred," said Harmony. "But my home is really just one large room with a tiny bedroom alcove and bath. However, I hope you, like Clyde, will stop by often. As the baron said, it's located on his ranch and isn't far out of town."

Dr. Brian came into the room and looked a bit startled to see Oswald but recovered quickly. "So, more visitors, I see. Have you figured out where you're going? I'd like to release the three of you."

"Yes," said Harmony, "I'm going home."

"But...," said Dr. Brian.

The baron laughed and said, "She's just trying to get a reaction. She is going home, but Oswald and I will be caring for her."

Dr. Brian chuckled and said, "I've never had a gryphon for a nurse, but I imagine she won't be able to get away with anything with you guys looking after her. Thank you. We nearly had a war here."

"She can be very stubborn," said the baron.

"Like you aren't," teased Oswald.

Everyone laughed, and Dr. Brian looked at Rya and Artemis. "You two are going to your uncle's still, I assume."

"Yes," said Rya. And then she added, "After all, that's our home while I'm his apprentice, so we too are going home."

"I get it," said Dr. Brian. He then proceeded to give them discharge instructions and also let them know when they'd need to return for follow-up care.

Emily, Chloe, the baron, and Oswald left the room after the baron said, "We'll meet you in the waiting room out front, once you're ready to go."

Oswald added, "We've got a cart for you to ride in, Harmony. Rya and Artemis, you can ride in it too if you want, and we'll drop you at Clyde's."

"Thanks, Oswald," said Rya. "That would sure be easier than riding on Jasmine."

Emily and Chloe stayed with the baron and Oswald while they waited for the patients. Emily brought them up to date with everything that had happened.

The baron said, "I know George Pontsby, and he's a real jerk and a bully with a vicious temper, but he's not terribly bright. I can see him shooting Chloe in reaction to his son's injuries, but finding Bertha and doing the kidnapping surprises me."

"And he wasn't at Bertha's cave," said Emily. "At least Harmony didn't see him."

"Have you talked with Patrick?" asked Chloe. "Has Rupert found out who his friends are?"

"You know what," said Emily, "let's see if we can talk to him now."

"Sounds like a good idea," said Oswald.

"Please keep us in the loop," said the baron as he noticed Harmony and the others coming down the hallway, both Harmony and Rya in wheelchairs and Artemis riding in Rya's lap.

"Wil do, and thanks for looking after Harmony," said Emily.

Emily and Chloe, with Shosty following, then stopped at the desk to ask Nurse Beatrice if they could visit Patrick.

"Yes," said Nurse Beatrice, "he's got his girlfriend with him now, but if you don't stay long, you can ask him a few questions. He's just down the hall from the room Harmony was in."

"Thanks," said Emily, and she and Chloe went in search of his room. As they entered they saw that Patrick was heavily bandaged on his arms and even had bandages on his face. There was a young, very pretty girl standing beside his bed. She had long blond hair and blue eyes; she was medium height and slender in build.

Emily said, "Hi, Patrick. Is it all right if Chloe and I come in and ask you some questions?"

"I guess," he said. "This is my girlfriend, Elise."

"Hi, Elise," said Emily. "You're a dragon rider apprentice, aren't you?"

"Yes," said Elise in a very quiet voice.

"You were chosen by a brown dragon at the last hatching two years ago, if I remember correctly," Emily continued.

"Yes," said Elise. "That's Cinnamon."

"Lovely name," said Chloe.

Elise only nodded.

Emily said, "Patrick, I know you know that you're in a lot of trouble. But since you're actions have only damaged you, we really aren't interested in punishing you. I think you've been punished enough."

Patrick didn't say anything, and Emily continued, "But we do need to know about your dad. Do you have any idea where he is?"

Patrick said, "No."

"When did you see him last?" asked Chloe.

"Right after I was brought here," answered Patrick. "He said he'd fix things."

"Do you know that he tried to shoot me?" Chloe continued.

"No," said Patrick. "But he gets mad easily."

"And have you been telling him about the dragon riders and their history?" asked Emily, looking at both Patrick and Elise.

"I don't know any of that stuff," said Patrick.

"What about you, Elise?" asked Emily.

"I didn't tell Patrick or his dad," said Elise.

Chloe caught a stray thought from her, and it so surprised her that she nearly shouted, "My telepathy is coming back," but instead she just said, "But you told someone, didn't you?"

Elise looked down at her shoes and said, so quietly that they almost couldn't hear her, "Maybe."

Emily looked at her and said as gently as possible, "Who did you talk to?"

"My parents," said Elise.

"Why would you do that?" asked Emily. "Weren't you told not to share that information with anyone?"

Tears started streaming down Elise's face, and she finally said, "Yes, but my parents said they didn't think I had it in me to be a rider, and they thought I'd make a fool of myself, and I guess I just wanted them to know some of the history, so they could understand. But I told them they couldn't tell anyone."

Patrick looked shocked and said, "But you wouldn't tell me anything. I could have helped my dad if you had."

"I'm sorry, Patrick," said Elise.

Emily looked at the two young people and thought, *Was I ever that young?* Then she said, "Elise, I'll need to see you in my office this afternoon, when your classes are done."

"Are you going to take Cinnamon away from me?" said Elise, crying now.

"No, sweetie, once a rider has bonded with her dragon, that can't be changed. But I do have to find out exactly what you said and whom you told. And I'm sure Jake will have extra discipline for you," said Emily.

With that, Emily and Chloe left the room.

"Well, that raises a lot of questions," said Emily.

"Sure does," said Chloe.

— 14 —

RANSOM DEMANDS

Once outside the hospital, Emily said, "I'd really like you to be present when I meet with Elise. If you feel up to it, that is."

"I'd like to be there as well," said Chloe. "I have to finish some paperwork to close out the school year, though. What time will she be there?"

"Afternoon classes end at four," said Emily.

"That would be perfect," said Chloe. "See you then."

Chloe and Shosty then set off for the library as Emily returned to her office.

Once inside her office, Chloe was eager to see if her telepathic skills really were returning. She looked at Shosty and said, *Can you hear me?*

Yes, said Shosty telepathically back to her.

"Oh thank you, Shosty," said Chloe aloud as Calliope answered, *You could have tested with me.*

Yes, I could, and we now have. Now let me try with Libby, answered Chloe.

Libby, can you hear me?

Yes, dear, and I'll refrain from saying, "I told you so."

Thanks, Libby, and I'm feeling a bit foolish but also more my own self. Have you been able to reach Bertha?

Nothing so far, replied Libby. *I'll let you know if I do.*

Thanks.

With that Chloe sat at her desk and pulled her paperwork out. The students were now officially on their summer break, but she was just finishing up on the extensive notes she put into each student's file. She'd completed seven of the nine and hoped to do the last two today. She knew she wasn't supposed to do a lot of reading, so she tried to limit herself to writing comments without proofing, and she took frequent breaks. She was pleased also to see that she could magic up a cup of tea for herself, and midday she also made some pasta and salad appear.

She finished the ninth report at three thirty. It felt really good to be on summer break herself now. She'd be able to devote all her attention to the kidnapping and helping Bertha.

"OK, you two," Chloe said to Calliope and Shosty, "I'm going to meet with Emily. Keep an eye on things here for me while I'm gone."

Don't worry, said Calliope. *I'll keep the library safe from this puppy's antics.*

"Hey, I don't do antics," protested Shosty.

Chloe laughed and said, "Play nice," as she headed to the front door.

She enjoyed the walk to rider headquarters. It was a lovely warm summer day, and she stopped to admire the various displays in the shop windows. Anita had put a fine selection of summer clothes in the window of her secondhand shop, and Mary had colorful yarn in her Sweaters and Yarn store, as well as a sign counting the days to fall, saying that if you started now, you could easily knit new sweaters to be ready for the cooler weather.

Chloe chuckled at that as she walked through the arch into the dragon riders' complex. *Not likely that I'd ever finish a sweater*, she thought as she walked up the stairs to the building that housed various offices and conference rooms.

Chloe found the door to Emily's office open and so walked in to discover that both Emily and Rupert were there, as well as Esmeralda and Whipper. The two lovely purple dragons, one female and one male, looked so magnificent, that Chloe just stopped to admire them.

"Hi, Chloe," said Emily, looking up from her papers. "Have a seat. Elise should be here shortly."

"Thanks," said Chloe, "and good to see you as well, Rupert."

"I've been investigating how George found out about the alternate timeline, and while I knew Elise was Patrick's girl-friend, I didn't suspect her. Her parents aren't happy with her being a rider," said Rupert. "At least that's what Jake told me. But they also don't have any connection that I've been able to find to George."

"Have any of Patrick's other friends been more promising?" asked Chloe, tipping her head in a questioning glance.

"No," said Rupert, "as far as I've been able to discover, Patrick has two other friends among the apprentices, but I can find no evidence that they've said anything that they shouldn't have."

"Let's hope we can learn something from Elise, then," said Chloe. "My telepathic skills have returned, as has my magic, but neither is up to full strength yet. I'm just glad to have them back."

"I can imagine," said Emily. "While I don't have magic, I cer-tainly can't think of anything worse than losing my telepathy, especially my link with Esmeralda."

"I agree," said Rupert.

"Won't ever happen," said Esmeralda, and Whipper nodded in agreement.

"Anyway," said Chloe, "the point is that neither Libby nor I can reach Bertha, and that is very troubling."

"I agree," said Esmeralda, "and various dragon patrols have been unable to locate her or her cubs. They just seem to have disappeared."

There was a tentative knock on the doorjamb to Emily's office, and Emily called to Elise to come in.

"Hi, Elise," said Emily. "Please have a seat." Emily motioned to the chair in front of her desk. "Would you like anything? Tea? Snacks?"

Elise sat in the chair and just shook her head.

Emily said, "You remember Chloe from this morning, and I don't know if you know Rupert?"

Elise just nodded yes.

"Well, then," said Emily. "We need to find out what's been going on with Patrick's dad, and apparently that involves you in some way."

"I've never talked with him," said Elise. "He doesn't like Patrick seeing me. He doesn't like dragons or riders."

"OK," said Emily. "I'd rather figure that out from George himself. How does Patrick feel?"

"Oh, Patrick really admires the dragons. He thinks they're beautiful."

"And so we are," said Esmeralda, stretching her long neck and looking at Elise.

Elise smiled and said, "I'd certainly agree with you."

Esmeralda said, "You're bonded with Cinnamon, aren't you?"

"Yes," said Elise, "and I love her, and I wouldn't do anything to hurt her or you or any of the dragons. Please don't take her away from me."

Esmeralda looked carefully at Elise before saying, "If I did, that would kill Cinnamon, so I'm not likely to do anything to hurt her, especially since she's done nothing to deserve it."

Elise started crying, and Chloe handed her a handkerchief.

Once Elise was a bit calmer, Esmeralda continued. "You know you aren't supposed to share our history with nonriders. I'm sure that was made very clear in your lessons."

"Y-y-yes," stuttered Elise.

"So then why did you?" asked Esmeralda.

"I got so mad at my parents, especially my dad, last weekend when I went home. I hadn't seen them in months because we don't get much time off," said Elise.

"And now, you'll get even less," said Esmeralda, "but continue."

"That's OK. I don't want to go home again," said Elise. "My dad was upset because I'd been chosen, and each time he sees me, he ridicules me, says that I won't make a proper rider. And maybe he's right."

"Are you doubting Cinnamon's choice?" asked Esmeralda in a very stern voice.

"No! No, not really. But she probably could have gotten someone better."

"Cinnamon doesn't think so," said Esmeralda. "I've already talked with her, and I agree: she made the perfect choice. But your hatching was less than three years ago, and rider training takes nine years. Cinnamon isn't fully grown even, and neither are you. You both have a lot to learn, and you will learn it together. So stop worrying that you are going to lose her, but you certainly have to tell me everything."

"Yes, Esmeralda," said Elise. "When I got home, well, my parents were just as upset as before, and my dad has never thought I was capable of anything, and then he started saying all sorts of horrible things about dragons, about how they were wimps and not necessary to Draconia, and all they did was pamper themselves.

"Anyway, I lost my temper, and I said that our planet would have been destroyed if it weren't for the dragons and their riders and that the planet chose them to save herself. I knew as soon as I said it that I'd goofed, but I was so mad," said Elise as she stared down at the floor.

Esmeralda smiled and said in a much gentler voice, "I understand why you would have gotten mad. And the young aren't good at self-control. The damage is done now, but what happened then?"

"Well, my dad wanted to know what I meant, but I'd come to my senses then and said that I couldn't say anymore. Both he and my mom tried to pressure me, saying that surely I wasn't meant to keep secrets from them, but I didn't say another word, I promise."

Esmeralda said, "That must have been hard, but it was the right thing to do. I'll speak to Jake about this. You will have extra duties and no more weekends home until Cinnamon can go with you, which won't be until your seventh year, but I do think you've learned a valuable lesson."

"Thank you," said Elise very softly.

Rupert spoke up then. "So how did Patrick's dad find out? Do your parents know him?"

"No," said Elise, "and I definitely didn't tell Patrick. He's never made me mad. My parents did have a big party when I was home, with lots of families with boys my age. I don't think they like me having a boyfriend in Havenshold. They live in Alfredsville, you know."

Emily nodded and said, "So what happened at the party?"

"I tried to stay out of any conversations," said Elise. "I really don't like parties at all. But I heard my dad shouting across the room to a friend that the dragons thought they'd saved the planet. I'd asked them not to say anything, but obviously they didn't honor that. The entire room went silent for a few minutes, and then the party resumed. I don't know most of my parent's friends, and I did my best to leave the party then, pleading a headache, so I don't know what happened after that."

"What do your parents do?" asked Emily. "Do you know anything about their friends?"

"My dad owns several buildings, and he rents out space to different businesses. He also has some apartments he rents," said Elise. "And my mom does alterations for people—you know, clothing."

"Ah," said Emily, "that might be a tentative connection to George, as he was making fabric."

"I don't think so really," said Elise. "My mom only alters clothes. She doesn't make them. And there is a small fabric shop in Alfredsville. I don't think Patrick's dad's fabric has reached that far yet."

"That's OK," said Emily. "You've given us some leads. And we'll follow up from here. You just keep your eyes on your studies and your mouth shut."

"Is it OK to visit Patrick?" asked Elise.

"As long as you don't talk about rider things: nothing about Cinnamon or your classes or anything," said Emily.

"I promise," said Elise. "I really feel sorry for Patrick. From what he's said, I think his father is a bully, and all Patrick has ever wanted is some love. His mother died when he was an infant, so it's just Patrick and his dad. I know what he did was wrong," said Elise in a rush, "but he was just trying to earn his father's approval. He and I have that in common: fathers who don't think we're worth anything."

"I am sorry," said Emily, "and I will take that into account. Patrick has some growing up to do as well, and we'll try to ensure that it happens in a positive way."

"Now you need to get back to your chores," said Rupert. "I only cleared it with Jake to have you here for an hour, and we've used all that up."

Elise stood and looked at them all before she said, "I won't ever mess up like this again, I promise."

And with that she left the office.

Once she was gone, Emily said, "So what do you think?"

"I think that anyone at that party could have heard," said Chloe. "We're going to have to think hard about keeping this under wraps. Maybe it's time to make the time shift public?"

"I really don't think that's a good idea," said Esmeralda.

"I agree," said Emily after a few minutes of thought. "Right now it's only rumor. I sure wish we could find Bertha. Or Boris and Berla. Or George. Or these mysterious guys."

"Well, that does have to be the first priority," said Rupert.

"Why is Bertha not contacting us?" asked Chloe. "I mean, she did blast me with her pain, but then she went silent."

"Could she be injured?" asked Emily.

"Possibly," said Chloe. "After all, I couldn't use telepathy at all when I was. But it takes a lot to knock out a bear, especially an angry one, and believe me, she was angry."

Hannah came running into the office then, shouting, "Guess what!"

Emily looked at her sister and said, "What?"

"We've found George, but you aren't going to like it. He's dead and has a ransom note attached to him."

"What?" said Emily.

"Yeah," said Hannah, "he was found just outside Havenshold. He'd been dumped at the side of the road. Someone had slit his throat."

"Who found him?" asked Chloe.

"We got a bit lucky there," said Hannah. "It was a dragon returning from patrolling in the mountains, so at least no towns-people know. The note said that George was too unreliable, and then it went on to demand that Bertha open her secret vault and give over all the information stored there, or else her cubs would meet the same fate as George."

"That's horrible," said Emily. "And we still can't find Bertha."

"The note said that the knowledge had to be removed from the vault and left inside Bertha's cave by day after tomorrow, or we'd get the cubs' bodies back just like George's," Hannah finished.

"That doesn't give us much time to find them or Bertha or the cubs," said Rupert.

Everyone was quiet for a few minutes, absorbed in their own thoughts. Finally, Chloe said, "Someone has to let Patrick know about his father. Does anyone know if he's apprenticed anywhere?"

Rupert shook his head and said, "No, he's been working for his dad. I gathered from talking with him and his friends that Patrick really has been at loose ends, not knowing what he wants to do. And now he won't even have a home."

Chloe said, "I'll go break the news, and maybe I can figure out a way to get him into Pathfinder or an apprenticeship. He's going to need something. Not today, obviously, but down the road."

Emily nodded and said, "Do what you can for him, Chloe. And I'm thinking that some public service for his arson attempt would be appropriate, so that might help him as well, if you can find out what his interests are."

Chloe stood to leave and said, "I'll go now. You know how news spreads in Havenshold. I don't want him to find out from someone else."

"And if you can," said Emily, "see if you can discover if his father has been hanging around anyone else. Maybe you can give Patrick the descriptions of the three men at Bertha's cave."

"I'll try," said Chloe. "Depending on how he takes the news, I may have to wait until morning for that, but I'll ask him just as soon as he can stand it."

Esmeralda stood then too, being careful not to knock over anything on Emily's desk. "I need to step up the patrols," she said. "We have to discover the whereabouts of some of these players, and so far they've eluded us. I know the mountains are treacherous, but even so, our dragons do know them pretty well, and I can't believe they've found nothing."

"And two bears the size of Boris and Berla can't be easy to hide," said Whipper as he also stood ready to follow Esmeralda out of the room.

"Keep us posted," said Emily as the two dragons left.

Chloe walked into Patrick's hospital room after first telling Nurse Beatrice that she was there to break bad news to him. Patrick was alone, and he looked small and vulnerable in the hospital bed. Chloe walked over to his bed and pulled up a nearby chair.

"Hi, Patrick," she began. "I'm afraid I have some very bad news."

"What?" he asked, looking apprehensive.

"Your father has been killed—murdered, actually."

Patrick looked absolutely stunned at this news. After a few minutes, he said, "Dad's dead?"

"Yes," said Chloe. "I'm really sorry. Do you have any other family?"

Patrick shook his head and then said, "No, it's just my dad and me."

"Are you up to answering some questions?" said Chloe. "It might help us find out who did this to your father."

"I guess," said Patrick. "I don't really know who would do this. My dad wasn't the easiest man to get along with, but he could take care of himself."

Chloe proceeded to describe the three men from Bertha's cave and then said, "Do any of these descriptions sound familiar?"

Patrick shook his head again and said, "Not really. The only people I ever saw at our place were the factory workers, and I don't remember any of them looking like what you've described."

"OK," said Chloe. "It was a long shot, but we're trying to find out what your father was up to, and we need to find those other men."

"What am I going to do now?" said Patrick, his voice rising in panic.

"Don't worry about that now," said Chloe. "We will help you once you're healed, but Nurse Beatrice said you would be here for a while yet."

"I can't run Dad's factory," said Patrick morosely.

"Nor should you," said Chloe. "You have to find something that works for you. Is there anything you enjoy doing?"

"Not really," said Patrick. "I've just done what Dad told me to do."

Chloe watched as a silent tear stole down Patrick's cheek. Then she said, "Well, don't worry. We'll help you figure things out. You shouldn't go back to your home now anyway. We don't know if it's safe."

"Guess I'm going to be one of those weaklings Dad was always yammering about—the ones who had to be helped by the riders."

"That doesn't make you weak," said Chloe, in a firm but kind voice. "We can all use some help from time to time. I think your dad was wrong about that, and I hope you'll come to see that in time as well."

"Maybe," said Patrick.

"Well, I'm going to go now," said Chloe, "but I'll be back tomorrow to see you, and I do have some ideas, so please don't worry. Just do your best to heal."

Patrick didn't answer but instead rolled onto his side away from Chloe.

Chloe stood and left quietly. As she went out to the front, Nurse Beatrice said, "Don't you worry. I'll keep a close eye on him. That young man has been through too much already, and even if some of it is his own doing, it doesn't make it any easier to deal with."

"Thanks," said Chloe.

— 15 —
SEARCH

The next morning Emily and Esmeralda arrived at the library just as it was opening. They headed into Chloe's office, and Emily said, "Morning. How're you feeling?"

"I'm doing fine," said Chloe. "My headache is now completely gone."

"Do you want to go to look for Bertha?" asked Emily.

"Don't you have a lot of riders out doing that?" asked Chloe.

"Yes, but honestly, I'm tired of sitting behind my desk in the first place. I feel so helpless. Time is running out. And you are closer to Bertha than any of the riders I sent out. Now that your telepathy is back, I thought maybe if we got close enough to her, you might be able to sense her."

"Possibly," said Chloe, "unless she is deliberately blocking herself."

"Anyway, I thought Esmeralda could fly us to Bertha's, and the three of us could start searching," said Emily.

"Four of us," said Shosty as he jumped off the couch. "You need me to track."

"You think you're a better tracker than I am, pup?" said Esmeralda.

"No," said Shosty quickly, "but I can get into smaller places, so I might pick up something you don't."

"I don't know, Shosty," said Chloe. "I don't want you hurt again."

Yeah, you weren't great the first time, said Chloe.

"I wasn't expecting George to jump out at us," said Shosty. "Now I'll be prepared."

"I don't think it would hurt to take him," said Emily, smiling at Shosty, "and it might help."

"OK," said Chloe, "but only if you promise to mind every command that Emily, Esmeralda, or I give you. And I mean mind instantly, without question or argument."

"Got it," said Shosty as he bounced up and down with excitement.

"And, Calliope," said Chloe, "you keep an eye on things here, will you?"

Of course, answered the cat as she stretched out on Chloe's desk.

Esmeralda flew out of Havenshold directly for Bertha's cave. Chloe sat behind Emily and held Shosty in her lap. While they were flying, Chloe asked, "How are things going at Ingrid's?"

"Really well," said Emily. "Now that George is dead, I've taken the guards off. Whoever is doing this has a larger agenda, and I don't think he will target just one shop."

"Yeah," said Chloe, "it sounds as if the problem with Ingrid was George's alone. I did talk with Patrick yesterday, and I'd planned to go back today. But he doesn't seem to know anything about his dad's business. He looks so lost at the moment."

"Well, we'll take care of him," said Emily. "He's another of George's victims, sad to say."

They arrived at the clearing in front of Bertha's cave, and Esmeralda landed. Emily vaulted down and then reached up to lift Shosty down so that Chloe could climb down using the bent foreleg that Esmeralda offered. Emily then showed them where the attack on Rya, Artemis, and Harmony had taken place.

"We found them over here," said Emily, moving to an area near the mouth of the cave.

Shosty made a big show of sniffing around, but he didn't find anything. Next they went into Bertha's cave and again didn't find any clues. The area had been examined so many times by others that the scents were confusing.

"I smell lots of different scents," said Shosty, "but I don't know which are relevant."

"I can do a bit better," said Esmeralda, "because I know the scents of the dragons and riders who were here, but I have to admit that Shosty is right. I can't get a strong scent for the villains."

They walked back outside, and then Emily asked Chloe, "Can you reach Bertha?"

Chloe tried for a few minutes and then shook her head. "I can't sense her at all, or Boris and Berla."

"OK," said Emily, "let's start moving in a circular pattern from this point."

Slowly and methodically the three of them began to circle the cave. It was hard work as the terrain wasn't even, and the cave itself was cut into the mountain cliff. Chloe offered to carry Shosty over the steepest parts, but he refused.

"I need to keep my nose to the ground," he said as he moved his short little legs up a particularly difficult patch.

They found a series of broken branches that might indicate someone coming through the area, but it was hard to tell who. Chloe kept calling out for Bertha, telepathically, but with no success.

After about three hours, they found themselves five miles from the cave, when Shosty barked and said, "I've got something."

He was sniffing under a prickly bush, managing to get his fur caught but refusing to move. Esmeralda stepped carefully over to the bush so as not to disturb whatever Shosty had found, and after sniffing herself, she said, "He's right. This smells of bear."

"And I found it," said Shosty proudly as Chloe worked to get him untangled from the bush.

"You certainly did," said Chloe.

"Nice job," said Emily. "Now let's see if this leads us to more information."

Neither Shosty nor Esmeralda found anything for a while, but then Shosty called out again. "More, here," he said. "I think it's bear again, and maybe one of the cubs is trying to mark a trail."

Esmeralda said, "I agree, and that trail leads off to the north."

They followed the trail for over an hour, but then it suddenly stopped. Try as they might, they couldn't pick it up at all.

"It's as if they just disappeared," said Emily.

"I bet the bear got caught," said Shosty. "I mean, someone was bound to notice that he or she was leaving a trail, peeing more often than usual."

"I'm afraid you're right," said Chloe. "And I can't pick up any stray thoughts from the kidnappers either."

"And what is Bertha doing?" asked Emily. "Why can't we reach her?"

The four of them kept searching for another few hours, taking a break every now and then for some snacks that Chloe conjured for them. But by the end of the day, they were tired and discouraged.

"I so wanted to find something," said Emily. "Not that I thought we were so much better than the others, but I really thought that our familiarity with Bertha would help."

"Me too," said Chloe. "I thought being closer would allow me to reach out to Bertha."

"And if we can't find Bertha," said Esmeralda, "there is no way to meet the kidnappers' demands."

"True," said Emily. "She's the only one who can open the secret vault."

They trudged back toward Bertha's cave, tired and discouraged. They had moved in circles, but now they took the shortest path to the cave. Shosty still refused to be carried, and they had to slow their pace to his, as his short puppy legs were definitely very tired. They didn't find any more evidence of the kidnappers, and by the time they reached the clearing in front of Bertha's cave, they were very discouraged.

However, all of a sudden, Shosty barked and raced into the cave. The others followed, and there, to their surprise, they found Bertha, tears streaming down her face.

"Bertha," exclaimed Chloe as she ran over to hug the bear.

Bertha looked up, and she seemed disoriented, unable to figure out who they were for a few moments. Then finally she said, "Chloe, what are you doing here?"

"Trying to find you," said Chloe gently. "We wanted to help."

Bertha seemed finally to take in Emily's and Esmeralda's presence as well. "Why are you here? And why are there so many dragons and riders on my mountain? They're in the way."

"They're looking for you and for Boris and Berla," said Emily. "Didn't you know we'd try to help?"

"You're messing up the scents," said Bertha. "I've been all over the mountain. I can't find them anywhere. I don't know what to do now."

Bertha put her head in her front paws and wept. Chloe put an arm around as much of Bertha as she could reach, and finally she said, "We know about the ransom demands."

"Then you know that I can't accede to them," said Bertha sadly, "even to save my own kids."

"What would happen if you did?" asked Emily.

"Then our planet would be in danger again," said Bertha. "That's why my ancestors and I were given the task of guarding the knowledge from the other timeline. It would be better to have that knowledge destroyed than to have it fall into the wrong hands.

"Generations of my maternal line have protected the secrets, as have yours, Esmeralda."

Esmeralda nodded and said, "Yes, I know, Bertha. And I would have to do as you are, but it hasn't come to that yet."

Emily said, "We got a ransom demand yesterday saying that the materials had to be left in your cave by tomorrow, or your cubs would be killed."

Bertha nodded, tears still streaming down her face. "I've been expecting that. I'm actually surprised they've waited this long."

"You know this mountain better than anyone," said Esmeralda. "Have you found no place where they could be hiding?"

"None," said Bertha. "I've looked into every cave I know. Nothing. I can't sense them at all, so they have to be drugged."

"I haven't been able to sense you either," said Chloe.

"That's because I deliberately blocked you and Libby," said Bertha.

"But why?" said Chloe. "Didn't you know we'd want to help?"

"Of course," said Bertha, "but there's nothing you could do, and I needed to concentrate on just finding Boris and Berla. But now I've failed, and I don't know where else to look."

"Could we make some false information," asked Emily, "something that could fool the kidnappers?"

"Maybe," said Bertha, "but not by tomorrow. Chloe, you've been in the vault. You know how many thousands of scrolls there are in there."

"Yes, but the kidnappers don't," said Chloe. "I could make fake scrolls. But unfortunately I wouldn't know what kind of information to put in them."

"That's the problem," said Bertha. "Our world hasn't become a technological one the way the other reality was. And that's something to be thankful for. That's why we don't have the pollution issues, the social poverty, the massive divide between those with power and those without. But it also means that we don't know how to fake the scrolls that the kidnappers want."

"We can't let Boris and Berla be killed either," said Emily.

"They wouldn't want to live at the expense of the entire planet," said Bertha. "They know what it means to be a seer, and Berla is just starting to have her seer powers awaken, so she'll already know what the stakes are. She'll have let Boris know, and he's sworn to protect her—and me, for that matter."

"Do we need this knowledge?" asked Esmeralda. "I always wondered why it was saved. Why did King Alfred bring it with him in the time travel?"

"I've just painted the worst picture of it," said Bertha. "There is also a lot of good that could come from it. Technology is neither good nor bad. It's the uses of it that caused so many problems before. But they had a lot of medical knowledge, for instance, that would be helpful."

"But who's to say," said Esmeralda, "that we won't develop that in time?"

"Remember that asteroid?" said Bertha. "Chloe needed the knowledge of the telescope to save the planet from its impact. True, Chloe had to do the actual work. But if she hadn't been able to learn about the asteroid until it was visible to the naked eye, it would have been too late.

"That's why the knowledge was brought back but guarded by the seers so that in the event of a situation like that the seer could release just the knowledge that was needed and no more."

"And a telescope is never going to be anything but a telescope," said Esmeralda. "It's never going to be a weapon, for instance."

"The kidnappers can't know what information is in your vault or even how much information," said Emily. "Can you release those scrolls that can't be misused?"

"It's not that easy," said Bertha. "The information isn't sorted, and there wouldn't be time by tomorrow to do what you ask. And to be honest, I don't think any of it should be released. My seer eye has searched all the possible outcomes, and releasing any knowledge always leads to a war or other disaster."

"So what actions give us the best outcome," asked Emily.

"Truthfully," said Bertha, "now that the news of the alternate universe has started to leak, I can only find one possible course of action. The vault has to be destroyed, and then the riders need to deny any alternate reality, saying that it's just a myth. Eventually, that's exactly what it will become, another legend about King Alfred, and nothing more."

"But what if we need that knowledge?" said Emily.

"Then we'll have to figure it out on our own," said Bertha. "The more I think about it, the more I believe that's what should have happened in the first place."

"Then we would have been smashed by the asteroid before I was even born," said Shosty.

"Would we?" asked Bertha. "Or would my foreknowledge have been enough to cause someone to develop the telescope or another similar device without the easy answer of plans dropping into the library? You can't say, and personally, I think that the risk surrounding the scrolls in the vault is too great.

"We've been really lucky so far that in over five hundred years no one has figured out what's here. But now that someone has, now that the secret's out, there will be more. Even if we stop these kidnappers, more will come after them."

"Remember that Elise said her dad had announced the alternate time to an entire roomful of people," said Chloe.

Bertha looked puzzled by this statement, so Chloe quickly brought Bertha up to date on George and his factory, as well as Elise and her slip of information to her parents.

"You see," said Bertha, "it's already begun without anything from the vault. George developed the first factory, and if that path is allowed to continue, well, we'll end up destroying the planet again without any help from the vault."

"So what are we going to do?" asked Esmeralda.

"I don't know," said Bertha.

Everyone was quiet as they all tried to think through options. Finally Chloe said, "I think the vault and its knowledge do need to be destroyed."

"I agree," said Emily.

"Me too," said Esmeralda.

"Well," said Bertha, "I'd already decided that, and after all, it's my decision and always has been. It was one part of my seer training. If discovery was likely, the vault had to be destroyed."

"OK," said Chloe. "But can we do it without letting the kidnappers know?"

"The vault can only be accessed, as you know," said Bertha, "from the back of my cave, so yes, the vault is fireproof, and so I just need to set a fire going inside and then seal it. There will never be a way to get inside again, and no one will know that it was ever there."

"I'd be happy to lend my flames," said Esmeralda.

"Thanks," said Bertha. "Might as well do that now."

"Right," said Chloe, "after which we'll see if we can find a way to get Boris and Berla rescued."

Bertha stood and went to the back of her cave. The others followed, and everyone but Chloe stood in amazement as Bertha waved a paw over the back wall, causing it to slide out of the way. A deep vault was revealed, shelves lining the walls and every shelf crammed with scrolls.

"I see what you mean," said Emily, "about not being able to fake this."

Chloe looked puzzled but kept her thoughts to herself. The vault seemed different from what she remembered.

"Ready, Esmeralda?" asked Bertha, after a quick glance at Chloe.

"Yes," Esmeralda said as she moved to the opening into the vault.

"Right then," said Bertha, "flame away. Everything has to burn."

Esmeralda took a deep breath and then sent flames into the vault, moving methodically around the walls until everything was turned to cinders. Once she was done, she stepped back away from the opening.

Bertha took a step into the space, checking to be sure that everything was indeed gone. Then she stepped back and swiped her paw over the back wall. The wall slid easily into place.

Bertha then said, "Esmeralda, can you please flame the wall? That will seal it so that it can never open again."

"Certainly," said Esmeralda as everyone else backed up into the front of the cave.

Esmeralda let her flames dance over the entire wall. The rock seemed to fuse, and once she was done, Bertha went back and swiped her paw across it. This time nothing happened.

"It's done," said Bertha in a quiet, sad voice.

Everyone was silent for a few minutes. The magnitude of what they had done was overwhelming even though they all agreed it was for the best.

Finally, Emily said, "We need now to figure out how to snare the kidnappers."

"Well," said Chloe, "they are planning to return tomorrow, expecting to find the scrolls. I was thinking I might be able to create the illusion of the vault. It wouldn't last long, and as soon as the kidnappers got close, they'd see that the wall was not open, but if we draw them far enough into the cave, then we can trap them."

"That's an idea," said Emily. "Are you recovered enough to manage that?"

"I think so," said Chloe. "I hope so. I think we all need to clear out of here now anyway, in case anyone is watching. Bertha, you keep looking, and don't change your pattern. We'll fly back to Havenshold, and I'll get a good night's sleep. Then we'll return tomorrow afternoon, and at that point, you, Bertha, need to return here, making sure you do it by the most open and direct route so that if they are watching, they will see you."

"Well, it's a plan at least," said Bertha. "And I don't have any-thing else to suggest."

"One more thing," said Chloe, "talk to Libby. And don't close yourself off again! We need to be able to communicate with you."

Bertha just nodded, and Chloe went over and hugged her. "Try not to worry. We will get Berla and Boris back."

Emily said, "Until tomorrow then."

Once they were in the air again, Emily said, "Do you think we really stand a chance? Can you do that illusion?"

"Of course she can," said Shosty.

"I don't know," said Chloe honestly, "but it's the only hope we have, so I sure hope so."

Esmeralda said, "I've always admired Bertha and the way she's cared for us all, but never more than today. That was a brave decision she made."

— 16 —

RODNEY'S PLAN

Boris and Berla sat in the cave, pretending to sleep, until the man who brought the food and water every day had left. Once they thought it was safe, Boris said, "I'm soooo hungry," with a pitiful moan.

"Me too," echoed Berla miserably. "And thirsty. And this cave is really starting to stink."

"My head feels a bit less fuzzy, but not much," said Boris.

"Same here," said Berla. "This drug is sure taking a long time to wear off."

Just then they heard scurrying sounds, and they stopped talking, fearing that one of the men had come back. But they quickly recognized Rodney, and they started to shout, "Rodney," until he shook his head and put a paw in front of his mouth. They bit off their greeting and waited as Rodney crossed the cave floor and climbed up onto Berla's leg.

"Did you find our mom?" asked Boris in a whisper.

Rodney shook his head and then started to pull at a pack that he'd carried in his teeth. Berla shook her head a bit and then said, excitedly, "I think I can hear your thoughts, Rodney."

About time, answered Rodney, who finally pulled his pack open and pulled out two loaves of bread.

"Food," whispered Boris. He took one of the loaves and swallowed it in a large gulp.

Berla did the same with the other, thanking Rodney. Then she said, "You couldn't find our mom, then."

No, thought Rodney, *I think she's out hunting for you, and I knew you guys needed food and water. I couldn't bring much, but I also brought some tools.*

"Tools," said Boris in a puzzled voice. "I can't eat them."

Berla laughed and said, "Hunger really has taken over your brain." Then she looked at Rodney and said, "So you're thinking you can help us get out of here?"

Exactly, answered Rodney as he proceeded to lay out what he'd brought.

Berla and Boris looked at his meager selection. There were some lock picks, a small pry bar, and an equally small saw.

Rodney watched them and, sensing their disappointment, said, *Well, I couldn't carry a lot.*

"No," said Berla, with as much enthusiasm as she could. "No, you did really well. I've just never learned to pick locks, and well, face it," she continued, not even noticing that she was using one of her mother's favorite expressions, "my paws aren't ideal for such a task."

Rodney laughed and answered, *But mine are, and you guys are stronger, so you can try sawing or prying at the chains. Between us, well, maybe it will work.*

Boris frowned, and after a few minutes he said, "You're right, Rodney. We have to try. Hand me the saw. Berla, you take the pry bar, and we'll work on the chain attached to my back leg. Rodney, you try to pick the lock on the chain attached to Berla's leg."

The three of them were silent as they worked. It was hard to make any dent in the chains, and both Boris and Berla were weak from hunger and thirst, but they were determined.

After about half an hour, the lock on Berla's leg clicked open. Berla quickly removed the clamp from her leg and said, "Rodney, you are truly amazing. Thanks! Can you do Boris's now?"

"Yeah," said Boris, "these small tools aren't making a dent in the metal."

Rodney said, *This should go faster, as I learned how to do it on Berla's.*

Boris and Berla held still while Rodney worked, and true to his word, in about fifteen minutes, Boris's clamp opened.

"Rodney, you are the very best," said Boris as both Boris and Berla stood and walked around unfettered by their chains.

Rodney cautioned them as they headed toward the cave opening. *There's a guard sitting on a large rock about twenty feet from the entrance, keeping watch.*

"Well, we're going to have to take care of him," said Boris.

What I thought..., said Rodney, and then he hesitated.

"Go ahead, Rodney," encouraged Berla. "You're our rescuer after all."

Rodney grinned and said, *What I thought is that I could sneak out and then move to the other side of the guard, the side away from the cave entrance, and make a distraction. I mean, I could chatter and swing from a branch and act cute, and if that doesn't work, I could pelt him with small stones.*

"And once he turns away," continued Berla, catching on, "Boris and I can grab him."

Right, confirmed Rodney. *Then we have to keep him in the cave somehow. Your leg cuffs would be too big for his ankles, but maybe they'd fasten to his waist or neck.*

"Well, we'll worry about that once we have him," said Boris. "We'll give you a few minutes to get into position, and after we hear you chattering, we'll keep watch."

Rodney nodded and headed out of the cave. He was very quiet and moved off to the right of the entrance before circling around the guard. He'd already spotted a suitable branch on the tree just beyond the guard, so he scurried up it quickly and began his chattering, turning somersaults on the branch.

The guard was obviously bored and tired, and he was very happy to watch a crazy squirrel. Rodney kept up his antics, glancing at the cave entrance as he landed from a somersault. It wasn't long before he saw Boris and Berla coming out, and he was amazed by how quietly and quickly the bears could move.

Boris grabbed the man and held his arms as Berla grabbed his legs. Rodney ran down the tree and followed as Boris and Berla carried the guard back into the cave.

"You can't do this," said the guard.

"I could be wrong," said Berla with a grin, "but I think we have."

"My buddies will be here any minute," the guard said.

"Don't you think we've figured out the drill," said Berla as Boris was checking the size of the cuff that he'd worn. "Your buddies only show up once a day, and they've already come. You're on your own."

As Berla kept her grip on the man, Boris looked at the cuff and then tried it on the man's neck. It wasn't very tight, but it definitely wouldn't go over his head.

"This should hold him," said Boris as the lock clicked in place. "I'm sure glad we didn't have to break the chains. Great lock picking, Rodney."

Once the cuff was in place, Boris, Berla, and Rodney stood back to admire their handiwork.

The man began shouting, "You can't do this to humans!"

"And you can't harm bears as we're a protected species," said Berla firmly. "Think on that while you wait for your buddies."

With that the three friends headed out of the cave. Boris and Berla looked around trying to figure out where they were. Finally Boris said, "I've never been here before."

"Me either," agreed Berla. "How did you find us, Rodney?"

Wasn't easy, answered Rodney, *but follow me, and I'll show you the way home.*

— 17 —

ILLUSIONS

Once they were back in Havenshold, Chloe decided to stop at the hospital to see Patrick as she'd promised. When she walked into his room, she found that Elise was visiting him as well.

"Hi, there," said Chloe as she entered the room. "Just wanted to stop by to see how you are doing, Patrick. Nice to see you as well, Elise."

"I can't stay long," said Elise, "as I now have extra chores, but Jake said a short visit would be all right."

"I agree," said Chloe.

"You know," said Patrick, "I've been trying to think about my dad's business. I really want to help, if I can."

"We appreciate that," said Chloe. "Have you thought of anything?"

"Not a lot," admitted Patrick. "But you know after the lava flow came across our land, well, my dad was looking for a new way to make money, and he found others who were also interested in what my dad called 'factories.'"

"Yes," said Chloe, "we knew that he'd set up one to make fabric."

"Yeah," said Patrick, "and so did our neighbor whose land was also wrecked by the lava. I think there were a group of them. My dad went to a meeting last week, and he came back all fired up about something, but he didn't share that with me."

"That's a start," said Chloe.

"And apparently this group found some large coal deposits," said Patrick. "My dad was bragging about how he could save us a ton by using coal and—how did he put it? Oh yeah, he said he could cut the dragon riders out of their slice of the pie."

"You think there are others doing this as well," asked Chloe.

"I do," said Patrick, "but unfortunately, I don't know any names." He stared down at his bandaged arms. "Guess I'm not much help after all."

"No," said Chloe quickly, "that helps a lot actually."

Elise looked thoughtful and then said a bit tentatively, "My dad mentioned something at that party."

"Oh," said Chloe.

"Yeah, he mentioned that his new investments were looking good. I have no idea what he was talking about, but he was talking to several business associates," said Elise. "I don't know more, unfortunately. I just heard it in passing when I was trying to get out of the room."

"Both of you have given me some leads," said Chloe. "Keep trying to remember whatever you can, and be sure to let Emily or me know if anything comes to mind."

Patrick and Elise nodded, and then Elise stood to leave. "See you tomorrow," she said as she left the room.

Chloe stayed a bit longer, talking to Patrick about Pathfinder Academy and what it could offer him. She was gentle and didn't push him toward any decision.

"I just want you to know that you do have options," she concluded. "And that you will find your own way. I'll come back and visit with you whenever I'm available. You aren't alone."

Patrick nodded and seemed more responsive to the idea of help. Finally he said quietly, "Thanks."

Chloe had a quiet evening and went to bed, where she got a full night's sleep. The next morning she went to Libby's for breakfast, so she could discuss her plan. Calliope and Shosty weren't about to be left, and when Chloe moved toward the door, they raced ahead of her. They enjoyed Libby's breakfasts too much to miss out.

Once the three of them had their food, Libby said, "It was so good to hear from that silly bear. I can't believe she didn't want to let us help her. Glad she's come to her senses."

"Yes," said Chloe, "I was so relieved to see her yesterday. But now we have to figure out how to save Berla and Boris. I need your help with an idea I had."

Chloe proceeded to explain about making an illusion of the open vault.

"I think that could work," said Libby. "Try to form an image of the vault on the other side of this room, and let's work on tweaking it, as well as sustaining it."

Chloe took a few moments to concentrate on remembering just what the vault looked like, and then she projected her image onto the wall to the right of the couch. The image flickered for a few minutes and then faded.

"Drat," said Chloe.

"I saw it for a second," said Shosty. "It looked just like Bertha's vault."

"Thanks, Shosty," said Chloe, "but it has to last a lot longer than that."

"It was just your first time," said Libby. "Have you tried doing this before, projecting any image?"

"No," said Chloe.

"Well, as you're discovering," said Libby, "it's not as easy as it seems. First, let's try something easier. Why don't you project an image of Calliope?"

Chloe took a good look at Calliope, and then, with her eyes on the cat, she projected the image onto the wall. This time the image was fully realized and didn't flicker at all. Except for the fact that Chloe didn't have anything for Calliope to sleep on, so it seemed as if she were floating in midair, the image was totally believable. Chloe maintained it for several minutes before it faded.

"Well done," said Libby. "Now, why was that easier?"

"I had Calliope right in front of me, so I didn't have to cast her image from memory," answered Chloe.

"Exactly," said Libby. "So you need to have a complete picture of the vault in your mind, a picture that seems complete and real to you. That picture has to be as real as Calliope is on that couch. So this time, try doing an image of Shosty, but don't look at him while you're doing it. Shosty, go hide behind the couch for a few minutes."

"OK," said Shosty. He jumped down off the couch and scooted behind it before saying, "I can see the wall, but Chloe can't see me."

Chloe thought hard about Shosty and then formed the image. It wasn't quite as complete as the one she'd done of Calliope, but at least it didn't flicker. It also lasted longer, nearly three minutes.

"Great," said Libby.

"That looked nearly like me," said Shosty.

Libby had Chloe practice on several more images, and she got to the point where she could cast an image of Esmeralda that was nearly perfect.

"Now, try the vault again," said Libby.

Chloe thought really hard about exactly how the vault looked, trying to focus on even the smallest detail, and then she cast again. This time the vault appeared three dimensional, and the scrolls looked as if they could be lifted off the shelves. Chloe was able to sustain the image for five minutes before it crumbled.

"Great," said Libby. "That will be enough to fool the kidnappers. I knew it was an image, and yet I believed that I could pick up a scroll. And five minutes should be enough to get the kidnappers to enter the cave and try to walk into the vault."

"Thanks, Libby," said Chloe. "I never could have done that without your coaching."

"Now you need to rest and have a good lunch before Emily and Esmeralda come to take you to Bertha's cave. I'll contact Bertha to let her know that you're ready."

"I will, Libby," said Chloe. "This just has to work."

A few hours later, Chloe, Emily, Shosty, and Esmeralda were once again in the air. Chloe updated Emily on what she'd learned the night before from Patrick and Elise, as well as how she'd trained with Libby to learn how to make the images.

"So, you think," said Emily, "that there's a group of people trying to manufacture things by machine using coal power?"

"I think so, and I think they're the ones trying to get the knowledge from Bertha's cave. I'm not saying that all of them are in on the kidnapping, but even if we do get Berla and Boris back—"

"Not if," said Shosty, "when!"

"OK," said Chloe, "when we get them back, we'll still have to deal with the use of coal and the pollution it will cause. We know, although now we can't share how we know, that the use of coal was a major contributor to the destruction of the environment in the alternate timeline."

"Agreed," said Emily, "but first we do have the major hurdle of getting Boris and Berla back."

Esmeralda was circling high about the forest, next to the clearing. "Where do you want me to land?"

"Good question," said Emily. "We can't take a chance on being seen, but we have to be close enough to act."

Esmeralda said, "I think I'm going to land down by the lake over there, and then we can hike through the forest to the edge of the clearing nearest the cave entrance."

"Sounds good," said Emily.

Once they'd landed and then crept into place, they could see Bertha returning to her cave as they'd suggested. She entered the cave, and Chloe moved so that she was within sight of the entrance. She wanted to be sure that she projected her image on the back wall, where the vault had actually been. And then they waited. And waited. Finally, when it was nearly dusk, they saw two men coming toward the cave. The men looked around in every direction before approaching the cave. When they got to the entrance, Bertha moved into view and said, "Where are my kids?"

"You'll get them when we have the information you promised us," snapped the tall, thin man. "Now, where is it?"

"Back there," said Bertha.

"Step out of the way," said the man who was obviously the leader. "Mac, watch her while I check it out."

As the leader started into the cave, Chloe formed the image of the vault and projected it onto the back wall of Bertha's cave. The leader took a few steps in and then shouted, "She's done it, Mac."

Just then Emily, Shosty, and Esmeralda crossed over to the entrance, and Bertha grabbed Mac by the arms. Chloe's image faded, and the leader turned around to find himself boxed in. "What's going on?" he asked.

"I could ask you the same thing," said Emily. "Where are Boris and Berla?"

"Wouldn't you like to know?" he snarled.

"Yes, and you're going to tell me," said Emily.

"Not likely," said the man, "and if we aren't back in an hour, Roy has instructions to kill the bears."

Bertha let out a howl of pain and in the process wrenched Mac's arm, snapping the bone.

As Mac screamed, Emily said, "I really don't think you want to find out what Bertha will do if you harm her cubs. Now, where are they?"

The leader looked alarmed and said, "Look, we just wanted the knowledge. You can't keep it for yourselves."

"Actually," said Emily, "there isn't any so-called knowledge. There never was. That was a myth that just got out of hand. You've been deceived, and now you'll be punished for kidnapping."

"What do you mean?" said the leader. "We got the information from the parent of a rider."

"Actually," said Emily, "from the parent of a rider in training, and that rider believed that the legend told in her history class was fact. This whole thing has been a major mix-up, and you fell for it. Unfortunately, you've become a kidnapper and a murderer with no hope of any gain."

"But I saw the room," said the leader.

"That would be my image," said Chloe. "I projected that fiction onto the wall so that we could trap you. Now we need Boris and Berla if you don't want to be torn apart, limb by limb, by a very angry mother bear."

The leader seemed to withdraw into himself before he said, "I had such hopes."

Mac was still screaming in pain.

"Take us to Boris and Berla," said Emily. "Chloe, can you look after this guy? Bertha is going to come with us."

"Certainly," said Chloe, "I might even splint his arm."

With that the leader took Emily and Bertha into the forest, while Shosty, Esmeralda, and Chloe stayed with Mac. Good to her word, Chloe fashioned a splint and fastened it to Mac's arm, which did ease his pain.

But it wasn't long before the three of them heard shouts of joy as Boris and Berla tumbled into the clearing, followed closely by Emily, Bertha, and surprisingly a squirrel. Bertha had a firm grip on a man who had to be Roy.

Bertha was laughing and said, "Guess what my smart twins did? They found themselves a rescuer and got out of their cave on their own."

The squirrel began chattering, and Bertha laughed before saying, "Yes, Rodney, with major help from you!"

"How did you do it?" Emily asked.

Berla began recounting how they'd figured out that they were being drugged and what steps they'd taken even before Rodney showed up. Then Rodney took over the account, with Berla and Boris, both of whom now had their telepathic abilities back, taking turns translating.

Rodney said, with much chattering and gestures, that he hadn't been able to find Bertha.

Bertha said, "Probably because I was always out searching."

Rodney nodded and told the rest of the story, ending by saying, "Then we ran into Bertha and Emily just a short distance from here."

Bertha looked at Rodney, Boris, and Berla, tears running down her checks, and said, "You guys really were resourceful! I'm so proud of you. And, Rodney, you're definitely part of our family now!"

Rodney bowed deeply and said, "Thank you. Glad I could help!"

"Thanks, Mom," said Boris.

"We just knew that we had to get back to you," said Berla.

"Now you all need some real food," said Bertha.

"Oh, yes, please," said both Boris and Berla, and the rest of the group laughed.

Emily then said, "We have captured all three men now, and Esmeralda can't carry them all, so I've called Hannah and Rupert to help with transport. They should be here in a half hour. Then, Chloe, you'll ride with me, you and Shosty, and we'll take the leader. Hannah and Rupert can then each take one of the others, after you, Rodney, show them the cave where you left the man you tied up."

"Sounds like a plan," said Chloe.

Bertha was feeling so much better now that her kids were home that she provided snacks for everyone, even the kidnappers, which they'd just finished when Hannah and Firebird, Rupert, and Whipper arrived.

"We'll get out of here now, Bertha," said Emily. "We'll be in touch tomorrow. I'm going to be sending these three off to Alfredsville so that Queen Clotilda and Matilda can decide their fate."

With that, the dragons took off from the clearing and headed for Havenshold.

— 18 —

CONSEQUENCES

Once everyone was back in Havenshold, Emily contacted Clotilda telepathically and arranged to have the kidnappers taken to the palace at Alfredsville. She asked Clotilda to try to get the leader, whose name was Munroe, to let them know of the others in the group who were trying to use coal, and Clotilda promised to get back to her as soon as possible.

Emily spent time thinking about the options facing her, and then she called Rupert into her office. "I'd like to have a meeting as soon as possible, with those of us who know about the alternate timeline and who are willing to figure out how we proceed to stop the use of coal. Can you ask the following to come: I'd like you, Hannah, Gregory, Chloe, Hazel, the baron, Oswald, Harmony, Clyde, Mildred, Aster, and Rya. I know it will be hard for Harmony, so it may take a bit to set this up, but if possible, I'd like to meet this afternoon."

"I'll get right on it," said Rupert. "I assume you'd like to meet in the conference room here."

"Yes," said Emily.

Rupert left, and Emily thought a bit more before deciding to head out to Gregory's office. As she entered the library, she waved at Chloe, who was in her office, and then headed to the back of the library, where Gregory's office was. She entered, gave him a big hug, and then said, "I need your help."

"Sure thing," said Gregory.

"I know it isn't part of your usual area as a volcanologist, but do you know where there are coal deposits?"

"Hmm," said Gregory as he stood and walked over to the wall in his office that held his maps. He pulled down the one for Havenshold as he said, "I'm of course most familiar with Havenshold, and we already know that George and his neighbor both found deposits when the dragons dug the trench for the lava. That will give me information that I should be able to extrapolate from."

"I really need to know just how much coal we are dealing with," said Emily.

"I'm suspecting that my dad will be able to help as well," said Gregory. "After all he has all those mines in Forbury."

"Definitely talk with the baron," said Emily. "And thanks. I'm trying to pull a meeting together, hopefully this afternoon, to discuss options. I'll let you know as soon as the time is set."

"I'll be there," said Gregory, giving her a hug as she left.

Emily then stopped at Chloe's office and let her know about the impending meeting.

"I'm on summer vacation now," said Chloe, "so my schedule is wide open. I'll be there whenever you say."

"We have to wait to see when Harmony can get there as her transport is the most difficult."

Chloe laughed and said, "Knowing Harmony, she'll be itching to get out, so I suspect you won't have to wait long. She'll get the baron to bring her for sure."

Emily agreed and then scratched both Calliope and Shosty behind their ears and headed back to her office.

Rupert succeeded in setting up the meeting for one o'clock, and he got snacks and beverages into the conference room before the participants arrived. Once everyone was settled around the large round table, Emily brought them up to date and then said, "So we have to find a way to stop the use of coal before it takes us down the path that it did before. Any thoughts?"

Rupert said, "Why don't we just pass a law making the use of coal illegal."

"We could," said Emily. "But that will put those who want to use it on the defensive and make them resentful." She paused to gather her thoughts and then said, "I'd like to review some of our past difficulties and look at how those were solved. If it's all right, I'd like to begin with you, Baron."

The baron nodded and said, "Certainly."

"As we all know," said Emily, "the baron had a very difficult time handling the loss of his wife, who died when Lance was born. He distanced himself from both Gregory and Lance, throwing himself into making more and more money and eventually trying to seize the throne from the then king Jacob, Rupert's father. He did this by kidnapping Rupert and then starting the Baron's War. Would you like to share with us, Baron, how that war ended with no casualties and how you were able to regain your true self?"

"Certainly," said the baron. "It was all thanks to my sons, who insisted on discussing our difficult history and making me realize how much I'd lost by shutting them out of my life. We healed as a family, and then I met this guy," said the baron, ruffling Oswald's fur, "when I walked into a gryphon sanctuary in Forbury. He nearly bowled me over as he demanded to know why it had taken me so long to find him. We were immediately bonded, about the oldest bonding ever to happen since I was fifty-one at the time. I always figured Oswald hadn't bonded at birth because he was born with only one wing and the other had to be amputated for his health and balance, but I couldn't have a better bonded mate."

"Nonsense," said Oswald, "I didn't bond with anyone else because I was waiting for you."

"In any case," said the baron, blushing slightly, "I realized that money and power aren't the be-all and end-all."

"Exactly," said Emily, "and so while you are definitely the richest man in Draconia and probably on the planet, you are also the biggest philanthropist, giving generously both here and in Forbury."

After a pause, Emily went on. "I'd like to move to Mildred now, if I might."

Mildred looked shocked and surprised.

"Mildred," said Emily, "you left home twenty-six years ago and remained estranged from your mother and brother, until Rya, your natural born daughter whom you'd allowed good friends to adopt, was in trouble. When her adoptive parents were murdered and Rya was threatened, you made sure that she was helped, eventually coming to me with the proof of her adoption. You didn't want personal contact at that point, but you agreed to telepathic communication not only with Rya, but also your mother, Harmony, and your niece, Aster. You would have had contact with Clyde as well, but he's the only one in your family who has no magical abilities.

"But when your mother cried out in pain, when she was attacked nearby in Bertha's clearing, you didn't hesitate. You went to find her and help with both Harmony and Rya. Even then, you could have just sent them off with the dragons, but you've chosen to accompany them back to Havenshold, a really big stretch for you. I don't expect you'll make your home here, as you are a reclusive artist, one who has not only stayed away from family, but any friends as well, a true loner. But I'm hoping you will continue to visit us all here in Havenshold as you feel comfortable."

"I plan to," said Mildred.

"But what caused the change in your willingness to reach out, especially to your mother?"

"I couldn't let anything happen to Rya," began Mildred. "I knew I was never cut out to be a mother, so I arranged for her to be adopted by close friends who'd never been able to have a child of their own. But when her world was threatened, I had to help, no matter what the cost to me. And honestly, I've really enjoyed the telepathic communication with all of them. I'd thought about meeting them in person, but that just seemed like too great a step.

"However, when I heard my mom crying out, well, that was the catalyst I needed. I had to help, and I'm so glad I did. I'm sorry, Mom, that you were injured, but that was the push I needed, and now I've gotten to see Clyde again as well. He was so young when I left."

"And I am glad, too," said Harmony. "A broken leg and a broken arm are well worth it to bring our family together."

Emily nodded and said, "So again we've seen problems solved by a development of relationships. And, Rya, you inherited significant wealth, but you chose to give it to the people of your village, Goldfog, with the proviso that it be used for the benefit of all."

Rya looked a bit embarrassed and then said, "Well, I didn't want it, and I thought maybe it would help repair the damage that was caused to Goldfog, both by the murderers and by the natural disasters that resulted from their actions. All I wanted was an apprenticeship with Uncle Clyde, and I've got that now."

"Again," said Emily, "a solution was found. And now there are two more examples of a more general nature that I'd like to treat. The first is the War of the Asteroid, where Chloe came into her full power as a mage. Chloe was only able to divert the asteroid from its path by using an energy net, which was formed by a linking of all the bonded pairs from all four nations. But that wouldn't have worked if it hadn't been for Hazel and her support team, providing those of us in the net with much-needed food when it was our turn to rest."

Hazel blushed and then said, "Well, I'd not always been the best mom to Chloe, so I was glad we'd reconnected and I was able to help."

Emily nodded and continued. "Finally, we have the recent crisis with Jaluhz. This time it was Clyde who brought us focus as he gave his perspective on the rift between those of us with magic and those without. He's the only one in his family with no telepathic abilities, and he shared just how hard it was for him to learn about Aster's power and then accept her bond with Jasmine. But he did it because of his intense love for Aster. His wisdom helped us to merge the dragon community with the rest of Havenshold, with all sorts of contests, thanks to the efforts of Oswald and Mary, who worked to keep sprits high, and ended up with us now having Jaluhz as our mascot, with shirts and mugs and so forth. Rya was put to the test communicating with Jaluhz, but with everyone pulling in the same direction and with a smaller energy net activated by Chloe, with Hazel's support group as well, the lava was rechanneled to a safer, less destructive path."

Emily paused and then said, "So can you see a pattern in all these solutions?"

Rupert spoke first. "I think I can. You weren't in favor of my idea of a law because that was an arbitrary and even abstract ruling. All of the examples you mention have been resolved by building stronger relationships between the parties involved."

"Exactly," said Emily. "And I think that's one reason why Hannah has discovered so few laws dealing with employment, for instance. When we told people about what George was doing, the universal answer from everyone was 'that's not the way we do things in Havenshold.' And they are right."

The baron said, "In each instance, the parties all benefitted, whether it was my family or the entire village of Goldfog. There really weren't any losers."

"Exactly," said Emily, "so people don't feel ill used if they get something of benefit to them. What we need to figure out now is what these businessmen are trying to get."

Emily stood and went to the whiteboard with her purple marker. "So what do they seem to want?"

"George is the easiest to figure out," said Hazel. "He and his neighbor tried to get better land from Clotilda when the drag-ons were digging the trench, but he lost out entirely. He had to allow the trench, but both he and his neighbor could no longer use their land as they had, so they were forced to find a new way to make a living."

"And that just fueled their hatred for dragons and their rid-ers," said Gregory, "so when they found an alternate fuel source with the discovery of coal on their land, they were all set to use it."

"So, cheap fuel," said Emily, "fuel that wasn't linked to the riders or the volcano." Emily wrote this on the board and then said, "What else?"

Hazel said, "George's hatred of Havenshold went way beyond cheap fuel. I mean, he did everything in his power to destroy Ingrid's quilt shop, from shoving her out of the building to making cheap fabric so that hers wasn't viable. As we know, he didn't just hurt Ingrid, but a major chunk of the business in Havenshold."

"Very true," said Rupert, "but do we know if the others feel the same way? We don't know what motivates all of the businessmen involved. They may have a common desire for, say, cheap fuel, but they may not all have the deep hatreds that George had."

"I suspect that's true," said Gregory, "and probably that's what got him killed. The others might have seen him as a loose cannon. But your point is good, Rupert. We just don't know enough about these people to surmise what they want."

"Well, we have to start somewhere," said the baron, "and one commonality seems to be the desire for a cheaper alternative fuel source."

"True," said Emily, "and while Draconia has depended on the use of thermal power, even exporting it to the other three nations in exchange for things we can't grow or manufacture here, as the population of the planet has grown, other options have developed."

The baron nodded and said, "Granvale has a very large wind field that produces significant power for them. And Sanwight has a fair amount of solar power developing."

"Those are both clean, nonpolluting sources," said Emily. "And near rivers, water power is being used as well."

"Even in Draconia," said Aster, "we've come across small landholdings that are using wind power."

"So if we could offer alternatives to these men," said Emily, "and do it in a way that would help them to become leaders in this, bringing them closer to the community, we'd have a solution that could help us all."

"The start-up for these powers can be pricey," said the baron.

"We can help with that with our funds," said Emily.

"Not all of them may be interested in taking your help," said the baron. "But I'd be willing to set up a trust to give grants to those who are interested in developing alternate sources of power."

"That's incredibly generous of you, baron," said Emily.

"After all," said the baron, blushing slightly and waving a dismissive hand, "it's in all our interests."

"True," said Emily, "and I really hope that Clotilda can get us the names soon. I'd like these men to see George's land before all that black smoke dissipates. It's still there even several days after his factory shut down. If we could show them the pollution, that would be much more powerful an incentive than just telling them."

"When will you hear back from Clotilda?" asked Rupert.

"She said she'd let me know as soon as she finds out anything," said Emily. "My guess is that she'll offer them incentives, such as less painful punishments, to motivate them."

Chloe said, "We could also talk to Elise's father. After all, that's where we think the original leak came from."

"Yes," said Emily, "but we'll have to be careful there as we don't want anything to lend credence to there being any truth in what Elise let slip. That story has to slide into myth and legend."

The assembled group nodded.

"When I get a meeting set up, I want to ask Chloe, Rupert, the baron, and Oswald to be there. I think if we are all there, it will be a bit overwhelming. And, Hannah, I'd like you there as well."

Hannah looked surprised. "Why me?"

"Well, you're our legal expert," said Emily.

"I'm beginning to think that there isn't much of a need for a lawyer, given what you've shown us about how things work best in Draconia."

"Maybe," said Emily, "but what I think you'd be really good as is mediator. You notice that every one of my examples involved people talking to each other. But sometimes that's really hard to bring about. If you trained as a mediator with legal knowledge, you could serve as a professional impartial bridge between parties."

"Hmm," said Hannah. "Mediator...I like the sound of that."

"And while it's possible that if this group has a lot of animosity toward the riders, they might not see you as impartial, we need to try, and you are already very good at sorting people out. Maybe that comes from being the youngest with five older siblings, four of whom are brothers, but you've figured out a lot already."

"OK," said Hannah, "I'll look up more resources as well. Chloe, do you think the library has anything on mediator skills?"

Chloe smiled and said, "I'd be happy to help you look."

Emily looked around the table and said, "Is there anything else anyone can suggest?"

There was a general shaking of heads, and the baron said, "I think I need to get Harmony back home. She's looking a bit tired."

"But it's been so good to get out for a bit," said Harmony.

"How are you doing?" Emily asked.

"Pretty well," said Harmony. "I do have to admit that Mildred and Clyde were right. I was being stubborn, and if it weren't for the baron and Oswald, I couldn't stay at home. They're looking after my rescue animals, cooking for me, helping me dress and take care of myself. It seems daunting to me, all they are having to do, but I'm very grateful, as without them I couldn't stay in my own space."

"We're very happy to look after you," said the baron as he stood to push her wheelchair to the door.

"Mom, I think I can make some modifications to your place," said Clyde, "which would allow you to maneuver inside your home better, and also I could build a ramp, which would allow you to get outside. If you'd like, that is."

"I would definitely like," said Harmony. "Thank you."

Rya stood as well, moving pretty easily with her crutches. "Trust me," she said, "stairs are not your friend. I have to sit my way up and down them, which is very embarrassing."

Mildred smiled and said, "Well, we did offer to make you a bed downstairs."

"I know, Mom, but there is something about sleeping in your own bed."

"I agree," said Mildred.

"Me too," said Chloe.

Gregory said, "Hey, Dad, could I pick your brain about coal deposits? Emily asked me to try to find out just how much coal we have on this planet, and that's not exactly my area of expertise. I've got some ideas, but I thought you and Oswald might have discovered something in Forbury with your mines."

"Certainly," said the baron. "Honestly we haven't come across much, and I don't think we've found any deposits that would provide any significant amounts of coal, but given our knowledge of the alternate timeline, there have to be deposits somewhere. I'll help as much as I can."

"Great and thanks," said Gregory.

With that the meeting broke up with promises to keep thinking of ideas to get these businessmen turned in the right direction.

— 19 —

INVENTIONS

Chloe heard from Emily the next morning that the meeting with the businessmen wouldn't happen for a few days, so she decided she'd walk to see Harmony. It was a beautiful summer morning, and she was in need of some exercise after all her paperwork.

"Want to go on a long walk, Shosty?" Chloe asked.

Shosty jumped out of his dog bed and said, "Walk! Of course."

You are so predictable, said Calliope with feline scorn from the top of the bookcase in Chloe's office.

Chloe laughed and said, "You keep an eye on the library for us while we're gone."

Of course, said Calliope, *and I'll visit with Arryn without your annoying interference.*

Shosty barely heard that last comment as he was already at the front door, eager for his adventure.

The two of them walked past Ingrid's Quilt Shop, and Chloe was glad to see a number of customers there. She and Shosty continued down the dirt road, passing a few houses before reaching the one that belonged to Emily and Gregory. It was a small, white two-story house with blue shingles. Chloe knew that both Emily and Gregory would be at work now.

About a half mile farther on, they were passing Amy and Todd's house. It was so distinctive. It had begun as a small rambler, but then as Amy became pregnant with each of their six children, Todd felt compelled to knock holes in the walls and add another room in a rather random way. Chloe thought fondly of the six years she'd lived there, and she thought that there wasn't a happier home on the planet.

She and Shosty continued on their way and reached the limit of Havenshold proper. The land then became more rugged and had small scrub bushes, which Shosty found absolutely fascinating, stopping at each and every one. This slowed their progress, but Chloe was content to let him enjoy his walk. They rarely had time during the school year to take such a long one.

After about an hour, they reached the baron's large ranch, the largest in Draconia, which his younger son, Lance, now managed as the baron spent most of his time in Forbury looking after his mining properties there. But Chloe couldn't help wondering if now that Harmony had relocated to Havenshold from her island off the coast of Forbury so she could be closer to her family, would the baron spend more time in Havenshold? Those two seemed to be very fond of each other.

When they reached the small trail that led to the cottage Harmony was living in, they turned right and walked down the short path. It was very nice of Lance and the baron to provide this for Harmony as she tried to decide whether she was staying here or returning to her island.

Chloe walked up the two steps to the front porch and knocked on the door. She heard Harmony call, "Come in," and they entered.

"Hi there," said Chloe as Shosty ran over to greet Harmony, who was stretched out on her couch. Chloe knew that as an animal person, Harmony would welcome the greeting, and in fact, two of Harmony's larger dogs who were sleeping next to the couch woke to join in the greeting.

Mildred stood up from the chair next to the couch and said, "How lovely to see you. Would you like some tea?"

"That would be great," said Chloe. "We don't mean to be interrupting your visit, though."

"You aren't," said Mildred with a chuckle. "We've been having a lovely time, getting reacquainted, and you're such a part of Mom's life now that it will be nice to get to know you better also."

With that she moved to the other side of the room to the kitchen area. Harmony's home was very small and compact, but it suited her. The room was painted a pale pink, and it contained both the living room and the kitchen/dining area. There was a small alcove tucked into one wall that held Harmony's bed, and between that and the main living area, there was a door that led to a small bathroom.

Mildred returned with tea for all of them, and once they were settled with that, Chloe asked, "So how are you feeling, Harmony?"

"Not too awful," she answered. "The pain is a lot less, thankfully, but the inactivity, not being able to tend to my sheep or milk my goats or gather the chicken's eggs, is driving me nuts."

"I bet," said Chloe.

"Mom never did take inactivity well," Mildred said, causing Harmony to chuckle.

"You've got that right," Harmony agreed, "and it's hard to ask for help or have people doing everything for me. I need help for everything."

This time it was Mildred's turn to laugh. "Well, you could have had it more easily if you'd stayed at Clyde's, you know."

Harmony nodded. "I know, but then I couldn't even have seen my animals. At least now I can see them out the window.

And I'm so grateful that you are part of my support team, Mildred."

"I'm glad too, Mom," said Mildred.

Just then they heard a loud ruckus outside, and Mildred went to see what was going on. Chloe and Harmony looked puzzled when Mildred burst out laughing. Then she returned to them and said, "You simply aren't going to believe this. You have a ton of visitors and a big surprise, I suspect."

Just then Rya and Artemis came in, Rya managing her crutches very expertly. Mildred immediately suggested that Rya take her chair, which Rya did gratefully. As soon as she sat down, Artemis jumped into her lap. Shosty had to come over to greet them as well, after which he returned to Chloe's side.

"Whew," said Rya. "We got to ride with Aster and Sasha on Jasmine, and that was an experience with my leg sticking straight out, but it felt so good to be moving without crutches."

"I know," said Harmony. "I rode on Oswald yesterday to get to the meeting, and I was really glad that the pain in my leg had lessened enough so that I could actually enjoy the ride. And Oswald was such a trooper, taking me, the baron, who insisted on holding onto me tightly as he was sure I'd slip off with my leg stuck out, and also my clunky wheelchair. We made quite a sight I'm sure."

"Well, we're here to help that," said the baron as he walked in, followed by Todd, Henry, Aster, Arryn, Oswald, and Sasha, who immediately ran over to greet Shosty as if she hadn't seen him for centuries. The baron went over to one of Harmony's windows and opened it so that Jasmine could stick her head in, since the small room would definitely not accommodate both her and Oswald. Once the two small dogs were curled up under Chloe's chair and everyone else had found somewhere to sit or perch, Harmony asked, "To what do I owe this wonderful visit?"

The baron went back to the entryway and rolled in a small chair on large wheels, which looked like a really weird contraption. There appeared to be some sort of shelf hanging down, and there were all sorts of levers and gadgets attached.

Henry got up and went over to show off all the finer features. He said, "The baron and Oswald came to Todd and me with an idea for you to give you greater mobility."

"Oswald actually designed it," said the baron, fondly ruffling Oswald's fur.

"But it was your idea," noted Oswald.

"Anyway, we built it together," said Henry. "It's narrow enough to get through regular doorways, and if you'd like to try it out, we can show you how it works."

The baron wheeled it over to the couch, and Harmony was able to lift herself in, although her leg then just stuck out into midair. Todd jumped up, obviously very eager to demonstrate the features of this remarkable chair, and said, "Don't worry, Harmony. There's a lever right here—see, on your left—so you can operate it with your good arm. Simply pull back on the lever..."

"Wow," said Harmony as the shelf she'd noticed earlier not only came up to the height of the chair but also unfolded so that her leg was now supported.

"Pretty slick, huh," said Todd. "I think Oswald could make a fortune off of that unfolding mechanism. It's all done with pulleys."

"And this lever," said Henry with just as much eagerness and pride, "makes a small shelf slide out so that your right foot has a place to rest, and you won't catch on anything."

"Clever," said Harmony.

"The best is yet to come," said Arryn. "Show her, Todd."

"Well, Arryn and I have been working on better solar batteries, ones that last a lot longer, and I thought this would be the perfect use for one. The chair is motorized. Obviously it would be really tough to move it with only one good arm, especially since we used such large tires, but if you just flip this switch, you'll go forward, backward, or turn."

"Todd, that is incredible," said Harmony.

Oswald moved closer, although the small room was really crowded, and said, "That's so you can go outside as well."

"What?" said Harmony in amazement.

The baron nodded and beamed at Oswald. "We wanted a way for you to be able to get outside by yourself. We know how much that has been bothering you. So that's why we put the larger all-terrain tires on the chair. It makes the chair a bit higher than a normal chair, but I think that will also make it easier for you to get in and out."

Oswald nodded and said, "In addition, you'll be able to get to your bathroom and your kitchen by yourself. You'll have to back into the bathroom, as there won't be room to turn around, but I think you'll get the hang of it pretty quickly."

The baron added, "The kitchen table will be easy to get to, so you'll be able to eat at it, but the sink and the stove are of course made for a standing height, so that still will be out of reach, quite literally."

"However," said Mildred, who was also getting into the spirit of it all, "I doubt very much that the baron is going to let you cook anyway."

"True," he said with a grin. "But at least we can all sit at the same table to eat."

"Oh," said Harmony with tears in her eyes, "this is just so wonderful. I'm overwhelmed by your generosity, not to mention your inventiveness."

"And we showed it to Dr. Brian," said the baron, "to be sure it was OK for you, and he is thrilled. I think he'll be asking for more as he needs them."

"Well, be prepared for more," said Todd. "It's a solar battery, as I said, so that means it needs charging about once a day. However, your porch faces south, so if you just sit out on your porch for an hour or so, it will charge. It won't, I need to add, charge while you are using it, so when you are chasing after your sheep and goats, that is not charging the battery."

Everyone laughed at this, and Mildred said, "You mean, Mom is going to have to sit still."

"But at least she can do that outside," said Todd, "and we're really lucky it is summer. I haven't quite figured out how to do portable solar batteries in the winter. The really large ones do pull in enough energy even on partially cloudy days, but obviously they aren't portable. But I'm working on spare batteries."

"Well, hopefully I won't need it by then," said Harmony, "but I do think you are really on to something, Todd."

Clyde then spoke up, saying, "I don't know if you've noticed the one hitch in all this yet, Mom, but we're here to fix that as well. You obviously can't roll down the two steps that lead to your porch."

"Those are a pain to navigate on crutches," said Rya.

"Right, well today we are going to ramp the front porch so that you can glide right out into your yard," said Clyde.

"That's my part of this," said Rya. "I had to design the ramp as part of one of my apprentice projects. Can't build it, unfortunately"—she looked down at the bright pink cast encasing her leg—"but at least you know it's my design, Grandma."

"Thanks, dear," said Harmony, "and us lame ducks with our pink casts need to stick together."

With that, Oswald, the baron, Todd, Henry, Arryn, and Clyde headed outside, where Jasmine was able to join them, and soon the others heard the sounds of sawing and pounding. The dogs decided it was too nice a day, and there was too much excitement outside to stay in, so they tore out the door. Artemis, however, was content just to stay in Rya's lap.

Chloe said, "So how are you doing, Rya?"

"Better," she said. "The crutches are getting a bit easier although my armpits are hurting. Mom suggested the padding that is over the top of them now, and that really helps."

"Are you able to get around OK?" asked Chloe.

"Stairs are definitely a nightmare," said Rya. "Nurse Beatrice did teach me the proper way to go up and down, and it works OK for a couple stairs like Grandma's porch, but a full flight, like getting up to my bedroom or back down again—that just seems too scary, so I sit my way up and down. Quite humiliating, but much safer.

"And Dad made me some space in the kitchen for my wood carving, since if I thought the upstairs were bad, well, the basement stairs are a real hazard, and I'd get splinters the entire way. But I'm able to carve, and you know that I really want to get into more artistic woodwork."

"Yes," said Chloe, "I remember the carving you made in Artemis's likeness as part of your graduation projects from Goldfog School. I thought that was pretty incredible, and it was only your first."

"Thanks," said Rya, blushing. "I've been talking with Henry to see if he could use figures with his toys, and he's really excited about that."

"Dad makes such great wooden toys, and I think he's branching out into dollhouses, as well as his trucks, boats, and trains," said Chloe.

"Yes, he seems to think that it would be really nice to have figures and maybe even furniture if he does dollhouses. He has a booth at all the festivals in Havenshold, and I'm hoping to work on some figures for the summer solstice, although that's only three weeks away. But I should have a lot of them by the winter solstice," concluded Rya.

"That's great," said Chloe, "and it will mean more apprenticeship credit, as well as being something to occupy you while that leg of yours heals."

"Our thoughts exactly," said Rya.

"It does make for a lot of wood shavings in the kitchen," said Mildred with a chuckle, "but us artists have to stick together."

"Yeah," said Rya, "Mom's doing a lot of sketching, and I'm using some of her sketches as models for my carvings. It's really fun." She was quiet for a few moments and then said, blushing a bit, "And Arryn visits a lot, which really helps."

Mildred laughed and said, "Those two can certainly giggle when they get going."

Harmony smiled from her chair, which she'd positioned near the couch, after a few false starts with directions. Chloe thought she looked extremely content, actually bursting with joy as she listened to Rya and Harmony. Chloe knew just how much family meant to Harmony and how much she was enjoying having all of hers together.

Harmony looked over at Chloe as if she knew what Chloe was thinking and just nodded at her.

They chatted some more, until Shosty came racing in, saying, "They're nearly done. Oh, it is so fun to run up and down it."

Chloe and the others laughed at this, and Chloe said, "So you think we should build a ramp for you?"

"Yeah," said Shosty, "right in the library, and I could chase Calliope up and down it."

That brought laughs from them all, and Chloe said, "Not sure how that would work out, but I'll take it under advisement."

The baron and Oswald entered, and the baron said, "So are you ready to take your chariot for a spin?"

"Definitely," said Harmony.

The others stepped back out of the way as Harmony, with very few false moves, got herself over to the door. She noticed that the men had modified the opening so that it was flat, and she could roll out easily. And then she saw the ramp, which led straight out from the door over the existing steps.

"What a wonderful design, Rya," she said as she noticed that her granddaughter had navigated her way out to the porch.

"Thanks, Grandma," said Rya. "I didn't want any corners, and your front yard has plenty of room for a straight ramp."

"Well, you can enjoy the benefits of your design as well," said Harmony, and with that she moved to the ramp and whizzed down it.

"Wow," she said, "That was fun and fast."

"Arryn checked the incline and calculated the speed that you would travel," said Todd, "and we decided that brakes weren't going to be necessary, especially since your land is basically flat (a Draconia anomaly, by the way)."

Harmony chuckled and said, "Yes, I do know that I was lucky to get such a good spot." Then she turned to look at the baron and smiled warmly.

"OK," said the baron, "let's see how your critters like this. The all-terrain tires are puncture proof, and you won't have any trouble unless things get really muddy. But that won't be a problem in the summer, at least."

Everyone watched as Harmony moved off into her pastures. It took her a few tries to position herself so that she could open the gate, but she was grateful that the others waited for her to figure it out and didn't just rush over to help.

Once she'd gotten inside, she latched the gate, and the others stood on the outside of the fence, watching and cheering her on. At first the sheep just ran away. Shosty seemed to feel that he should herd them back, but they paid no attention to him. However, Harmony's two dogs were used to this, and they rounded up the sheep in no time. Sasha stayed outside the gate with Jasmine and Oswald.

Harmony started crying when she could finally rub her sheep, and the baron entered the yard to take a handkerchief over to her. The goats were next, and they enjoyed being scratched under the chin. The baron joined her and said, "You won't be able to milk them, but you can be right here when I do. And you can hold the basket for the eggs when I gather them."

Harmony reached out and took his hand, kissing the back of it, and said quietly, "You're so good to me."

The baron bent down and kissed her as the others out at the fence pretended not to notice. But Clyde looked over at Mildred and smiled, and she smiled back. Chloe thought they made the perfect picture.

Finally, Harmony admitted to being tired, and so they headed back inside her home. Once she'd demonstrated to everyone's satisfaction that she was able to get around on her own, most of them said their good-byes and headed out. The baron and Oswald remained, saying that they would get lunch and then see that Harmony was settled for a well-deserved nap.

Harmony moved to the front door once the rest of them were outside and said, "Thank you all so very much! You have given me an extraordinary gift. I have maneuverability and the ability to look after myself, at least mostly. Thank you from the bottom of my heart."

There were many shouts of "You're welcome" as Aster helped Rya onto Jasmine's back, before handing up first Sasha and then Rya's crutches. Then she leaped easily onto Jasmine's back with the agility of a sixteen-year-old experienced rider. Chloe and Shosty stood back as Jasmine took off. Clyde, Henry, and Todd got onto the wagon they'd brought to transport not only the chair but all the lumber and building supplies for the ramp, and then they left.

Finally, Shosty and Chloe started walking back to the library. Clyde had offered them a ride, but she and Shosty decided that it was too nice a day to miss the walk.

— 20 —

MENTORING

Chloe and Shosty got back to the library in the late afternoon, and both were ravenous. In all the excitement at Harmony's, they'd missed lunch, and then they'd also exercised a lot more. So they were looking forward to heading home for an early dinner.

However, when they walked into the library, they found a very disgruntled Calliope.

Where have you been? Do you know how long you were gone?

"Sorry, Calliope," said Chloe.

And I didn't even have Arryn as I thought I would. And with all that's been going on and you getting hurt before, well, I was worried.

Chloe went over to Calliope and picked her up for a big hug. "I know it's been long, and I should have contacted you telepathically to let you know what was going on. Arryn got to spend the day with Rya, and I'm sure she'll be here tomorrow."

"We did lots of fun stuff," said Shosty, "but I'm hungry."

Yeah, I didn't get my lunch either.

"OK," said Chloe. "What do you say that we head home, and I'll make us an early dinner, and then I'll tell you all about our day."

Everything?

"Yes, absolutely everything," said Chloe, scratching Calliope behind her ears the way she loved.

The three of them walked through the library, through the stacks, to the door at the rear that led into Chloe's apartment. Once they were home, Chloe was good to her word, making sure that Calliope got fed first and then Shosty, after which she made herself a dish of pasta with mushrooms and marinara sauce and a fresh sourdough roll. She put her dinner on the side table next to her place on the couch and then waited for Calliope and Shosty to jump up and nestle with her.

As she ate, she told Calliope everything, with a lot of help from Shosty, from the walk out and back, to the events at Harmony's. When they were done, Calliope seemed greatly mollified. *It does sound like an exciting day. I wouldn't have liked the walk or all the dogs or the noise, so I have to admit that I think it's better to hear about it than to experience it.*

Chloe laughed and rubbed Calliope's head. "And after all, you are the library cat. You're really needed here, even when we don't have anyone in here. You may not see Libby most days, but I know she enjoys your presence."

And I'm beginning to feel something strange about the library. I think Arryn's right. I think something is going to happen. So you do need me here.

"Always," said Chloe. "Besides, you know you hate going outside, even if it isn't for a trip to see Sylvester at the animal clinic. I just want to thank you again for your tremendous bravery when you did go out to rescue Shosty and me. That was amazing, and I don't like to think how we would have managed without you."

As Calliope purred loudly, Shosty added, "You were very brave. And you did what I couldn't. You may be a cat, but you're pretty darned cool, and I'm glad you're my cat."

I'm not your anything, dog. After a pause she said, *But you're not so bad yourself.*

With peace restored to her family, Chloe picked up the book she'd been reading, and the three of them enjoyed a quiet evening on the couch together.

The next morning Chloe decided she'd better do some work. She knew that Emily had said it would be several days before the meeting could be arranged with the businessmen, and she decided to take advantage of the brief hiatus. She'd received a number of inquiry letters from parents and students asking about Pathfinder Academy, and even though it was summer, she needed to give some thought to those so that the selection of new students could be accomplished.

In addition, she wanted to visit Patrick again, as she not only saw him as a potential Pathfinder student but also felt that he needed some support. Since she hoped that she could enlist Elise in helping her present options, she decided to visit him during the lunch hour, as she knew that Jake let Elise take her lunch at the hospital with Patrick.

With a plan for at least the first part of the day made, Chloe showered, dressed, and fed the three of them. They then walked through the kitchen door into the library heading through the stacks and the long hall to her office.

As they passed Gregory's office, which was located on the right immediately past the stacks, they noticed that he was already hard at work. Chloe stuck her head in to say, "Good morning. You're looking very industrious."

Gregory looked up from his maps, running a hand through his brown hair, and said, "I'm trying to figure out just how much coal our planet has. Emily needs that information for her meeting, whenever that happens."

"How's it going?" Chloe asked.

"Well, slowly. My dad and Aster will be here later. My dad knows a lot more about what's underground in Forbury, of course. And Aster told me that some of her history books might shed some light on how long the coal lasted in the alternate timeline."

"Well, we'll leave you to it," said Chloe, "and good luck."

"Thanks," said Gregory, his attention already focused back on his maps.

Once they were settled in her office, Chloe opened the file she had with inquiry letters. Of course, just as soon as she had the pile spread out on her desk, Calliope sat on the papers, but Chloe was used to this "assistance" and knew how to work around it.

The morning sped by as Chloe answered the inquiries. Some were from parents who were determined to help their child find his or her calling. They knew that while their offspring had finished the mandated schooling, they didn't really have any idea where to go next. Chloe knew this wasn't uncommon for thirteen- or fourteen-year-olds, the age they usually were when they graduated. It was true that many students came from families with farms, ranches, or other businesses where they would naturally be expected to work.

But that wasn't always a good fit. Others had offers for apprenticeships in areas they were interested in, and so they'd spend the next six to nine years learning their trade.

Nevertheless, that still left a percentage who were in need of something different. Chloe was always happiest to receive letters from parents who were supporting their students in finding a good fit. Too often students were told what to do, rather than being listened to. So Chloe found the parents' letters the easiest to answer, and she wrote replies to about a dozen of them. Many of those would decide on something other than Pathfinder, but Chloe felt that whatever they did, it would be in their student's interests, and that was gratifying.

Once those letters were written, she turned to the half dozen she'd received from the students themselves. These were always harder, as they came from students who felt trapped and not heard. They were frequently being forced into a path they had no interest in or talent for. Chloe was thankful for a couple of things when she had these students to answer. The first was that Pathfinder Academy was becoming better known in Draconia, and teachers in the local schools were more apt to let students know about the alternative options Pathfinder offered.

The other thing that Chloe was very grateful for was the Draconia statute that gave students the right, once they'd graduated, to go out on their own. This meant that they didn't have to have parental permission if they decided to attend Pathfinder. Therefore, Chloe was able to write directly to the students and let them know what their options were.

It took her longer to craft these six letters, but she finished the last just before lunch.

"Well, that's a good morning's work," she said to Calliope and Shosty, both of whom had napped the morning away.

They lifted their heads briefly, without interest, until Chloe stood and grabbed their food dishes. Today, they wouldn't miss lunch. Chloe always tried to give them each a bit of kibble mid-day. Calliope didn't exactly need it as she was a bit plump, but she certainly enjoyed it. Shosty was still a growing puppy, and he did benefit from a midday snack, and after all, it didn't seem right to Chloe to feed one and not the other.

Once her family was set, Chloe decided to head for the hospital. She'd already decided to have her lunch after her visit, since she really wanted to catch both Elise and Patrick.

"I'll stay here with Calliope," said Shosty. "I'm sure she'll appreciate the company."

Right, said Calliope with a bit of sarcasm, but Chloe knew she was really glad for the company.

"And maybe Arryn will come in," said Chloe. "Anyway, I shouldn't be more than a few hours. I'm going first to the hospital, and then I'll grab my lunch out, maybe at Stella's Coffee Shop. Be good, you too."

Chloe walked down the stairs outside the library's front door, turned right, and walked past several businesses, including Anita's Second Chance Shop and Mary's Sweaters and Yarn Shop, before turning through the large archway that led into the dragon riders' compound. She then headed through the front doors of the hospital and greeted Nurse Beatrice at the front desk.

"Here to see Patrick?" Nurse Beatrice asked.

"Yes," said Chloe, "I feel very sorry for him."

"Me too," said the nurse. "I wasn't sure at first how I felt about someone who would try to burn a house down, especially knowing that someone was inside, but now, I just think he's a good kid at heart who's had a really rough time. I sure hope you can help him."

"Me too," said Chloe, "and thanks for your read on him. That's my take as well, and I do have some ideas. Is Elise with him, I hope?"

Nurse Beatrice nodded and then said, "She just got here on her lunch break. She's a really sweet young girl, and she's the best medicine Patrick gets. I'm really glad that they have each other."

Chloe nodded and headed down the hallway to Patrick's room. As she walked in, she heard Patrick laughing, and that raised her spirits. She hadn't seen so much as a smile from him since she'd met him.

"Hi, you two," Chloe said. "Mind if I join you for a bit?"

"No, not at all," said Elise as Patrick merely said, "OK."

Chloe pulled up a chair on the other side of the bed from Elise and then said, "Remember, I told you, Patrick, that we were all here to help you and that you had options?"

Again, Patrick only nodded.

Undaunted by his lack of enthusiasm, Chloe said, "Well, don't worry. No one is going to force you into anything. But I just wanted the chance to tell you some more about Pathfinder and also about other options that might appeal. And I want to get to know you more first. It's hard to help when I don't know what your interests are, or whether you have any dreams."

"My dad wasn't much on dreams," said Patrick quietly.

"I'm sorry," said Chloe. "Before we go much further, Emily asked me to check with you about what you wanted to do for your father's funeral. Do you have any thoughts?"

Patrick looked over at Elise, and she took his hand in hers. Then he looked back at Chloe and said, "I thought he should be cremated and then his ashes scattered in the lava river."

Chloe nodded and then said, "And how did you come to that plan?"

Patrick looked down at the hand Elise was holding and then said, "Well, it seems to me that the lava river is a real turning point in my family. That's what started all the trouble with my dad, not that he was ever an easy man. But he really turned when he didn't get new land and when the trench was dug across our land so that Jaluhz's lava could journey to the sea."

Chloe nodded but remained silent, giving Patrick the space to continue.

"And I understand from Elise that Jaluhz's lava flow will last for a long time, twenty or more years."

Again Chloe merely nodded.

"So I think it's a good place for his ashes to be scattered," Patrick said. "Because that river is also my turning point."

"Can you explain that?" said Chloe.

"Well, as I say, my dad was always demanding," began Patrick. "He never cared what I was interested in or anything like that, just how well I did what he told me too. And somehow that was never enough. I was never good enough for him."

Several tears slipped down Patrick's cheek, and Elise used a handkerchief to wipe them away before Patrick continued. "That's why I did what I did. I thought that would make him happy. For once, he'd see that I could get something right. But of course, it wasn't right, and it didn't turn out well.

"But I figure this is my turning point now, my chance to decide how I want my life to go. I can continue to feel miserable and think I'm a failure, or I can see this as a chance to become my true self. At least that's what Elise has been saying, and I think maybe she's right."

Chloe smiled and looked over at Elise, who nodded and said, "Patrick and I aren't that different really. Oh, I wasn't ever abused the way he was, but I was always just a pawn in my parents' plan for a life, more money, more of everything. When I was chosen to be a dragon-hatching candidate, my parents were furious. They kept hoping I wouldn't be chosen, and you already know how they reacted to the most wonderful day in my life, when Cinnamon hatched and staggered directly to me, told me her name, and demanded food.

"I was so happy. I knew I was where I was supposed to be and that Cinnamon was my soul mate. And when Hannah and Jake took us, the new dragon rider apprentices, to our new homes, the caves in the complex, well, I was so happy. Others in my hatching class had parents and friends crowding into their caves, congratulating them and cooing over their baby drag- ons. But Cinnamon and I were alone. My parents just stormed out of the hatching and went back to Havenshold. I didn't learn until later that they tried to get Jake to remove Cinnamon and give her to one of the candidates who wasn't chosen."

"That's horrible," said Chloe.

"Anyway, even though I was alone, I wasn't. I had Cinnamon, and she had me, and that was more than enough. I've never felt so fulfilled, so alive, so present in my own space. I know that Patrick can find something to make him feel like that. And just as I had no idea who I was until I met Cinnamon, I know that Patrick's never had the chance to discover who he is. And he's really a good sweet person, Chloe. Truly he is, in spite of what he did."

Chloe smiled and looked at both of them before saying, "I know he is, Elise, and thank you for sharing your path with me. We all have them, and sometime I'll share mine with you both. Some paths seem to be pretty easy and smooth, but others, like ours, are very rocky indeed. But at some level, I think that maybe those rocky paths are better because once we find our true path, well, I think it means a lot more."

Everyone was silent for a few minutes, and then Patrick said, "Can I say something?"

"Of course," said Chloe.

"Well, it may sound weird, but I'd really like to thank you, for putting that protection spell on Ingrid's house," he said. "Without that, well, I don't know if I could have lived with myself if my arson had connected, especially if Ingrid had been badly injured or died."

"When I put the spell on the house," said Chloe, "it was with the intent of protecting any perpetrators also, so that they would have the opportunity to feel what their actions delivered. I wasn't sure that they would understand or have a change of heart, but I felt they deserved the chance. So I'm very glad you did, and you're welcome.

"Back to your dad's funeral then," said Chloe after a moment. "Did you want to have the cremation on your property?"

Patrick nodded and said, "Yes, and I'd really like to have a dragon do it."

Chloe looked surprised at this, and Patrick continued, "My dad had no time for dragons or riders or their whole idea of service to the planet. But I'm beginning to think that he was all wrong. I've gotten to know Elise and Cinnamon, and I've also watched how all of you have treated me, someone who didn't deserve anything but cruel punishment, and I think that maybe there are other ways to act."

Elise said, "If Cinnamon were older, she'd do it, but she hasn't grown enough to have even a tiny flame yet."

Chloe smiled and said, "I'm sure that Emily and Esmeralda would be honored to help with this. And we'll do it where the lava river crosses your property. I've already spoken with Dr. Brian, and he says you are strong enough to attend if we keep it short. It will need to happen tomorrow, if that's OK. It's summer now, and not to put too fine a point on it, your father's body doesn't need to linger."

Patrick said very quietly, "That's fine."

Chloe then said, "Now, onto the future. As you've said so eloquently, you're at a turning point. You have inherited your father's property, so that may help."

"Not really," said Patrick. "He'd gotten loans for everything, and the ranch and factory are actually now owned by others. I don't think there'll be anything left once the creditors are done."

"I'm sure that Emily will help you handle those details, and maybe if you're up to it, we can help pack up your clothes and personal possessions after the funeral."

"But where will I go?" said Patrick, a note of desperation in his voice.

"That's really the main reason I'm here today," said Chloe. "I have ideas that I'd like to run past you."

She began by once again telling him about Pathfinder and what opportunities would be available if he chose that route. Then she explained about the foster homes she arranged for Pathfinder students.

"If you chose to enroll in Pathfinder Academy, then I have a number of families who have offered to foster students. Some of our students come from situations like yours, where they are on their own, for a variety of reasons. Some live too far away to commute, so they stay with a foster family during the school year and go home on holidays and vacations. There are as many variations as there are families.

"If you don't choose Pathfinder but want to seek an apprenticeship, then it will be up to your teacher to provide you with room and board. So, whatever you decide, you will have a home. Now, can you tell me if you've got any idea of a direction or interest you might want to explore?"

Patrick took a few minutes to think once Chloe was finished. Finally he said, "You know, I've really been thinking about Pathfinder since you first mentioned it to me. Elise has been kind enough to ask about it as well and share that information with me. I really don't have any idea what I want to do, so Pathfinder seems as if it would give me the best chance to explore options."

"I'd have to agree with that," said Chloe, smiling, "but then I am not exactly unbiased. It is true that if you signed an apprenticeship agreement, you'd be forced to fulfill it. That isn't a good option if you are unsure."

"And I don't want to promise something that I can't fulfill," said Patrick. "This is my turning point, as I said, and I really want to do it properly."

"Excellent," said Chloe. "Now, can you tell me if you ever have found anything that you did enjoy, no matter how small or insignificant it might seem to you?"

Patrick looked at the covers on his bed and then said, very quietly, "I've always liked animals. My dad had some sheep (well, before the lava), and I love to help with the lambing. My dad didn't like helping a ewe. He was quick just to cut her open and yank a lamb out and then kill them if they didn't survive. But if I could get there first, I discovered I could help the ewe. It gave me a lot of joy to bring that new life into being."

"I'd say that was something major that you enjoyed," said Chloe.

Patrick laughed and said, "And you know lambing always happens in the early spring, and it seemed it would always be windy, cold—snowy even—but I didn't care. As I got older, my dad wouldn't even bother to come out, but that was fine by me."

Chloe thought for a moment and then said, "I'm thinking that once school starts up, I'll have you hook up with Sylvester at the animal clinic as part of your studies. And maybe, if you're open to it, I'll ask him to stop by here while you're still in the hospital, just to give you another visitor. You guys can then chat informally."

Patrick said hesitantly, "I guess."

"He's not got a lot of time, but my guess is that when I tell him how you've done with lambing, he'll jump at the chance to meet you," said Chloe, "but the choice will still be yours. Next we need to discuss housing options. Dr. Brian has said that you can be released from the hospital by the end of the week if you have a good place to go. So, can you tell me, do you like or do you think you'd like to be in a large family or small? Do you have friends?"

"When I was in school, I was always a loner," said Patrick. "I never seemed to find anyone to hang around with, and also my dad had me working every minute I wasn't in school. It's always just been him and me."

Chloe nodded and said, "OK, then, I'll find a home with just a couple, probably retired. Is that OK? Do you remember any grandparents?"

"Not really," said Patrick. "My dad's died before I was born. My mom's lived in Granvale, and they tried to visit me, after my mom died, but my dad made them so uncomfortable that they finally gave up. They died a few years ago."

"I'm sorry," said Chloe. "Well, what I think I'll do is contact some of the people on my foster list, and if I find what I think might be a good match, I'll see if they can come by to chat with you here. Then you can let me know what you think. The final choice will be yours, and I want you to remember that. From now on, you're in the driver's seat, and you will direct your life. I'm here only as support and a mentor, and you will have others to help as well, but the choices will always be yours."

Patrick stared at her, looking a bit overwhelmed. Elise patted his hand, and then he finally said, "That seems a bit much, but also kinda good."

Chloe laughed and said, "Well, one step at a time. And we won't ever throw you off a cliff. So let's get through the funeral and then find you a home. Those are the first goals."

Chloe stood and said, "Now, I've taken up most of your lunchtime, so I'll get out of here and let you have a few minutes anyway, but it was great meeting with you both."

As she turned toward the door, Patrick said, "Thanks, Chloe, and thanks for caring."

"You're most welcome," Chloe said as she left.

LIBRARY EXPANSION

Chloe let Emily know about the funeral for George, and as Chloe expected, Esmeralda was willing to do the cremation. Later in the afternoon, Emily had gotten back to her to let her know that the funeral would be the next day, at nine o'clock in the morning. Dr. Brian would bring both Patrick and Elise, after Jake agreed to give Elise the time off for just the funeral. Dr. Brian wanted to keep an eye on his patient. Emily suggested that Chloe fly there with her on Esmeralda, and Chloe happily agreed.

The next morning Chloe got going promptly, and after making sure that Calliope and Shosty were taken care of, she walked to the riders' compound. She found Emily and Esmeralda already out in the courtyard, and Esmeralda had a bundle strapped to her back.

"Morning," said Emily. "Are you ready?"

"For sure," said Chloe.

It only took a few minutes to fly to the Pontsby property, and Esmeralda landed at the edge of the lava river. Chloe helped Emily lift the bundle down off of Esmeralda. She found out that it was the bag with George's body, as well as a folding trestle table.

Emily set up the table, which had a shallow metal tray for its top, and then lifted George out of the bag, placing him carefully into the tray. They'd just finished setting everything up when Dr. Brian arrived in a wagon with Patrick and Elise.

The small group gathered in front of the table, and Emily asked Patrick if there was anything he wanted to say.

Patrick, looking extremely pale and uncomfortable, and holding tightly to Elise's hand, said, "I don't know what to say." He stared at his father's corpse and finally said, "You were my dad, and you raised me. I hope you're in a better place now. Thanks, Dad."

Patrick then turned to Emily, who said, "That's fine. Now then, Chloe said that you wanted Esmeralda to do the cremation."

Patrick nodded and then said, "Please."

"It would be my honor," said Esmeralda.

Everyone stepped back a few paces to give Esmeralda space, and then, after bowing first to Patrick and then to George, she inhaled a large breath and then blew orange and yellow flames onto the corpse. It didn't take long, given how hot her flames were, and when she was done, she turned and bowed to Patrick again.

The metal tray now contained only ashes. They waited a few minutes for the tray to cool, and then the tray was tipped so that the ashes could be swept into a glass container, which Patrick held.

Emily then said, "You want to scatter these ashes in the lava river then?"

Patrick nodded and walked to the edge of the river, where he stood uncertainly. Esmeralda came up to him and said, "If you would like, I could lift you so that you would be over the center of the river. It would make it easier to scatter the ashes."

Patrick took his eyes off of the river and turned to Esmeralda. He then said, "You'd be willing to do that?"

"Of course," said Esmeralda, "if it's what you want."

Patrick held tightly onto the jar with the ashes, and Esmeralda gently lifted him by the waist, using her front two legs. She flew to the middle of the river, hovering just above the lava, and Patrick tipped the ashes into the center of the river. Then Esmeralda flew back to the others and gently placed Patrick down.

Patrick then bowed to Esmeralda and said, "Thank you so much."

"You are most welcome," said Esmeralda.

Dr. Brian said, "We need to get you back to the hospital, Patrick, but I understand that you need to gather up your belongings first."

Patrick nodded and led them toward the house. He went up the stairs to a small bedroom, followed by Emily and Chloe, and walked in. Emily had brought a couple duffle bags to use, and she opened them on the bed. Patrick pulled his clothes out of a small dresser and then grabbed a couple small items from his bookcase.

Chloe looked over at Emily, and she could tell that they were both thinking the same thing. Patrick had almost no posses-sions at all to show for his fifteen years. It seemed a sad ending to things, but Chloe could only hope that Patrick was right, that this was a turning point for him and he would soon be in a much better space.

Patrick and Elise, along with Patrick's possessions, went with Dr. Brian in the wagon back to the hospital. Emily and Chloe folded the table and tied it onto Esmeralda before they flew back to Havenshold.

After saying good-bye, Chloe returned to the library. As soon as she stepped through the front doors, she saw Bertha, along with Libby and a very excited Arryn.

It was Arryn who spoke first. "I told you that something was going to happen with the library! Look!" She pointed to another level of library stacks sitting above the current stacks and below the second floor, which held the astronomy observatory.

Chloe stared in amazement. It was as if there was an extra floor between the first and the second floors. And it was filled with shelves, shelves that were crammed with books.

Chloe then ran over to Bertha, gave her a big hug, and said, "This is your doing, isn't it?"

Bertha said, "Yes, it is. And we need to talk about it—you, me, Arryn, and Libby."

And me, said Calliope forcefully. *I am the library cat.*

"Yes, and you, and yes, and you too, Shosty, as I know you are the library dog," said Bertha with a smile.

Libby said, "Why don't we all move into my apartment. I'll then be able to provide food for all of you, and we can discuss this and find out what Bertha has been up to."

With that they moved to the back of the main floor, where a door, to the left of the one that led into Chloe's kitchen, suddenly materialized. Libby opened it and ushered them all in. Once they were in Libby's apartment, the door vanished.

Bertha sat on the floor while Arryn and Chloe sat on Libby's couch. Calliope and Shosty jumped up onto the couch with them and Libby sat in her chair. A large plate of sandwiches appeared on the coffee table, along with two small bowls of kibble. There was also hot tea for Chloe and Arryn.

Once everyone was settled, Libby said, "So now, my friend, why don't you tell us what you've been up to."

"Before she does that," said Chloe, "how are Bertha and Berla?"

"They're fine," said Bertha. "I explained to these guys before you arrived that it took a day or two before the last of the effects from the doping they'd been given wore off. And they're also being a lot more careful now, not that there should be any danger. Bears are protected after all. But we saw how much good that did."

Chloe nodded and said, "Well, I'm sure glad they're OK and back home again."

"You and me both," said Bertha. "I don't ever want to go through that again. But to answer Libby, I did know something was going to happen several months ago."

"What?" said Chloe. "What kind of something?"

"You may remember from when you had to battle that asteroid that my abilities to see into the future are limited, and the further away the event is in the timeline, the less I know about it."

Chloe nodded and Bertha continued. "I didn't see the danger to Boris and Berla at all, to my shame. What I did see was a vague threat to the cave's store of knowledge.

"And so I began thinking about that. I had some tough decisions to make. As I said before I destroyed the materials on the shelves in my cave, that knowledge is a two-edged sword, and I have wondered if we weren't better off without it.

"That being said, there had to be a reason why King Alfred brought it back to our reality and why he chose my distant maternal ancestor to guard it. So I've been thinking long and hard about this over the past couple of months.

"By the time of the kidnapping, I'd managed to sort through the materials, dividing them into subject matter and then further setting things apart that were only destructive, like weapons and bombs."

"And I'm betting," said Chloe, smiling, "that those are the materials you actually destroyed in front of us. I thought the storage room looked different from what I remembered."

Bertha smiled and nodded and then said, "Got it in one. But I've been looking at this present crisis, over energy and rider control and so on, and I realized that our world is changing. Technology is developing, and that's actually a good thing, in some ways."

Bertha grabbed another sandwich and after swallowing it in one bite said, "So I had to figure out what to do. I don't think it's my place to try to control the knowledge. And I think letting the idea of an alternate reality drift into the realm of myth and legend is a good one.

"But face it, Libby," Bertha went on, "before Chloe came along, you'd pretty well fallen into slumber because no one was interested in the library. King Alfred had built it—or should I say, *you*—and the building has always been a stunning landmark in Havenshold, but rarely did anyone enter it."

"Very true," said Libby.

"But now," continued Bertha, "thanks to Chloe, Pathfinder Academy, and now Arryn, the library is starting to be used, and used for more than just Gregory's and William's offices. Arryn mentioned when I first got here that people are actually show-ing up to see if there are books about various things they are interested in."

"That's true," said Arryn. "Hannah was in here trying to find legal books immediately after we learned about George, for instance."

"Exactly," said Bertha, "and I know that you, Chloe, are hop-ing to encourage more academics. So it seemed to me that the logical thing to do would be to move all the books King Alfred brought, minus the weaponry and bomb materials, here. No one will be likely to realize that they haven't always been here, so no timeline confusion.

"And Arryn is going to make a very fine librarian, so she will be able to oversee the collection," said Bertha. "Our nation and indeed our planet are just going to have to keep an active watch on itself. Because many technological or sci-entific advances can also be used to gain power or hurt oth-ers. Knowledge isn't good or evil, in and of itself. It's how it's used. So while I've sifted out the knowledge that seemed to me to be purely destructive, there's still a lot that could easily be misused.

"However, there's also a lot that we could benefit from, especially medical knowledge. So my challenge was to figure out if we could keep any of what King Alfred brought back without disclosing the alternate reality and without causing harm to this one. I'm not entirely sure I've managed that, but my seer sense tells me that the immediate danger has passed, so I certainly hope I've found a good solution."

Chloe laughed and then said, "So you just stuck another floor into Libby and then filled it with shelves lined with books."

"Yep," said Bertha nonchalantly, "that's about it."

Libby smiled and said sweetly, "She did ask me first. We talked this over after Berla and Boris were rescued, and I said that I thought her solution made a lot of sense. Our world is starting to take off in new directions, not just in Draconia, but in all four nations. I don't like the idea of censorship. No library ever would. That being said, I really don't think we need materials on how to make bombs or weapons of mass destruction. If we're going down that path, then we need to figure it out for ourselves, and I, for one, hope we never do."

"Agreed," said Chloe.

"And I now have so many books to arrange," said Arryn with an excited gleam in her eyes.

"First you have to figure out how to get to them," said Bertha with a chuckle as she grabbed two more sandwiches.

"What do you mean?" asked Arryn.

Did no one notice that there is no way to reach those new stacks, not even for me? said Calliope.

"Oh," said Arryn as she pictured the new level, "that's right. What are we going to do?"

"Not we," said Libby with a smile. "What's our mage going to do?"

"All right," said Chloe, "I get it. I'm going to make design changes. So let's all go back out into the main room, and I'll entertain suggestions."

Once they were all back in the main room and were staring up at the balcony level, as Chloe thought of it, especially since it wasn't a full floor, ideas were thrown out. Arryn suggested stairs, and that made some sense as, especially, a spiral staircase wouldn't take up a lot of room.

Then Shosty shouted, "Ramps! You said we could have ramps!"

The others laughed, and Chloe said, "I'm not sure how practical that would be. Ramps take up a lot of space."

Bertha said, "Maybe, but the main reading room does have a fair amount of space."

Libby smirked and said, "And of course you can make more space as well."

"Ramps, please," said Shosty as he ran around the room.

Chloe held up her hands and said, "OK, let me think about this."

Everyone quieted down as Chloe imagined where ramps might go, how the room might need enlarging, and how the ramps would affect the current use of the space. Finally, she started moving her arms, and as Arryn and Shosty watched in amazement, the library started shifting. Bertha, Libby, and Calliope merely nodded since they'd seen Chloe do this before.

Chloe designed ramps leading to the right and left side of the new balcony. The ramps then angled across the main reading room, with seating below them in their higher spots. The library also seemed to get wider to accommodate the ramps, so nothing ended up crowed or unusable.

Once she was done, including handrails on the sides of the ramps, Shosty and Calliope took off, with great glee. They could chase each other up one side, across the balcony in front of the stacks, and down the other side. As the two of them enjoyed their antics, Chloe said, "Bertha, I think you sent these materials here just so that I'd make ramps for Shosty and Calliope."

Bertha shrugged and said, "Maybe. After all, they certainly are having a wonderful time."

"And think of all the exercise they're getting," said Libby, who was definitely enjoying her new look.

Chloe laughed and said, "OK, you two, I'm convinced."

Bertha looked thoughtful for a few moments and then said, "I'm wondering now if this wasn't what King Alfred had in mind all along, or him and our wonderful sentient planet who managed to save herself with the alternate timeline. We were given lots of information, and then it became imperative that we decide how to handle it."

"Maybe," said Chloe, "but part of me thinks that if the kidnappers and others interested in this knew what you'd destroyed, they might not be very happy about it."

"Yes," said Bertha, "that was my call, and I do think it was the right one, for all the reasons I gave you at my cave. Don't forget, in our world we have magical creatures bonded to humans in service to the planet and all life. We also have a mage, and we have a seer, so it seems to me that we do have the responsibility to take action."

Chloe thought for a moment and finally said, "I have to agree. And thanks!"

— 22 —

ENERGY GRANTS

Once Clotilda got the names of the businessmen involved from Munroe, she sent the list to Emily. Armed with the names, Emily had finally succeeded in setting up a meeting with the businessmen, who had agreed to show up after lunch, and they were all touring George's factory before the meeting. Emily just hoped that there were still evidences of the air pollution for them to see. She doubted that these men would be easy to convince. This morning she was trying to gather all the information she could to persuade them to abandon the use of coal.

Emily looked through her lists and then made an outline for her presentation. As she was working on that, Gregory walked in with a sheaf of papers.

"Here's everything I've been able to find on our planet's coal deposits. I've also included Aster's estimates from her history books as to how long coal was a viable energy option," said Gregory.

"What's the overall summary?" asked Emily, staring at the thick stack of paper.

Gregory smiled and said, "Bottom line, the planet does not have much coal, and it all petered out after about three hundred years, but by then, the use of coal had greatly altered the environment."

"That's not very long in the grand scheme of things," said Emily. "I just hope that I can convince those who are looking for something quick. I'm worried that I don't really have a lot of ammunition to use to persuade them."

"Want to review with me what you do have?" asked Gregory. "Maybe I can offer some suggestions."

Emily nodded and then went over everything she'd planned to talk about, from the pollution issues, to the success of the various alternative energy sources not only in Draconia, but the other three nations as well. It didn't take her long to share the main points of her outline. When she was done, she looked discouraged.

"It doesn't seem like much, does it?" she said.

"You'd convince me," said Gregory, "but then I'm already convinced."

"And I don't know how much these men resent dragon riders, either. If they're like George, then they won't be interested in listening at all. They'll just be preparing their negative responses," said Emily.

As Gregory was trying to find something positive to say, there was a knock on the door, followed by the entrance of his father, Emily's father, and Oswald.

"Hi, Dad. Hi, baron, and hi, Oswald," said Emily. "Good to see you, but I'm really busy at the moment."

The baron nodded and said, "We suspected as much, and we also suspected that you were worried about this afternoon's meeting. And we think we can help."

"I don't know that there is any help," she said, sighing heavily, her voice filled with obvious worry.

"Of course there is," said Todd, not at all worried by his daughter's discouragement. "May we show you something?"

"I guess," said Emily. "It certainly can't hurt."

Oswald stuck his head out in the hall and said, "Now, Harmony." Then he came back into the room and moved over to one side.

Emily watched as Harmony entered her office in a moving chair. Emily had heard something about what her father and the others had been doing, but she hadn't imagined anything like this. "Hi, Harmony," she said. "Nice to see you moving around."

Harmony smiled and said, "We thought that maybe this might just be the leverage you need to get those men at your meeting on board."

Emily frowned, puzzled, and said, "How?"

The baron looked at her and said, "Glad that you asked. You see, you're trying to make a case for alternative energies, right?"

"Yes," said Emily.

"Well, what Todd has done has never been done before. Harmony's chair is powered by a portable solar battery," the baron said.

Oswald added, "And that's something that coal just can't do."

"Right," said Todd. "I've been working on a number of ways to make portable power, and this is the best—so far, at least."

Emily's eyes began to light up. "So you're saying that you have something unique and also something that could become a moneymaker, since that's obviously all these guys seem to be thinking of."

"Yes," said the baron, "I'm sure Harmony isn't the only one who could use a motorized chair, but even beyond that, Todd's portable power source could definitely have many other applications."

"True," said Emily, "and maybe if we can get them thinking about new, more creative avenues, they will at least open their minds to trying something other than coal."

"Exactly," said Oswald, looking very pleased with himself.

"So how do you want to use us?" asked Harmony.

Emily thought for a moment and then said, "Well, I could start with my presentation as planned, with Gregory there as my expert on coal. And then Todd and Harmony could enter the room. I think that would make a really impressive entrance, and if we make that entrance before any of them gets a chance to open their mouths, I think we may take the wind out of their sails."

The baron said, "I think your plan is excellent, and since we can communicate telepathically, I can let Todd know when you are about ready. That way you won't have to be distracted."

They went over a few more points and then decided that they were as prepared as they were going to be. Chloe arrived just as they were ready to set up the conference room. As they put out snacks and beverages, Emily updated Chloe.

"I like the plan," said Chloe. "And I think it should work. Seems to me that if these men are looking for new sources of income, things like the chair our dads and Oswald designed should be just the thing."

They all headed back to Emily's office, where Todd and Harmony would wait until it was time for their grand entrance.

Once the meeting time arrived, Emily, the baron, Oswald, and Gregory went into the conference room to find it filled with businessmen discussing their plans. They went quiet as soon as Emily and the others entered.

"Thank you all for coming," said Emily. "Please help your-selves to any snacks or beverages that you'd like, and let's begin."

Once everyone was settled around the table, Emily began. She followed the outline that had been agreed upon. As she detailed the problems with coal, she noticed several of the businessmen getting restless. A couple of them came close to interrupting several times, but Emily just shook her head and said, "Please let me finish. You'll then have plenty of time to state your position."

As she got to the end of her presentation, she gave a small nod to the baron, and with perfect timing, as she concluded, the door opened, and Todd and Harmony came in.

All eyes turned to Harmony as she maneuvered her chair into the room to a space Gregory cleared for her by removing the chair he'd been sitting in. Then Todd said, "I thought you guys might be interested in this invention of mine."

He went on to explain all the benefits of the portable solar battery and how it could be used, not only for this one item, but for many other uses as well.

"I'm sure others will be able to develop different uses for the portable solar battery, and this is something that coal simply can't do," Todd concluded. "Solar power is much cheaper, once it is installed, and I know Emily's already told you about how it's being used in various places. The same is true for wind power. And those are both resources that are unlimited. We won't run out of wind or sun in three hundred years, and neither of them will produce the thick, black, smoky air that coal does."

He looked around the room, and he could tell that the advent of something new and unique had caught the interest of these hard-nosed businessmen.

"But neither wind power nor solar power is cheap to set up," said Al, who seemed to be the group's spokesman.

"I know," said Emily. "And that's why the dragon riders will be offering energy grants to anyone, anywhere in Draconia, who wants to convert to one or the other."

"Why would you do that?" said Al. "It'll cost you a lot."

"Because," said Emily, "we are not out to make money. Our mission is to preserve the planet and all life on it. This will just be another of our service outreaches."

"What if we don't want help from you?" said a large man across the table from her, one whom she had noticed had frowned the entire way through her presentation.

"Fair enough," said Emily. "And you are?"

"Bill," he answered, "and I don't want anything to do with dragons or riders."

"OK, Bill," said Emily, "that is certainly your right. But we also have a number of civic leaders who are also willing to provide energy grants for the conversion. You don't have to discount the entire idea just because you don't want to work with us."

"Who'd be fool enough to do that?" said Bill with a snort.

"I would," said the baron. "And I have friends who also will. You see, there are some of us who see beyond the making of money to something more fundamental. I know that the air had cleared noticeably at the Pontsby factory by the time you saw it, but you should have seen the black cloud that hung over the entire area when the factory was in operation."

"So what!" said Bill. "Big deal. Coal is cheap and available."

The baron nodded and then said, "The people who worked there were coughing, trying to breathe, and over time, they would get sick."

"So we put factories out in the boonies," said Bill, "and only the workers have to deal with it."

"Do you think you have an unlimited supply of workers?" asked the baron.

"And don't the workers deserve proper working conditions?" asked Oswald.

This brought a round of laughter from the men as Al said, "Honestly, no. We pay as little as we can to any factory workers, and they just have to be glad they have jobs."

Emily looked at Chloe in horror and said, *This is worse than I thought.*

Chloe answered back, *I was afraid of something like this. We need to appeal to their need for profit. Changing their views on the workers isn't going to happen, at least not right now.*

The baron seemed to come to the same conclusion since he said, "OK, you're only interested in profit. So once your factories were set up to run on wind power or solar power, you'd have basically no overhead for the energy."

"Except for any replacement parts," said Al. "But my coal is free as it's on my land."

Gregory set up a map of Draconia and then said, "You may have coal deposits. I've found a number of them. But, as Emily said in her presentation, the truth is that none of them are very large. It might be free now, but it won't last. And it takes billions of years to make coal. The reality is that once it's gone, it's gone. And at that point, you'll have to find another resource."

"So," said Bill, "we'll worry about that when it happens. I, for one, won't be around in three hundred years, so what do I care?"

Todd looked at the group, trying to keep a look of disgust off his face, as he said, "But wouldn't you like to make even more money?"

"Well, yes," said Al, "that's why we are in business."

"So if you could corner a market on something that was in great demand, that would do it?" Todd said.

"Definitely," said Al. "That's why we've set up our factories."

"So what if you had this solar battery, one that could be used for any devices you care to develop?" Todd asked.

"That'd be great," said Al, "but you already have it."

"I'd be willing to give the specifications over to any who take advantage of these energy grants and convert their factories to wind or solar or water power," said Todd.

"But you'd be giving away a gold mine," said Bill.

"As Emily said," Todd said, "we're not in this for the money. I care about this planet, and I care about factory workers, as well as my own family. I don't want anyone breathing that black soot."

The men looked at Todd with total bewilderment in their eyes. They all knew that he was a retired dragon rider, and most of them were still leery about having anything to do with them. And they really couldn't understand anyone who wasn't out for a profit. There had to be a catch somewhere.

Todd continued, "And truth be known, I'm an inventor, and the fun I have is in making something new. I was really glad that my work with the portable solar battery turned out to have such a wonderful practical application for Harmony here," he said, nodding to Harmony, "but I'm not looking to manufacture either the batteries or the chair."

Al said, "How practical is that battery? How long does it last?"

Harmony answered this question. "I sit outside on my porch for an hour each day, and I use this chair to get around from the time I wake up until I go to sleep. I use it in my home, but I also use it to go out in the fields with my sheep, goats, and chickens. I've never even come close to running out of power."

Al looked stunned. "Solar power can do that?"

Todd nodded and said, "In Sanwight factories are using solar power exclusively in several canning facilities. Of course, those are much larger installations. A portable battery couldn't begin to provide that kind of power. But then there are many different uses, many different needs.

"And in Granvale, factories are doing the same thing with wind power. It's important to remember that we can get power from a lot of sources. Why, even waste materials can be used to generate power. I have a friend who is doing experiments with poop, for instance."

That brought a chuckle to the room. Todd continued once the laughter had died down. "Jaluhz has been supplying the bulk of our world's power since the dragons and riders established Draconia. As we all know, this country doesn't have all the natural resources that the other nations have. We have a volcano and a lot of not very good land, sitting on lava, so we did what we could. It has worked well over the years. Exporting energy in trade for wool, gems, fish, grain, and so forth has served Draconia well.

"But we are evolving. This entire planet used to be very rural, with no major needs for energy. That is changing, and personally I think that change is good. But with the change comes responsibility."

Todd paused and looked carefully around the table. He could see that he had captured the interests of most of the men. After a moment, he continued, "I will be honest with you when I say that what George did fills me with dismay on several levels. We've already talked about coal and how environmentally destructive that is. But his labor practices are just as destructive. If you enslave workers, you will never gain their loyalty or their full talents. The minute George died, his laborers took off, and why wouldn't they? There was no incentive to stay. They had no personal investment in the factory. They were there only because they had nowhere else to go.

"Do any of you remember back to what has been called the Baron's War?"

Several men nodded, and Todd went on. "Havenshold was barricaded so that we couldn't get anything in or out. The riders offered all nonriders safe passage out of Havenshold so that they wouldn't suffer. We promised that their jobs would be kept safe, and when the situation was sorted, they could return.

"Not a single person left. And why? Because in Havenshold rider and nonrider alike are treated with respect and reasonableness.

The result is that our workers, wherever they work, find personal fulfillment in their jobs."

Al snorted and said, "That isn't always possible."

Todd shook his head and said, "Did you hear about the grants Emily is offering? Where do you think we get the funds to offer those grants (which by the way will be considerable)?"

Bill said, "Riders always get the top take on everything—that's how."

Todd shook his head and said, "Not true. We run our compound just the way you might run a factory or the baron runs his ranch and his mines. The truth is that enslaving workers in lousy conditions may get you a short-term profit. But for the long haul, you'll see a much greater profit if you treat people fairly."

"Todd's right," said the baron, "and I had to learn that the hard way. Before I started my thankfully unsuccessful bid to take over Draconia, I worked rather like you. I hope I was never as bad as George, but I didn't care whether my ranch hands had decent quarters or food. I just cared about how hard they worked, and I was quick to fire anyone who didn't meet my exacting standards. And I did very well financially.

"But now, I have so much that I can't begin to use it all. Those who work for me work much more productively because I also allow them a percentage of the profits. I provide comfortable housing for those who need it. If a worker gets sick or has a family member sick, I help.

"I was called a fool, just the way the riders have been called fools, but I learned that in doing the decent thing, I ended up making much more profit."

Al just shook his head.

Emily said, "Remember, when we started, I said that just passing laws about coal wasn't appropriate because you needed to feel that you were getting something in return for switching energy sources? This needs to be a win-win, or else it will fuel resentment, breaking of laws, and so forth. Well, try thinking about your employees the same way. If you can provide an environment where they gain as you gain, as both Todd and the baron have said, you will discover that your gains are enormous.

"But we won't solve all this today. I would just encourage you all to consider what's been said here. And after today's meeting, I will be publicizing the energy grants, allowing anyone interested to participate. I expect the demand to be heavy. If you want to be seen as leaders, at the forefront of what happens in Draconia, I'd encourage you to commit to the change sooner than later. I'll then publicly acknowledge you as part of the change for a cleaner, safer Draconia, and as I'm sure you are much more aware than I am, the publicity will help you promote whatever you're making."

"When do we have to decide?" said Al, who had been jotting down lots of notes throughout the meeting.

"I suppose if we don't decide fast enough, the grants will run out," said Bill, with a very nasty tone in his voice.

"There is no time limit," said Emily, looking directly at Bill. "And there is no limit to the number of grants. Each and every person who wants to try the alternative energies, whether they are currently getting thermal energy from Jaluhz (an energy without any harmful effects and totally renewable) or whether they are using coal (which really we would like to eliminate), they will all be eligible. It also doesn't matter whether they want the grant to energize their home or a large factory."

The men looked at her in stunned silence. Finally, Bill said, "Is this being set up to keep us from getting the knowledge that George said you were hoarding? What are you hiding?"

Chloe laughed and that brought the focus to her. She said, "You know, sometimes people just get the wrong end of the stick. Todd mentioned earlier about how our society was changing. When Draconia was first established, it took every ounce of effort just to survive. But even so, King Alfred had the library built. And for over five hundred years, that building has been noted as a lovely landmark, but not used. That was understandable because people didn't have time for reading or learning outside of what they needed on a daily basis. But the books and scrolls have always been there.

"Now that our society has developed to a more secure place, there is more leisure time. I'm getting students coming to Pathfinder who are interested in things like history, geology, law, and so forth. I even have one student who wants to be a librarian, and she is beginning to catalog and arrange all the information that King Alfred stored there years ago.

"So if any of you want this so-called hidden information, you only have to walk through the library doors and ask. It's always been there. And you may find resources concerning energy production. The library is open to all."

Bill's mouth dropped open. "But, I thought…"

"The reality is that," said Emily, "George was a bitter and misguided man. Let's not follow his example." She stood and said, "I think we've given you enough to think about. My door is always open, whether you want to apply for a grant or just ask questions."

The meeting broke up after that, and a few of the men did stop to talk with Todd, the baron, or Emily. Once the business-men had left, Emily sat down in the nearest chair and said, "Well, did we convince them?"

Gregory said, "Only time will tell, but I do think you've won some converts for sure."

— 23 —

A NEW HOME

Chloe started the next day in her office, looking through her list of potential foster homes for Patrick. She went over all the names, even those with children, so that she was very sure she didn't miss a potential home. She concluded, given what she knew about Patrick, that none of the homes with children were likely to provide a good fit. That left her with only three homes to choose from, since most of those willing to foster for Pathfinder also had children of their own and adding one more was apparently easier than adding a student to an all-adult household.

With her list of the three potentials in hand, Chloe left Calliope and Shosty in charge of the library and headed out to call on the couples. She started with the home that was closest to town, but when she explained Patrick's situation, the husband all but slammed the door in her face, saying they would never take someone who'd done what Patrick had.

Chloe was taken aback by the near violence of the man's reaction. She'd been very careful to explain why Patrick had tried what he had, but apparently that made absolutely no difference.

Once she was out of sight of the home, Chloe stopped and made notes on her clipboard, vowing to remove that couple from her list. Patrick had made a huge mistake for sure, but then didn't all people make them, especially young adolescents who were trying to find themselves? Certainly Chloe had, and she wouldn't want one of her students in such a rigid and stifling environment.

The second home wasn't as hostile as the first. They at least invited her in for tea and listened to all she had to share about Patrick, but then they too said, with at least a degree of reluctance, that they didn't feel up to the challenge of helping a young man from such a difficult background.

As Chloe walked to the third prospective home, her heart was heavy. She knew Patrick was a good person, who'd taken a few steps down his father's path but now was determined to turn things around. If Amy and Todd weren't already fostering Arryn, they would have been the perfect choice, and Chloe was sure that they could foster two students, but she wouldn't ask that until she'd tried all her other options. Arryn's early years had been just as rough if not rougher than Patrick's, and she was flourishing so well with Amy and Todd that Chloe was reluctant to change that balance.

Chloe had reached the third home, which was about a fifteen-minute walk from the library. It was a light blue home with dark blue shutters and a dark blue front door, a classic wood-framed two-story home, well cared for and inviting. Crossing her fingers, Chloe knocked on the front door.

A silver-haired smiling woman answered the door, exclaiming, "Chloe! What a pleasure."

"Thanks, Alma," said Chloe. "I hope you and Bruce are doing well."

"We are," said Alma. "Please come in. We were just sitting down to our morning tea."

Chloe followed Alma into their large kitchen, and as she entered, Bruce stood from his seat at the wooden kitchen table. "Chloe," he said, holding out his hand to her, "I haven't seen you in quite a while."

Chloe shook his hand, and then once everyone was seated and had tea, Chloe said, "I've come to ask a favor." She then proceeded to tell them all she knew about Patrick.

Both Alma and Bruce listened intently, with no signs of rejection that Chloe could see. When Chloe finished, Bruce said, "That poor young man. I'd heard something about an arson attempt at Ingrid's new place, but I had no idea."

"We haven't made most of the details public," said Chloe. "I've spent quite a bit of time with Patrick, and I must say, I like him. He is genuinely remorseful, and of course, he only ended up hurting himself."

"With a father like George," said Bruce, "his life can't have been easy. I heard about George's murder, and it didn't surprise me at all. Thankfully I've not had any dealings with him, but I've heard about him, and he was a very unpleasant man."

"I feel so sorry for this young man," said Alma. "And from what you've told us, he does seem determined to turn his life around now."

"I think he genuinely does want something different," said Chloe.

"And he has a dragon rider apprentice as a girlfriend?" asked Alma.

"Yes," said Chloe, "and Elise has been there every day to visit him, whenever she can get time off from her studies and chores."

"Well," said Alma, "I doubt very much that her dragon would permit that if there were anything bad about Patrick."

Chloe thought that was probably true, although she herself hadn't thought about that.

Alma looked at her husband, and Chloe saw him give her a small nod. Alma then said, "We'd like to meet Patrick and let him meet us. I think this might be a good fit, but he'll have to decide."

"Thank you," said Chloe, letting out a big sigh of relief. "When would you be free to come to the hospital with me?"

"Why not now," said Bruce. "No time like the present."

And so the three of them walked back into town to the riders' compound and into the hospital. Nurse Beatrice looked up from her desk as they entered and immediately her face lit up in a smile as she said, "Alma and Bruce, what a pleasure. Are you here to meet Patrick?"

Alma said, "Yes, we are if this is a good time."

"It definitely is," said Nurse Beatrice. Then she turned to Chloe and said, "You know the way, and you should also know that Dr. Brian is prepared to release Patrick if he has somewhere to go. He doesn't need to be here full-time. He'll just need to have his bandages checked and then return for follow-up visits."

"Good to know," said Chloe, and then she led Alma and Bruce back to Patrick's room.

As they walked in, Chloe thought how alone Patrick looked, sitting in a chair, staring out his window. But as soon as they walked in and Patrick saw Chloe, his face brightened, and he said, "Hi, Chloe. You'll never guess who stopped by last evening."

Chloe, Alma, and Bruce walked over to Patrick, and as they were pulling up chairs, Chloe introduced Alma and Bruce as her friends, not wanting to put any pressure on any of them, and then said, "So who stopped by?"

"Sylvester," said Patrick, smiling broadly, "and we talked all about animals, and he seemed to think I'd done something remarkable when I told him about some of the lambs I'd saved."

Bruce said, "You've helped with lambing?"

Patrick nodded and said, "Yeah, I've done it now for a couple years." A shadow passed across his face as he said, "My dad didn't think it was worth it. The lambs could either survive on their own or die. Same for the ewes." Then he gave himself a bit of a shake to bring himself back to the present and said, "But Sylvester said that's just not true, that we all need help at times and that humans have midwives or others to assist, so why shouldn't sheep or anyone else? He's just great."

Chloe smiled as she heard the pure joy in Patrick's voice and thought that she'd be sure to visit Sylvester and thank him. "I'd certainly have to agree with that," she said.

"And for you to be able to figure that out by yourself," said Alma, "that's pretty remarkable."

"I'll say," said Bruce. "I've never lived on a farm myself, but I wouldn't think it would be easy."

Soon Alma, Bruce, and Patrick were chatting back and forth as if they'd known each other for years, and Chloe marveled at how easily Alma and Bruce drew Patrick out of himself. They got him to talk about everything, leaving no secrets, from his childhood abuse to his misguided arson. Chloe thought this was smart on Alma and Bruce's part. She knew they already understood what Patrick had done, but she also knew that Patrick needed to tell them his story himself.

They'd been there for over an hour when Elise walked in. Alma and Bruce met her and quickly included her in their conversations, making the two young people feel at ease and comfortable. After Elise had to return for her afternoon classes, Alma said to Patrick, "So how would you feel about coming to live with us? You don't have to decide right now, but we'd love to have you."

Patrick's jaw dropped and then tears formed in his eyes, which he hastily wiped away with the back of his hand. Finally, he said, "You'd want me?"

Bruce smiled and said, with humor in his voice, "You never know when we might meet a pregnant sheep."

Alma gave a playful slap at her husband and said, "Stop kidding." Then she turned to Patrick and said, "Yes, Patrick, we would. We live a quiet life, but we have plenty of room, and we're big supporters of Pathfinder. We've lived in Havenshold all our lives, raised four children who are all married now and who have moved to the capital, and honestly, it would be nice to have some young energy in our home. If you think you'd be happy with us, we'd very much like to have you."

Patrick looked over at Bruce, who merely smiled and nodded. Then Patrick looked at Chloe, who said, "The decision is totally yours, and as Alma said, you don't have to decide right this minute. You have had a lot to deal with lately."

"No—I mean, yes, I would like to go with you, if you want me," said Patrick. "I promise I'm on a new path, and I won't let you down."

"Now, none of that," said Alma with mock severity, "you just be who you are. We can see all the goodness in you. We all make mistakes, and sometimes we have to get through some really hard times."

"We aren't offering you a home," said Bruce, "in order to get you to be someone different or someone we think you should be. We're offering you a home because we think that the three of us could make a family, looking out for each other, helping each other, and just enjoying the company."

Patrick was now sobbing, and Alma went over and put an arm around him. It was obvious to all three adults that Patrick had never had love or a family, and Chloe couldn't help but think that this foster placement would be the making of him.

Once Patrick had calmed and mopped his face with the large handkerchief that Bruce produced nonchalantly for him, Chloe said, "Why don't I find Nurse Beatrice, so you can get your discharge instructions. Then I think the three of you can head back home."

Patrick stared at her and said, "Really? Right now?"

"If that works for you," said Bruce.

Patrick looked stunned and said, "Well…Well, yes, please."

Chloe laughed as she left the room to find Nurse Beatrice. "We need to get the discharge instructions for Patrick," she said once she'd found Nurse Beatrice.

"I so hoped so," said the nurse. "I know Alma and Bruce, and I think they'll be the perfect foster parents for Patrick. Nice placement."

"Thank you," said Chloe, "and I agree."

Nurse Beatrice grabbed her clipboard, and she and Chloe headed back to Patrick's room. It didn't take long for her to go over all the instructions. Once Beatrice was sure that both Alma and Bruce understood about changing dressings and what to look for and once she'd given them Patrick's follow-up appointment for three days later, she headed out of the room.

Bruce helped Patrick pack his meager belongings, and then the four of them left the hospital as Alma said, "It'll take about fifteen minutes to walk to our home. Are you up to that?"

Patrick nodded and said, "Yes, it will feel good to get some activity."

"But not too much at once," said Bruce. "We don't want you back here as a resident."

"Good luck, Patrick," said Chloe. "I'll stop by and see you in a day or so. Meanwhile, if any of you need anything, you know where I am. Have fun settling into your new home."

Patrick turned to Chloe and then suddenly gave her a big hug, saying, "Thank you so much! Not everyone would take a chance on me; I know that."

"My pleasure," said Chloe.

With that the new family walked down the road, and Chloe heard Bruce saying, "Anyone interested in an ice-cream sundae? The ice-cream parlor is right on our way."

Chloe chuckled and then decided she'd swing into the animal clinic and see if Sylvester was free.

Chloe opened the door to the animal clinic and then held it, as a mother, her daughter, and a small puppy who obviously had no clue what a leash was for were trying to exit. The mother looked a bit harried, but the daughter, who appeared to be about eight, smiled broadly and said, "I just got a puppy."

Chloe laughed and said, "You sure did. Good luck."

Once the trio was through the door, Chloe entered and found that Sylvester was just handing over a file to the attendant at the front desk. He looked up as she walked in and said, "Hi, Chloe. Great to see you."

"Hi, Sylvester," said Chloe. "I was just walking by and thought I'd stop in to thank you for taking time to visit Patrick."

"I couldn't resist," said Sylvester. "Anyone who could teach himself to help with lambing, without any guidance—pretty incredible. I've got a few free minutes before my next patient. Want some tea in the break room?"

"That'd be nice," said Chloe. She followed Sylvester down the hall to a small room with a table and four chairs. She saw that there was a teapot on a stove next to the sink.

"Have a seat," said Sylvester, "and I'll just heat this water."

Once they both had their tea, Sylvester said, "Patrick said he's going to attend Pathfinder in the fall."

"Yes," said Chloe, "and I've just gotten him fostered with Alma and Bruce."

"Great," said Sylvester. "They've got strong connections to the community here. I think both of them come from families who have lived here for generations. I suspect it was hard for them when all their children married spouses from Alfredsville. I kinda expected them to relocate, but I'm glad they didn't."

"They've taken other fosters for me through the years," said Chloe. "Somehow I expect that this foster will be particularly good on both sides. I hope so anyway."

"What are you thinking for Patrick?" asked Sylvester.

"Well, I'm not sure what he'll pick, but his interests and abilities with animals seemed a logical place to start," said Chloe.

"He has a real gift," said Sylvester, "at least from what he's said. And we talked for quite a while. I wanted to be sure he wasn't bragging or exaggerating what he'd done, but he's the real thing."

"I was wondering if you'd be able to give him some community service this summer, once he's healed," said Chloe. "Emily's made that a condition of his acceptance, and I think it's very appropriate. He'll be doing some of his hours at Ingrid's since that's the place he tried to burn. But that's not going to be terribly exciting for him."

"No, certainly not," said Sylvester, "but his community service should be onerous at some level. However, I agree, and I can certainly find work for him that is equally onerous but, at the same time, something he'll need if he decides on a career path that involves animals in any way."

"Thanks, Sylvester," said Chloe. "I'd also like to be sure he has positive male role models, since his dad was such a bully. Between you and Bruce, he'll be well cared for."

"Well, thank you, ma'am," said Sylvester as he stood and gave her a mock bow.

Chloe laughed and stood as well. "I'd better let you get on with your day. I'll be sure to let you know when Patrick's been cleared to start on his community service. And thanks for taking yet another Pathfinder student under your wing."

"My pleasure," said Patrick as the two of them headed to the front desk.

— 24 —

EXPLOSION

Chloe walked through the main doors of the library and immediately noticed that the room looked different. Arryn called out, "What do you think?" as Chloe stepped farther into the room. She saw that Arryn had made signs and posters, which she'd then displayed. Some of the signs were directional, such as "Fiction" with an arrow pointing to the appropriate portion of the stacks. Others were more general in nature, such as the poster that diagrammed the stacks on each level with listings detailing what subjects could be found where.

There was a big sign proclaiming "Welcome" hung above a new central desk, which was labeled "Information." There was even a really funny poster listing the ten most commonly asked questions, and Chloe couldn't help but smile to notice that the first, third, and tenth were identical and read, "Where is the restroom?"

As Chloe took it all in, including new signs identifying William's, Gregory's, and her offices, she smiled and then turned to Arryn. "This is brilliant," she said, "but what brought all this on?"

"Well, you told me about yesterday's meeting and how you'd told everyone that the information they thought was so secret had been here all the time," said Arryn, "so I got to thinking that some of those people might decide to show up here to check it out."

Chloe said, "Makes sense, and I hope they do."

"So do I," said Arryn. "Libby and I've been working hard the last couple days. Well, Libby's done all the actual work magically, but I had to decide how to arrange the materials. So now, all the practical topics, such as cooking, woodworking, even knitting and sewing, as well as all the science information, are arranged by subject on the first floor, because I thought that those fields would be most in demand.

"Then things like fiction, history, psychology, education, poetry, and art are up on the middle level. Libby agreed that my arrangement made sense, and so she blinked a couple times, and it was all done. She's really amazing."

Chloe laughed and said, "Yes, she is, and yes, I agree that you've come up with a very sensible arrangement. And I like all the signs as well. You've done a great job."

"Now we just have to see if anyone comes," said Arryn.

"They will," said Chloe, "whether immediately or through time. We already have more people stopping in than we did when I first came here."

"I'm trying to think of ways to let people know what we have. I've been amazed at the collection myself. I thought maybe I'd show Mary the knitting books and Ingrid and Hazel the sewing and so on. And once Todd finds out what's here in the practical sciences, I think he'll be a steady visitor," said Arryn.

"I think for now," said Chloe, "we should restrict use of the materials to the library. Once we have everything listed, maybe we can allow people to check things out for short periods, but I'd hate to lose something we didn't even realize we had."

"I agree," said Arryn, "and so does Libby. She says she can monitor the exit so that no books or scrolls leave."

This really made Chloe chuckle. "That will be interesting. If she catches someone, how do we explain the locked doors. I assume that's what she'll do. But seriously, that's a great plan."

The next morning Arryn's predictions proved true. As Chloe sat in her office and looked out through the glass partition onto the main library room, she saw Arryn helping several of the men who'd attended Emily's meeting. She was especially glad to see Al there.

As far as Chloe could tell, Arryn pulled several books for Al and showed him to a workstation just outside Chloe's office. He worked industriously for over an hour before returning the books to Arryn. Then he came over to her office door and knocked.

"Come in," said Chloe.

Al walked in and said, "I just wanted to thank you. I had no idea all this information was here."

"It's available to any who want to use it," said Chloe.

"I can see that now," said Al. "Funny how rumors start and information gets twisted."

"Indeed," said Chloe.

"Anyway, I'll be back, and I'll let my friends know as well," said Al. "Also there are a number of us who are seeking those energy grants. Not all of us are as stubborn as Bill and poor George."

"I'm very glad to hear that," said Chloe. "Change is never easy, but working together, we can make things better for everyone."

"Possibly," said Al. "I'm still not sold on the employment practices the baron and Todd were advocating, but I'm willing to listen."

"That's a good starting spot," said Chloe.

Al turned to go as he said, "Again, thanks!"

Calliope stretched across the papers on Chloe's desk and said, *I'm sure Arryn is really excited to have people coming in, but it does make for a noisier library.*

Shosty stood and said, "It also messes with our ramp time."

"Listen, you two," said Chloe, "we need people to use the library. And if that messes with your sleep or recreation, so be it." Then she ruffled the fur on both of them.

By the end of the day, Chloe was beginning to wish for the quieter atmosphere as well, but Arryn was so excited.

"I've helped so many people," she said. Then she paused and said, "Well, maybe not that many, but at least ten, and that's lots more than we usually have."

Chloe laughed and said, "For sure, and at least we are dispelling the rumor that we're hiding knowledge."

"I'm learning a lot about energy sources," said Arryn, "which is great as well."

Later that afternoon Emily stopped by Chloe's office. "Wow, things are really busy here," she said as she dropped onto Chloe's couch. "And I like Libby's new look."

Chloe smiled and said, "Yes, I think Bertha had a great solution to the dilemma of King Alfred's information from the other timeline."

"How's that old bear doing?" asked Emily.

"She's stayed in Havenshold to work with Rya since obviously Rya can't get to her now. I think it's working out well, although I'm sure Clyde must be feeling overwhelmed with both Bertha and Mildred staying with him."

Emily laughed and said, "I'd think so. But it's so nice to see that family healing. Anyway, I've been receiving a lot of requests for energy grants, and the baron says he also has gotten a number of queries, so I think things are working out. I'm a bit concerned because I've heard nothing from Bill, but I'll give him a few more days."

"Hopefully he'll come around," said Chloe.

"Oh, and thank you for taking Patrick under your wing and finding him such a wonderful foster situation," said Emily. "I'm going to work with Alma and Bruce, as well as Sylvester and Ingrid, to line up community service for Patrick, but he seems so eager to make amends that I think that will be easy and that everyone involved will benefit."

"I'm glad something good is coming out of all this," said Chloe.

"Actually lots of good," said Emily, smiling. "Patrick now has a chance to become the person he wants to be. Ingrid has paid back the funds we advanced her and her business is thriving. And Mildred has been reunited with her mother, daughter, brother, and niece. Our energy grants are very popular, and the changes will benefit the entire planet."

"Gads," said Chloe, "when you list it like that, it is impressive."

Emily nodded and then stood. "Well, I'd better get back to processing all those grant requests. But it was nice to have a bit of a break, and thanks for the tea."

"Anytime," said Chloe.

As Emily was leaving Chloe's office, she nearly ran smack into Bertha.

"Oops, sorry," said Emily as she backed up.

"No problem," said Bertha. "Glad to find you here with Chloe."

As Bertha moved into the office, Emily and Chloe could see that Mildred was with her.

Once greetings had been exchanged, Bertha said, "We wanted to say good-bye before we head out."

"You're leaving?" asked Chloe.

Mildred said, "Yes, it's time to get back. I have a big show coming up, and I'm behind on getting ready for it. Mom and Rya are both doing fine, and honestly, I'm exhausted by being around so many people all the time."

Bertha chuckled and then said, "I sure understand that. And I need to get back to Boris and Berla as well. I've given Rya enough coaching so that she can handle any more natural disasters she may foretell, although I don't really think there will be anything as major as Jaluhz's eruption in the near future. But she feels more comfortable and has a better understanding of her abilities as a nature empath, and that was all I needed to do."

"Well, don't be strangers," said Emily. "Either of you."

Mildred laughed and said, "That's what Mom said, and we're going to communicate a lot more telepathically now, so that's a real plus. I can't believe I waited so long to make real contact with her and with Rya. So, yes, I'll be visiting a lot more frequently."

Just then there was a very loud explosion, which shook the teacups in Chloe's office.

"What was that?" asked Chloe.

Calliope and Shosty both ducked under Chloe's desk as Emily said, "An earthquake, maybe?"

Bertha shook her head and said, "I don't think so."

"Well, we'd better figure out what it was," said Emily. "It can't be good."

Emily, Chloe, Bertha, and Mildred headed out of the library, after Chloe had reassured both Calliope and Shosty that they were safe. Once outside they saw that people were heading toward the riders' headquarters, and the four of them followed suit.

When they reached the arch that opened into the riders' compound, Emily found Rupert and Hannah doing their best to answer questions from worried citizens. Emily joined them and said, "We don't know what the explosion was, but we're going to find out. Have there been any injuries here in Havenshold?"

No one had heard of any, so Emily said, "I'd suggest then that you all head back to your normal routine, and we'll make an announcement as soon as we discover what's happened."

As the crowd dispersed, Bertha looked at Chloe and said, "I don't think you need me for this, and Mildred and I want to get on our way back to a saner world." She smiled as she said this, and Mildred chuckled.

Chloe gave each of them a big hug and said, "Stay in touch, and when I know what's happening, I'll let you know, but yes, I suspect your gifts aren't needed at the moment. Take care and don't be strangers."

Once Bertha and Mildred had left, Chloe went over to Emily and said, "How can I help?"

"If you're free, could you fly with us?" said Emily as Esmeralda arrived in the courtyard. "You might be able to detect something we might miss."

"Certainly," said Chloe.

Once they were airborne, Chloe, sitting behind Emily, asked, "Any ideas about where the explosion took place?"

Esmeralda said, "Early reports are coming in from the west, so we'll head there first."

It didn't take long to find the spot. Smoke was rising from a large gash in the side of a cliff, and as Esmeralda circled, Chloe said, "Isn't that the coal mine George and Bill were operating?"

"I think so," said Emily. "Esmeralda, can you find a safe place to land?"

"I'll try," said Esmeralda. "But look, the river of lava is flowing into the gash."

Chloe said, "You're right. We're soon going to have a lake of lava with the river flowing in and then out the other side."

Esmeralda finally found a spot near a gathering of miners. Once she'd landed, Emily went over to them. "Anyone know what happened here?" she asked.

"All we know is that Bill told us to show up today," said one of the miners. "He said he was going to reopen the mine and that we'd all have all the work we wanted."

"Where's Bill now?" asked Emily.

The men just shrugged, and finally one of them said, "We think he was in the mine."

"What?" said Chloe. "He was inside?"

"We're not sure," said the first miner. "We heard the explosion while we were still a mile away. But he isn't here."

"OK," said Emily. "We need to get help here and figure out what happened. Any of you men who want to assist are most welcome, and yes, we will pay you for your time. I'm also sending out a call to dragons and their riders."

The men huddled to discuss the options, and finally the first miner said, "We'll stay. We did know the mine, although that explosion may have ripped it all apart. Still, we know the land better than anyone else."

"Thanks," said Emily.

It took a while to get more help to the site, and Gregory, the baron, and Oswald came as well.

"Thanks," said Emily to the three. "We definitely need all the experts we can get. Bill and maybe others could be trapped inside."

The baron went over to the lead miner and conferred. He came back and reported, "They say there was another entrance that was no longer used. It was closer to the factory, but the coal there had already been mined. But it might give us better access."

252

The miners were happy to show them where the other entrance was located, and the dragons began digging very carefully. Once they'd cleared a path into the old opening, there was a rush of escaping gas. Everyone stepped back, and the baron said, "Looks as if Bill didn't have this mine properly ventilated and the methane gases built up."

Gregory nodded and said, "And there is a volcano vent located in this area. If he hit that, the heat and lava from the volcano would ignite the gases, and the explosion would be unstoppable."

"What are the chances that anyone could still be alive in there?" asked Emily.

Oswald just shook his head, and the miners looked equally glum. The baron finally said, "Given the size of the crater, the way the lava is pouring into it, and the gases escaping out this side, I'd say there was no chance that anyone in there could have survived."

"Looks as if Bill discovered another reason against using coal," said Chloe, "but how sad to find out that way."

Emily said, "Well, we need to work on the cleanup of this explosion now."

It was nearly a month later when those working to make the explosion site safer discovered the charred remains of one body. The final report stated that Bill had been in the mine by himself, apparently determined to find new richer deposits, and as Gregory surmised, he hit one of the vents into the volcano. The vent was now allowing lava to flow out into the new lake, and that proved to be a fine solution as the extra lava wasn't enough to disturb the lava river heading to the sea.

Emily called a meeting with those businessmen whom she'd met with before to deliver the final report. When she finished, she said, "Any questions?"

Al looked at the others and said after a brief pause, "It's sad that Bill had to die that way. He just couldn't listen to any new ideas, especially if they came from the riders.

"I think many of us also felt the same way at first, but now..." He paused and looked at the others before continuing, "Now I think we're beginning to see that there are better ways."

Emily smiled and said, "I'm glad. And working together I believe we can ensure that this planet has enough safe, clean energy for all our needs. I want to thank each of you for being willing to give other options a chance. Please, my door is always open if you have questions, ideas, or just want to talk."

With that, the meeting broke up, and several of the men stopped to give Emily their personal thanks.

— 25 —

NEW BEGINNINGS

The next morning Chloe decided that she needed a walk. "Want to come with me, Shosty?" she asked.

"Of course," he answered.

"Keep an eye on things here, Calliope," said Chloe as she and Shosty headed for the door.

Naturally, Calliope replied before she stretched, turned herself around on Chloe's papers, and plopped down, closing her eyes.

Chloe and Shosty headed out along the road toward Ingrid's Quilt Shop. As they passed the place where they'd been attacked, Shosty said, "I'm sure glad Calliope was on the ball that day."

"Me too," said Chloe, "and glad also that the bad guys have been taken care of."

They walked into Ingrid's shop, and Ingrid welcomed them. "So glad to see you both," she said.

"Is it all right that Shosty comes in?" asked Chloe.

"Totally," said Ingrid, with a smile. "We're an animal-friendly establishment."

Hazel came into the front of the store from one of the side aisles and said, "Great to see you here."

"Hi, Mom," said Chloe. "Nice to see that you're still working here."

"Oh definitely," said Hazel. "Now that I don't have this big house to take care of, I have a lot more free time. And just being with all this great fabric is inspiring."

Ingrid laughed and said, "And she really knows her way around fabric. She's been making some great suggestions on expanding our offerings."

"And I understand from Emily," said Chloe, "that your business is back on an even footing."

Ingrid nodded and said, "The community has really rallied. I couldn't believe it, but I'm very lucky and very grateful."

Chloe and Shosty headed back out on their walk after touring the shop. "Shall we go see how Harmony is doing?"

Shosty said, "We won't have to wait long. I hear them coming."

"Who?" said Chloe.

"Hmm," said Shosty, "sounds like Harmony, Rya, Clyde, Oswald, and the baron."

Just then the five of them came into view, and Chloe said, "What keen ears you have."

Harmony was moving along in her chair, but Chloe noticed that her leg, while still in a bright pink cast, was bent rather than sticking out. Rya was no longer on crutches and also had a shorter walking cast. Chloe waved to the group as they approached.

"We were just on our way out to see you, Harmony," said Chloe.

Harmony laughed and said, "We're heading into Havenshold for a doctor's appointment. Want to tag along?"

"Certainly," said Chloe, "and it's good to see you both doing so well. Is your arm healed, Harmony?"

"It's a bit weak, but I got that cast off last week," she said.

"That's when I got my walking cast," said Rya.

"You can't slow these two down," said the baron.

Clyde nodded and said, "Rya's determined to be back to work now that she's off crutches, but we're trying to make her take it easy."

"Good luck with that," said Chloe.

That brought laughs all around. Chloe then said, "So Mildred stopped by on her way out of town with Bertha. Have you heard from her since they left?"

Harmony smiled and said, "Yes, she now contacts both of us telepathically on a regular basis, and her work for her next show is coming along really well."

"The show will be in Alfredsville," said Rya, excitedly, "at the end of summer, and we're going to go see it."

"That's wonderful," said Chloe.

"We're all going to be there," said Clyde, "to support her, and Aster, Sasha, and Jasmine hope to be able to come as well."

"I gather they're back on their ambassador duties now," said Chloe.

"Yes, they had to go about the same time as Mildred," said Clyde. "The house really seems empty now, but I know they'll all be coming back when they can."

"And now I, too, have to leave for a bit," said the baron. "I need to check on my Forbury holdings."

"We've always spent more time in Forbury than here," said Oswald, "and I do miss my home country."

The baron ruffled Oswald's fur and said, "He's right. And I think that Lance manages my affairs here very well, and he's probably tired of us hanging around. Now that Harmony is getting more independent, it's time for us to head back to Forbury. But we'll be back before too long, and we also are planning on going to Mildred's show."

"But this depends," said Oswald, "on Harmony getting a walking cast today. That's what's supposed to happen, but we won't leave until it does."

"Truly, you two," said Harmony, "I can manage now even if I don't get the new cast."

"Hard to milk a goat when you can't get close to them," teased the baron. He turned to Chloe and said, "The goats are still skittish around the chair."

"Maybe," said Harmony, reluctantly.

"Well, I have a new student," said Chloe, "named Patrick, who will be doing community service this summer. I could check with Emily and Sylvester and see if he could give you a hand. He loves animals."

"That would be nice," said Harmony. "I could use some help, even with the new cast."

By this time they'd reached the library, and Chloe said, "Well, good luck at the doctor's, and if you get the new cast, then stop by on your way back, and I'll give you a tour of our new expanded stacks."

With that, Chloe and Shosty went up the front steps, waving to the others and shouting, "Good luck."